BY BARBARA RASKIN

*Loose Ends*
*The National Anthem*
*Out of Order*

# OUT OF ORDER

## BARBARA RASKIN

SIMON AND SCHUSTER | NEW YORK

Published by Simon and Schuster
A Division of Gulf & Western Corporation
Simon & Schuster Building
Rockefeller Center
1230 Avenue of the Americas
New York, New York 10020
Manufactured in the United States of America

1 2 3 4 5 6 7 8 9 10


Library of Congress Cataloging in Publication Data

Raskin, Barbara.
    Out of order.

    I.  Title.
PZ4.R2247Ou  [PS3568.A69]  813'.5'4  79–12061
    ISBN 0–671–24281–4

*For My Mother and Father*

# CHAPTER ONE

"Am I hurting you, honey?"

"Oh, no. It feels great," Coco lied with a sweet synthetic sigh.

Actually she was feeling a little bit guilty and wanton making plans to seduce another man while her husband was stretched out on top of her, moving rhythmically up and down so that his face drifted like a dream before her eyes in the darkness.

Still, she had so little time for herself lately, Coco was forced to take advantage of any kind of privacy. The psychogenic aspermia—or delayed ejaculation dysfunction—from which Gavin suffered afforded her an unusually long uninterrupted opportunity in which to think about other things.

Sliding his fingers beneath her buttocks, Gavin grabbed several gulps of Coco's flesh inside his hungry hands.

"Hmmmm," Coco murmured, shifting her knees into Pap-smear position so as to relieve some internal pressure.

Tomorrow Coco was going to transcend the tedium of her routine existence by accelerating a mild flirtation into an intense affair. Tomorrow, instead of resenting her husband, rebelling against her boss, or scolding her children, Coco Burman was planning to launch a luscious romance that would make her feel giddy, heady, high, and unencumbered. She was going to summerize the winter of her discontent by letting yeast-like yearn-

9

ings swell her soul until all the domestic details which oppressed her were totally obliterated.

Breathing heavily, Gavin pivoted into a more north-easterly position and made a direct strike at Coco's right Fallopian tube.

"How's that?" he asked.

"Fantastic," Coco whispered, hoping to encourage him since he still showed no signs of approaching climax.

Throughout the hour during which the Burmans had been having intercourse, Coco had been mapping out a strategy for seducing John Canada, Princeton professor, chairman of the Social Science Institute's Board of Directors, and recently nominated director of President Carter's Council of Economic Advisors. Since Canada was scheduled to arrive at the Social Science Institute early the next morning for the first 1979 Board meeting, Coco had the entire day in which to signal her sexual availability and snare her man. Although sex was the last thing she needed, Coco wanted an extramarital romance for the same reason she had craved a hobby in high school. Exasperated by the banalities of life, Coco ached for an engrossing diversion.

"Are you getting tired, honey?" Gavin inquired solicitously as he switched into a circular motion that spiraled him up toward the tip of Coco's cervix.

"Not really, Gav."

Actually, the idea of having an affair with the tall, handsome economic development expert had been edging—erratically and erotically—through Coco's mind for the last three months, delightfully distracting her attention whenever she chose to indulge herself. From the moment they'd met, Coco had been aware of Canada's sexual interest in her even though they had only talked briefly at three previous Board meetings.

"Jesus," Gavin commented approvingly, as he continued to pummel Coco's body with piston-like precision.

In hopes of accelerating his progress, Coco made several sounds to suggest she was having a peak sexual experience. Although Coco had lost any vital interest in the proceedings after her third orgasm, she still felt obliged to participate actively. As if in a frenzy, she provocatively punched her pubis against Gavin's pelvic bone and elevated their three hundred consolidated pounds of flesh (of which only one hundred and fifteen were hers) off the bed into an airborne position.

That made Gavin initiate a series of staccato-style stabs in response.

Coco moaned as a sharp cramp constricted her vagina. At the moment, Coco's vaginal walls felt like a pair of skinned shins and this worried her because she had always believed that a dry vagina—other than the original virginal variety—was a sign of old age. The fact that she was beginning to lose her elasticity and lubricity at the early age of thirty-seven and a half made her wonder if some sexual atrophy symptoms were actually psychological and if her decreased discharge might be caused by an unconscious hostility toward her husband. It was quite possible that Coco was staging a retaliatory cutback just as the Seven Sisters had withheld oil reserves during the 1973 energy crisis so as to put a tighter squeeze on their consumers.

Encouragingly, Coco stroked Gavin's back.

Although she had been incredibly busy, both at home and the office, Coco had taken off an entire afternoon right before Christmas to do some research on the mysterious malady that afflicted her husband and discovered that Gavin's inability—or at least reluctance—to ejaculate was a type of male impotence which Dr. David Reuben, in his encyclopedically informative best seller, *Everything You've Always Wanted to Know About Sex—But Were Afraid to Ask*, admitted was "very rare." Dr. Reuben called psychogenic aspermia the "fourth form of male impotence" and said it was characterized by a:

> . . . complete inability to ejaculate in spite of prolonged intercourse. Sometimes the proceedings draw on for an hour or more with no prospect of orgasm for the male. Finally, in pain, boredom, and desperation, everyone gives up. Incidentally, nobody claims this is normal. . . . People who suffer from premature ejaculation sometimes think they would rather have this condition. Once in a while they get it; they change their mind immediately.

While the doctor had described Gavin's condition in accurate detail, he made no effort to explain its cause, so Coco had energetically tried to identify the source of the problem on her own. She finally concluded that Gavin had developed P.A. (Dr. Reuben's abbreviation for the fourth form of male impotence) from the meaninglessness of the 1970s. Because life since the '60s had become a holding pattern devoid of any meaning or motion, Coco decided that Gavin had become sexually retentive and was holding himself back—at least in terms of sperm—in retaliation.

Although superficially it appeared that Gavin was sitting on top of the world—possessor of a wonderful family, a good career, and a reasonable amount of disposable income—Coco knew he was experiencing the 1970s with extreme discomfort. Since she spent her days editing the Social Science Institute's National Infelicity Index, Coco knew that outward signs of success meant nothing and that personal felicity could only be measured in terms of self-esteem and satisfaction. For the past five years, Gavin's most common facial expression resembled that of a girl riding a boy's bike and anxiously anticipating the bar biting into her crotch at each bump in the road.

After the dazzling dialectic of the sixties, the politically alienating 1970s had an adverse effect upon Gavin's gonads. Without any sense of mission, Gavin had lost heart. After fifteen years of running a public-interest law firm which had fought all the great equal rights fights of the sixties, Gavin and his partners now spent their time fighting inflation. As public and private grant money evaporated, Gavin had to accept boring civil cases which brought him little satisfaction and gradually diminished his organic capacity for orgasms.

When Gavin transferred his attention from world affairs to household ones, his sexual congestion seemed to increase in direct proportion to the disorder around the house. Every faulty fixture and ailing appliance disrupted Gavin's tranquility. Missing faucet handles, torn screens, loose window sashes, sticky doorknobs, jammed locks, broken lampcords, lame-legged chairs, wiggling bannisters and broken electrical appliances—needing now discontinued parts—enraged him. When he was not banging Coco on the bed, he was berating her about the condition of their home.

"Do you want to turn over for a while?" Gavin asked.

"Not yet," Coco answered coyly.

Of course, after so many years, Gavin knew Coco inside and out. Indeed, he had discovered the particular fail-proof position which triggered her orgasms and, after fathering four babies, took a practicing-gynecologist's interest in Coco's reproductive system. Basically he understood her particular pink organs—her periods, her pregnancies (false, tubal, complicated, or completed), her headaches, her bladder, uterine or Fallopian tube troubles and all her fungus or yeast infections. He had a protective, proprietory interest in all her gynecological conditions and the cures that had been prescribed.

Still, Coco knew it was Gavin's psychogenic aspermia that was creating a climate for cancer in Coco's cervix—a kind of cancer which she had never had to worry about before since it was a scientifically established, though still medically mystifying, fact that Jewish women showed the lowest incidence of cervical cancer in the U.S. What every Jewish woman knew—and what every Jewish doctor had psychologically repressed and suppressed—was the obvious fact that Jewish ladies didn't develop cervical cancer at the customary rate because Jewish husbands didn't irritate their wives' cervixes as frequently or forcibly as other ethnics, thus lessening the irritation down there and decreasing the women's chances not only of cancer but also of pleasure.

But Gavin's psychogenic aspermia—a form of impotence traditionally uncommon among circumcised couples of Jewish descent—was clearly a carcinogenic threat to Coco whose now battered cervix could easily be irritated into a precancerous condition which might metasticize and make her a statistical aberration which

14

would push the Jewish cervical cancer curve way up on the national charts.

Still, Coco conceded, sliding into a soft undulating total-torso twist, which she hoped would have a succoring, suctioning effect upon her husband, she really didn't have any right to complain about this particular health hazard since her life was packed full of other environmental risks, such as the stockpile of 2,555, to be exact, Ortho-Novum Sequential birth control pills which she had dutifully swallowed daily for seven years, along with all the Ortho Pharmaceutical Company assurances that those pills had been proven perfectly safe in a rampantly racist experiment carried on in Puerto Rico, where Coco's Hispanic sisters had been imperially subjugated and sequentially subjected to those carcinogenic contraceptives before their introduction into U.S. uteri.

And, gullible as Coco had been back in the early sixties, she believed all the pharmaceutical propaganda about the women of San Juan not suffering any detrimental effects from those Ortho-Novum Sequentials—and had never ever wondered whether that country's rather sluggish struggle toward independence might be a negative by-product of those bitter pills which possibly prevented the conception and birth of some Puerto Rican Che Guevera who might have liberated his island by now.

Coco looked up at her husband. Illuminated by the light of the crime prevention spot hinged to the window, Gavin looked as tired as if he had just finished his daily quota of fifty push-ups. Coco firmly believed her husband's prowess at push-ups was related to the fact he practiced appropriate warm-up exercises on top of her all night long so that he was always limber by morning. Coco also believed that the reason women couldn't do push-ups easily was because they were an exercise based on an exclusively male motion—an innately masculine movement—foreign to females who just naturally pushed upward from below in the opposite direction.

"You really are getting to be a stud," Coco whispered, nibbling on the fleshy part of Gavin's shoulder.

Gavin kissed her affectionately and then, with a sudden burst of renewed energy, unexpectedly propelled himself up Coco again with so much enthusiasm that their king-sized bed went skittering against the wall, banging into the rusted radiator that served as a pillow-prop when they read in bed.

"Jesus," Gavin groaned, idling inside her. "If we don't do something about this bed, we're going to roll right out the window, Coco. Don't these goddamn Hollywood frames have any brakes on them?"

"Well, there's a lock on each wheel," Coco explained, "but they don't work unless there's a rug on the floor."

"But we've *got* a rug on the floor," Gavin objected.

Coco didn't answer. She didn't have the heart to confess that the do-it-yourself-carpet squares, of a burnt umber color she'd selected because it wouldn't show cigarette burns, didn't continue beneath the bed because she had falsely economized by leaving that unseen area bare.

"Next week I'm going to get some wooden blocks from a lumber yard to jam under the wheels," Coco said solemnly. She felt especially bad about the bed being in perpetual motion since she had invested a great deal of time, money, and imagination at the Hecht

Company's January white sale where she had impetuously purchased thousands of square inches of daisy-design, form-fitted and flat, noniron sheets plus an $85 dollar dacron-filled, velvet-backed, color-coordinated comforter that now lay in a heap on the floor.

"Don't worry about going out to a lumber yard, Coco," Gavin said testily, "just take care of some of the other stuff."

He slid out of her like a stick of margarine melting on a stove.

"What other stuff?" Coco inquired, smoothing any snarl out of her voice.

"Aw, come on, Coco," Gavin groaned. "You promised you were going to get an eight gang, round-hole, push-button light-switch plate for the front hall."

"Well, I am," Coco said, "but all the new ones have rectangular openings for up and down switches, so I have to find a hardware store that carries antique fixtures from the 1920s."

"Well, while you're there, get a ceramic handle for the faucet in the second floor toilet," Gavin said, stretching out flat on his back a little farther away from her.

Tentatively Coco closed her legs, hoping that Gavin's impatience with her would prevent any further sexual contact.

"And don't forget the toaster," Gavin warned. "The damn crumbs keep catching on fire."

"Yes, I know," Coco said, "but the man at Dauber's thinks they can fix that." Superstitiously, Coco crossed both her fingers and her legs to ward off any fallout from her falsehood.

"And you've also got to find someone to reinforce the back porch stairs and put a lock on the gate and remount the mailbox before we lose some really important letters, Coco." Gavin's irritation and frustration were mounting. "And you've got to get someone to adjust the thermostat and give us an estimate for painting the bricks and dry-walling the basement and retarring the roof and flashing the gutters before the damn house collapses. Also we have got to get the plumbing fixed. It's possible we might even have to change all the pipes from lead to copper because the risers are leaking."

"I've been planning to do some of those things, Gavin. But it takes time to find all those different workmen and I am working under a deadline, you know. I mean, I have to finish the report by May 1."

"I know *you're* working, Coco," Gavin agreed condescendingly, "but absolutely nothing else around here is. The doorbell, the dishwasher, the garbage disposal, the vacuum, the mailbox . . . everything's broken. And the back bedroom ceiling is still leaking."

"I had the roofer repatch that section of the roof, Gavin."

"Yeah, I know, but it's *still* leaking, Coco."

"Well, what did you want me to do, Gavin? Rent a helicopter and hover over the house while he was up there to make sure he was fixing it right?"

"There has got to be a way, Coco. You promised you would take charge of getting all that stuff repaired."

"I know," Coco responded reluctantly, suppressing an urge to come back at him with some sexual countercharges. "But it happens to be harder than it sounds."

"And if someone takes a shower the water seeps between the tiles and drips through to the second floor which is going to bring down the ceiling and the chandelier. Also, you've got to get the hot water tank adjusted. There's hardly enough hot water for two showers in a row. And that's why the dishes come out of the dishwasher dirty and why I have those little black spots on all of my shirts."

Coco felt her upper right eyelid begin to tremble and the inside of both elbows begin to itch.

"Those little black dots on your shirts come from an oil leak in the Bendix engine, Gavin, *not* from the temperature of the water. That's why I take your shirts to the laundry now. But if you want to buy a new washing machine . . . that's up to you, Gavin. The fact of the matter is those spots only show up on white clothing."

Coco fell silent, convinced that any man who was a total failure in the upkeep and maintenance depart-ment—a man who had developed a dysfunction in his own sexual plumbing—had no right to act like a quality-control agent criticizing Coco's managerial efficiency. A man who never shut the door of an airconditioned room, who never turned off his stereo, his desk lamp, or the car radio, who had never successfully changed a diaper, a bulb, a spare, or an appointment, a man who didn't know how to set an alarm clock, an oven-timer, a delivery date, a dinner table, or a firm bedtime for the kids properly, certainly had a lot of chutzpah complain-ing about Coco's inefficiency.

Still Coco didn't really want to fight about it. One of her New Year's resolutions had been to stop quarreling with Gavin and to remember he was feeling spiritually bereaved during the last year of the decade—just like the rest of their generation who had once tasted glory and now hicupped trivia.

"Well, it just so happens that all my shirts are white, Coco," Gavin finally responded after an unreasonably long silence. "And we spend enough goddamn money on all those maintenance contracts that you should be able to keep the stuff in working order."

"But Gavin, someone has to be here to let the repair people in. GE and Sears and Woodies won't even tell you what time their service people are coming out. They won't even attempt to guess whether it will be A.M. or P.M."

"Well, I'll be glad when your job is finished," Gavin said nastily. "Then maybe you can get the house back in shape."

Coco decided not to make any recriminatory remarks about money, but she knew there wasn't enough cash to do the job right. Certainly Coco understood that her home was an unpolished gem, and that buried beneath heavy layers of dirty interior paint handsome brick walls and beautiful broad ceiling beams waited to be exposed. She was sure that beneath soiled window sills and doorframes luminous old wood strained to surface. Often she imagined lavish living spaces liberated by the removal of nonbearing walls which circumscribed cloisterish rooms. Convinced that some childless young couple would buy her house and replace its conventional supports with handsomely weathered, three-story-high telephone poles that would soar upward toward some still unemancipated cathedral ceiling, Coco hung onto her home and her hope of someday being able to afford to repair, restore, and renovate it—along with the rest of her dilapidated life.

Maybe that was why an affair with John Canada seemed so attractive. It could be executed immediately and didn't cost any money. In fact, one of the first things that had attracted Coco to Canada was his look of practical proficiency. Unlike Gavin, Canada was obviously a natural-born trouble shooter, which was probably why Jimmy Carter had selected him to replace the previous Council of Economic Advisors chairman who had been caught selling dope to several Cabinet members.

At times Coco was uncertain whether she wanted a lover or a repairman, but it was perfectly clear that John Canada would be a terrific man to have around the house. Certainly he would know where to insert and which way to turn a key to bleed a radiator. Clearly he, unlike Gavin, would know which bloated object down in the basement was the hot-water tank and where on its belly to find and adjust the delicate Hot-Hotter-Hottest knob. John Canada even looked like the kind of man who would know how to deal with the wasps' nest over the Burman's back door and the pigeons who lived inside Coco's bedroom air conditioner.

With a man like Canada, an affair could have positive practical benefits.

Silence enveloped the Burmans and surreptitiously Coco glanced over at her husband, thinking he had fallen asleep. Instead, she caught him looking at her with the speculative expression of a surfer eyeing an epic wave in anticipation of an exhilarating ride into shore. Without a word, he rolled over, relaunching the bed so that it drifted back into the wall once more, causing a loud crash as it upset the rusty water container hooked over the radiator to humidify the air—something Coco's mother insisted upon for health reasons.

Feeling sexually skittish for the moment, Coco relaxed and listened to the song inside her loins, but after a while Gavin's movements became monotonous and she recalled another descriptive passage from Dr. Reuben concerning P.A. or "psychogenic aspermia":

Everything about the man's sexual performance is
flawless except that he never ejaculates. Not only does
he fail to ejaculate, he never reaches orgasm. It is the
male equivalent of female frigidity. The erection is
rigid, sensation is more or less intact (except for sore-
ness after the first hour) but for the man there is no
end. Ironically, a man with P.A. is in the same sexual
boat as the one with absolute impotence—neither of
them can complete the sexual act.

Increasingly desperate, Coco twisted her torso tor-
ridly against Gavin's body hoping to overcome his re-
sistance to petting which stemmed from his fear of finding a lump in one of Coco's breasts. But Gavin ignored
her silent invitation to diversify the action and main-
tained his repetitious, rhythmic routine.

In a last-ditch effort to organize an orgasm for him,
Coco initiated a hula-hoop hip action interspersed
with little pelvic burps, while she wondered if the fruit-
less friction of flesh rubbing against the new contour
sheet might cause it to fray. Indeed, it was clear that
the quilted mattress cover that she had bought (defiantly rejecting the rubberized style her mother recommended for economy and super-protection against
sperm spots or unexpected nocturnal flash floods of
menstrual blood), was superfluous since there was a
much greater danger of the new linens wearing out
than of Gavin staining their brand new Beautyrest.

Rising up to grind against Gavin's groin, Coco considered the possibility of putting the mattress cover on
top of the bottom sheet, rather than beneath it, so as to
preserve her new set of linens, but she quickly rejected
the idea, realizing such an improvision might deflate
Gavin's already low confidence quotient.

"Gavin, I'm getting a little sleepy, honey," Coco said.

"Aren't you ready for another one," he inquired softly. "Do you want to get on the pillow?"

"Oh, no," Coco protested, gripping the edge of the mattress to secure herself. "I really couldn't, Gav. Really, I've had it."

"Oh, come on," he cajoled, trying to turn her over as if rolling up a rug to be sent out to Bergmann's for drycleaning.

"No, please," Coco protested. "I mean it."

The authenticity of her desperation returned Gavin to his original abrasive assembly-line attacks. Depressed, Coco began to wonder if she and Gavin would remain locked together in an eternal embrace like Happy and the male cocker spaniel from across the alley who had gotten stuck in a post-coital spasm that necessitated Coco telephoning the fire department to send out an engine so the fireman could separate the dogs with a cruel stream of ice-cold water from their high-pressure hose.

"I just don't know what's the matter," Gavin complained. "I can't understand what's the matter with me." He sounded quite exhausted even though he was still rubbing Coco's vaginal walls like an earnest archeological student on a summer dig.

"Actually I think it's because of the bed," Coco commiserated kindly. "I think it's the bed moving around that's causing our problems."

"It's not *your* problem," Gavin assured her.

"Well, if I'm not part of the solution, I'm part of the problem," Coco quipped bravely, remembering Dr. Reuben's positive prognosis for people with psychogenic aspermia: "The one advantage for the P.A. sufferer is that with expert psychiatric help, normal sexual functioning can be restored rapidly. Curing other forms of impotence may take longer." Although Coco often recited those reassuring words to herself, she didn't dare suggest Gavin see a shrink since he was firmly opposed to psychiatry on the grounds it was elitist, extravagant, and ineffective.

"Anyway, if this is a problem, I'm all for it," Coco said seductively, as she began to accelerate her hips and rotate her bottom more robustly.

Somewhat reassured, Gavin increased his tempo for a while but, after a few minutes, the momentum slackened and though he was still breathing more briskly, nothing happened.

Coco sighed. Her thighs were sore from being stretched apart and the backs of her knees ached from pumping, just like when she pedaled her bike up a steep hill. Tossing her head, as if in a paroxysm of passion, Coco looked at the illuminated alarm clock on the bedside table. It was almost two o'clock and there was still no sign of success. How would she get up at six to get herself ready for the Big Day? How would she prepare herself for her big seduction scene without any sleep?

Suddenly Gavin gripped Coco's shoulders and began hurtling himself against whatever psychic barrier was blocking him. Hovering above her with intimate sounds of excitement, he put the bed and ceiling into motion again as he began moving more and more quickly.

"Oh, Gavin, I really do love you," Coco assured him, carefully aiming her words into his sexually sensitive left ear.

Then, as usual, when it started to happen, it happened so quickly that it seemed absolutely effortless,

24

and a moment later Gavin collapsed beside Coco with a look of surprised satisfaction on his face.

A few minutes later—just like in the movies—they fell asleep with their arms entwined about each other, looking exactly as if they were going to live happily ever after.

# CHAPTER TWO

The alarm clock rang at six.

Shivering, Coco sat up, retrieved her nightgown from the floor and pushed her feet inside the slippers that she compulsively parked beside the bed to avoid walking barefoot in the dark and smashing any unseen dog doo-doo into a flat tortilla beneath her feet. Moving quietly so as not to awaken Gavin, Coco walked down the unlit hallway to the bathroom, turned on the light, gathered her nightgown up around her waist, and sat down on the ice-cold toilet seat.

The bathroom was a mess. Committed to cleaning everything within arms reach while sitting on the toilet, Coco collected some discarded underwear, crumpled towels, and wet washcloths off the floor to toss inside the open hamper. Then she removed a flat blob of toothpaste, stuck like a mint Lifesaver to the side of the sink, and dropped it between her legs into the toilet. Bending sideways, she dislodged a stale slice of pink sponge from beneath her claw-footed bathtub and ran it along the ledge of the sink, collecting all the evenly cut whiskers Gavin had left strewn across the porcelain like freshly mown grass flung off a lawnmower.

Upset by such untidiness, Coco tugged at the tail of the toilet paper so impatiently that the roller went whirling into orbit, cascading the remaining tissue onto the floor. Groaning, she released the wooden rod from its niche, set aside the empty cardboard cylinder to save for Nicky, who used the empties as model-car filling-station pumps, and excavated a fresh roll of paper from the reserve depot beneath the sink. Then, compressing the spring, Coco wedged the refilled gadget back into the wall with a silent curse.

She was sick of maintenance and upkeep.

Spending her mid-late thirties in the mid-late seventies working, running errands, and trying to keep her small electrical appliances alive was just too demeaning. Turning twenty in 1960 had been perfect, for that kept internal and external demands in sync. Even becoming thirty in 1970 had seemed appropriate, but the Carter era had produced only menopausal politics and the thought of turning forty in 1980 was terribly distressing to Coco. The constant demands of her job, home, and family had deleted any passionate mystery or meaning from her life. Working at the Social Science Institute all day and then rushing home to cook dinner, clean the kitchen, help with the kid's homework, and administer to her husband's needs had totally depleted her energy and imagination.

The seventies had been so sterile that Coco's vitality was evaporating and it was clear she needed an exciting adventure to restore her natural vigor.

After flushing the toilet and jiggling the chain to stop the rush of water, she stationed herself in front of the medicine chest mirror which sported a spray of suspicious looking spots. As Coco's eldest son approached adolescence, the vanilla blots on the bathroom looking-glass increased in height, diameter, and density. Reluctantly, Coco rinsed the whiskers off the sponge and began to wipe away the toothpaste and other unhygienic sprinkles that soiled her reflection just as the general disarray of her home spoiled her self-image.

The windshield wiper strokes of her hand across the

glass reminded Coco of a marooned motorist flagging down help for a disabled vehicle. In fact, she seemed to be sending out dainty distress signals from her self to her reflection.

Leaning closer to the now clean mirror, Coco inspected herself critically, but finally concluded that fatigue had lent a certain existential elegance to her features. Stress and strain was illuminating her like a soft spotlight on an Italian actress in some grainy, grey, post–World War II movie. Coco was definitely acquiring that textured quality which one could view either as weary exhaustion or sexual magnetism depending upon the subtitles.

Pleased, she shook her head theatrically to flare out the framing edge of her long black hair and smiled in a particular way so that the wrinkles around her eyes crinkled up inside the laugh lines.

There.

Now if she'd just remember her recent New Year's resolution to dismiss frivolous First Worldly concerns about weight and age she'd be all right.

Absently, Coco riffled through the Wisconsin cheddar cheese jar which held the family bouquet of toothbrushes.

All she had to do was adopt an affirmative attitude, a mature approach, and a positive sense of direction to make John Canada succumb to her mature charms.

Inflating several deep dents from the midriff of the Colgate toothpaste, which bore above its brand name the magic-marked autograph of Michael Burman (proving Mike had actually brought back home, unlike his clothing, the same toothpaste he took to camp), Coco brushed her teeth.

Then she bent over the old-fashioned bathtub to remove the loosely woven web of human hair that covered the drain like a small imported area rug and tossed it into the toilet. Perching on the sulky lip of the ledge, Coco turned on the water and began to erase the rings running around the circumference, unconsciously identifying them like a forest ranger dating a tree. Since Gavin was heavier and displaced more water than the kids, his circular signature, punctuated by several commas of pubic hairs left high and dry after the water drained out, ran around the top of the tub, while the other rings descended according to the size of each child.

Although usually upset by such marked inconsideration, Coco decided that the chance to take a bath and make herself squeaky clean for John Canada was worth the work. Also, since she was leaving an hour earlier than usual, Gavin had to launch the children, so she felt that cleaning up the tub repaid him in advance for his substitute services.

Too impatient to wait for the tub to fill up, Coco climbed in after several inches of water had accumulated. Then, from her new perspective, she involuntarily inventoried the deterioration of the lower half of the bathroom and studied the paint peeling off the tiles around the toilet where male members of the family constantly splattered a strong spray of spirited urine drops.

Coco could hardly believe the paint was coming off the floor, for it was only six months since she had conscientiously tried to improve the house cosmetically and economically by painting it totally white. Determined to eliminate the disorder that triggered most of the Burman's marital squabbles, Coco had made a monumental effort to get her domestic act together and initiated a massive cleanup campaign during the first, still sultry days of September. Drafting her children into duty, Coco assigned them areas to paint, according to their heights, so that Josh did the floorboards, Nicky and Jessica the bottom halves of walls, Mike all the woodwork, and Coco the upper walls and ceilings with a roller attached to an extension pole.

Gradually, fingerprints, food marks, shoe scuffs, toy and trike gouges, sprinkle spots from shook-up Cokes, crayon scrawls and wall drawings (which offered circumstantial evidence as to the identity of each artist), inkblots, Scotch-tape marks, dimples from bouncing balls, craters from champagne corks catapulted into the ceiling, bike-fender dents, unused picture hooks, nail-holes, Wackypack-sticker stains and other sore spots disappeared beneath uneven, but heavy coats of white paint. By the end of the week the Burman house looked clean except for the floors, where paint had sprinkled off the rollers, the glass window panes, which had gotten smeared, and the bathtub, into which Coco had dripped while painting the ceiling and neglected to clean until the spots had dried into Braille-like bumps that hurt the children's bottoms when they bathed. Now the paint was coming off where it was supposed to stay, while still clinging to places it didn't belong.

After a quick wash, Coco wrapped herself in a bath-towel and hurried back into the bedroom. In the dark she burrowed through her bureau, kinetically hunting for a pair of relatively new underpants, and then pulled her black corduroy jumpsuit out of the closet. Dressed, she carried her boots so as not to wake the children as she hurried down the stairs, snagging her kneehigh nylons on the rough nailheads that erupted like poison ivy from the floorboards each winter when the wood contracted from the cold.

The first-floor hallway was crowded with ten-speed bikes the kids had left leaning against any convenient wall or chained to the stair banister as a precaution against home burglaries. Coco pulled on her boots, retrieved her thriftshop fur jacket from the pile of coats on the hall chest, and then plodded through the foyer where generations of outgrown baby and toddler boots still mingled with contemporary ones.

A scarf of bitterly cold winter wind wound around her as she stepped outside. There was a sense of snow in the air, and Coco inhaled deeply as she hurried along the icy ribbon of sidewalk, tieing back the red-brick Victorian rowhouses, hunting for the Burman's car which Gavin had parked in some unknown place late the night before. Keeping alert for any early-morning muggers who might take advantage of daylight savings time, Coco jogged up to 19th Street and then retraced her path back to 18th where she finally saw her 1971 teal-blue Monte Carlo Chevrolet. Quickly unhooking the combination bicycle lock she used to secure the front hood against battery thieves, Coco climbed inside, shoved the chain beneath the driver's seat, and turned on the ignition.

While waiting for the engine to warm up, Coco noticed that the fuel gauge hadn't moved. Hoping it was stuck from the cold, she knocked on its plastic cover but the marker remained stationary.

"Shit," Coco cursed, outraged that Gavin had left her an empty gas tank.

Seething with resentment, she sped down 18th Street to the Rock Creek Park Gulf service station on Columbia

Road where a legion of foreign students was standing around the gas pumps. The shortest of the three men, a dusty brown Iranian student from Howard University, detached himself from the group and trotted over to Coco's car as soon as she cut off the engine. He was wearing a pair of Levis and a plaid lumber jacket over his Gulf coveralls so his stocky body looked shorter and squatter than usual. Reluctantly, Coco rolled down her side window.

"Hi, Izzat," she said.

"How you been?" Izzat asked, inspecting Coco's face with his petrol-black eyes.

Since Izzat had worked at the station for several years, Coco knew he felt compelled to flirt with female customers and to tease any little children tucked in the back seats of the cars he serviced.

"You want regular . . . or super?" he asked, sounding like an obscene caller phoning long distance from the Middle East.

"Just regular," Coco answered briskly.

Izzat disappeared and then reappeared in Coco's outside rearview mirror, rounding the back of her car with the gasoline hose extended in front of his groin like the squared-off organ of an Arabian stallion. Slowly he inserted the nozzle into an invisible, but intimate, orifice somewhere along the rear flank of Coco's left fender and locked it firmly in place. Smiling, he moved around to the front of the car and raised the hood as if he were lifting up and looking under Coco's skirt.

Coco gnawed her bottom lip. Obviously her illicit intentions toward John Canada had heightened her sexual sensibilities so that in her overstimulated state even the most innocent of objects—the normally neuter nozzle of a gasoline hose—took on the qualities of a circumcised phallic symbol. Sexually entranced, Coco watched Izzat slide the dipstick up and down inside her oil tank. Finally he extracted the stick and, tenderly wrapping a dirty rag around it, gently slid it up and down between his fingers with the distant air of a man jerking off.

Beneath her corduroy jumpsuit and fur jacket, Coco felt a neurodermatological itch in the crook of her left elbow. Her recently diagnosed case of eczema was acting up just as her dermatologist had predicted when he explained that the skin was the body's largest organ and extremely sensitive to stress. Certainly Coco's eczema was a symptom of the seventies—although not as serious a reaction as Gavin's psychogenic aspermia. Still, it made Coco wonder how she could consummate her affair with John Canada if she had an angry red rash rushing around her largest organ.

Izzat plunged the oil dip back into the tank once more and then walked around to Coco's window.

"Your oil dip just broke," he reported, extending the amputated stump forward for her inspection.

"Where's the other half?" Coco asked.

"I think it's in the tank."

"Can't you get it out?"

"Nope."

Coco felt anger gather in her chest like a storm.

Looking over at Izzat's two compatriots still standing beneath the Gulf Oil standard, she saw the taller man check the zipper of his coverall fly and hitch his genitals from one side of the crotch seam to the other.

Coco decided not to make a fuss.

"Okay, Izzat. Just get me a new one. I'll buy a new one."

"We don't carry Monte Carlo dipsticks here," Izzat

33

said soberly. "You have to order one from the Chevrolet company."

"I just don't believe it," Coco complained bitterly. "I've never even heard of a dipstick breaking ever before. If you hadn't been . . . messing around with it, this wouldn't have happened."

"You're also down a quart," he announced.

"How would you know?" Coco asked coldly, suddenly understanding America's obsessive urge to achieve self-sufficiency in gas and oil production. "How can you measure it with only half a stick?"

Izzat retucked his heavyweight lumberjacket into the waist of his Levis, took an oilcan off the top of a pyramid display pile, and made another big production of inserting a funnel into the oil tank. Then he began wiping the windshield with a paper towel, looking into Coco's face as frequently as possible, until he reached the lower, right-hand corner of the window where the Burman's D.C. Motor Vehicle inspection card was glued. There he began to gesticulate toward the permit with exaggerated excitement.

"What's the matter now?" Coco called through her window.

"Did you know your deadline is the 26th? That's Monday. Don't you want us to check out your brakes and wheel alignment before you take it through inspection?"

"Oh, shit," Coco groaned looking at the date punched out on the sticker. Did she really have to worry about passing a municipal motor vehicle test on Monday when she had so many other things on her mind? Did she really have to get into that endlessly long line of cars crawling through the inspection center where she would, most certainly, fail some item on the check-list? Now? Right when she had so much to do?

"Can your mechanic check it today?" she asked with grim resignation.

"Oh, sure. For you—anything."

"OK, Izzat. I'll leave it and come back after work." Coco signed the Gulf charge slip and then left her car, with the keys in the ignition, in front of the garage door.

Now totally disoriented by the unexpected loss of transportation, Coco walked along 18th Street trying to avoid the sluggish stream of suburban traffic splattering slush against parked cars and pedestrians. Eventually a taxi already carrying three rush-hour passengers picked Coco up and, after pursuing a circuitous route, finally deposited her on Massachusetts Avenue.

Cutting across the driveway of the Brookings Institute, Coco hurried into the adjacent building. The main reception area of the Social Science Institute was still empty and Coco felt grateful that she could avoid any pretense of joy at the sight of the plump receptionist who spent the day pulling the long rubbery teats of the switchboard like a milkmaid.

Plucking a deck of pink telephone message slips out of her mailbox, Coco hurried down the central hall, double-breasted with offices, reading her messages until she reached the sanctuary of her own cubicle. Then, slamming shut the door, she sat down at her desk which was piled high with chapters of the National Infelicity Index.

"Hi."

Diana Whitcomb inserted her blown-dry blond head into the office.

"Hi," Coco answered, picking up a mimeographed copy of the January 23, 1979, Board of Directors' meeting agenda that had been left atop her desk.

"Guess what I'm going to do?" Diana said, sinking into the visitor's chair and looking at Coco with the cool competitive eyes of a college coed tracking some sorority sister's tan at the beach. Diana was always inspecting Coco for signs of weight gain, split ends or uncoordinated separates—a scrutiny based both on hostility and admiration.

"What are you going to do?" Coco asked suspiciously.

Despite all her fervent feminist feelings, Coco had never liked Diana Whitcomb's well-washed-Waspy good looks and manners. Indeed, Coco resented the elegantly emaciated, emancipated young woman who was a decade younger and a generation different from her. Diana Whitcomb was the perfect product of the Women's Movement—an unencumbered young woman, opportunistically using her position as Lionel Hearndon's administrative assistant to establish her career while practicing marriage with a series of progressively more attractive partners.

"I'm going to invite the Board and our whole staff over to my apartment for a wine and cheese party after the meeting today," Diana announced.

"Oh. That sounds nice," Coco said thoughtfully.

"I'm going to leave here around four to get everything ready," Diana continued with consummate confidence.

"Well, maybe I can break away a little early and come by to help you," Coco offered, since Diana had unwittingly solved Coco's problem. An intimate gathering at Diana's apartment would afford Coco the chance to make a move on Canada in a congenial setting. "What's your address?"

The telephone rang and Coco picked up the receiver. "Hello?"

"I'd really appreciate it if you would come early," Diana said, scribbling her address on a piece of paper which she shoved across the desk to Coco.

"Coco?"

It was Gavin.

"Hi."

"Bye, bye," Diana said, as she slipped out through the doorway.

"What's wrong?" Coco asked.

"Nothing serious," Gavin answered reassuringly. "I just can't find any student bus tokens. Do you know where they are?"

Coco looked at the clock. It was 8:15.

"There's probably some down in the lint catcher of the clothes drier," she said. "They fall out of the kid's jeans pockets while they're drying. Tell Jessica or Nicky to run down to the basement and look." She felt mildly irritated that on a morning when she had work to finish before the Board meeting everyone was conspiring to delay her. "But listen, Gavin. It's really getting slippery outside. Tell the kids to wear their boots and to put some kosher salt in their coat pockets so they can sprinkle it ahead of their feet if they have to run across Connecticut Avenue to catch the bus. It's getting late and it's already very icy."

"God, Coco, you know they won't do that," Gavin said irritably. "Anyway Nicky wants to know if we have any striped paper."

Coco sighed. "Yes. There's some lined notebook filler on top of the ironing board in the pantry. And please remind Jessica to take her gym shorts to school. They're on my desk. Oh, Gavin," Coco said casually, "Diana Whitcomb is having a cocktail party for the staff and the Board people right after the meeting, and I think I should stop by there for a little while because she asked me to help her."

"You mean you're not coming home after work?"

"Well, I was wondering if you could get home a little early today and start supper. Diana just decided to have the party this morning which is why I didn't know about it before."

There was a long, heavy pause from Gavin. "OK, Coco, I'll have to change an appointment but I can get back around five."

"Great, Gav. Thanks," Coco said.

He hung up.

Quickly Coco gathered her possessions and hurried down the hall to the little room where the huge IBM machine stood winking its red "Ready" eye. Setting down her stack of papers and clearing space on which to collate final copies, she inserted her first page into the machine. With the copies dial at 1 and the size on "legal," Coco pushed the A button and watched the paper drift under the lip of the IBM. Expectantly she waited for the familiar electronic sound of reproduction.

Silence.

Nothing happened.

The page had slid inside the machine and disappeared without initiating any organic reproductive clatter. As the intimidating "call key operator" sign lit up, demanding the expert services of a trained technician, the door opened.

David Macintosh, the thirty-year-old research director of the National Infelicity Index project, appeared, holding a pile of papers and looking upset at finding the IBM in use.

"Oh, hi, David," Coco smiled.

David walked inside. Although he didn't carry a purse, he still exuded a smug air of homosexual superiority that made Coco feel gross in his presence. Despite the fact that Coco considered David the best and brightest person at the Social Science Institute, she found him sexually confusing and was glad he spent his lunch hours rewriting his Harvard Ph.D. dissertation into a textbook so she didn't have to eat with him.

"Are you just beginning?" he asked, with the plaintive expression of a single golfer aching to play through a foursome.

"Yes, but the damn machine won't start," Coco complained.

"Here, let me see," David suggested. "It might just be out of paper."

Coco gratefully stepped aside to make room, although David had no trouble slipping through the narrow corridor of space between Coco and the IBM since he virtually had no hips.

Coco leaned across the machine, letting her breasts rest on the surface like an extra pair of elbows, while she watched David wrestle with the giant paper roller. When the clamp sprang open it shook the machine violently and David, inadvertently looking up, saw Coco's mammary flesh vibrating atop the IBM cover. Inevitably, Coco's breasts, like two children from a previous marriage determined to disrupt a new relationship, had a way of disturbing David. Straightening up, she moved away from the machine until David finished reloading it.

"Coco, there's something I've been wanting to talk to you about," he said, surreptitiously moving into loading position and sliding his papers on top of Coco's. "The Self-Reports of Satisfaction and Happiness figures I finished this week are a lot higher than I expected." He began inserting his papers into the IBM. "I have the feeling they were much lower when I spot-checked the returns, state by state, back last fall. Remember those random samples we looked at?"

Coco nodded and sat down on a large cardboard carton of duplicating paper. One of the things that had been troubling her over the past few months was the discrepancy between the professed happiness of the American people, as reflected in the National Infelicity Index, and the obvious unhappiness of everyone she knew. Unable to explain the contradiction, Coco had tried to ignore her doubts and chalked up her discomfort to the fact that she was a dissatisfied consumer and disaffected citizen whose discontent discolored her view of the universe.

Anyway, since Coco had only been hired to translate David Macintosh's Harvardese into English, she didn't feel responsible for the validity of the study. Basically, Coco's 1960-ish skepticism about statistics made her disapprove of the five-million dollar, five-year-long national survey on which she was working. When she had first started editing the report she felt she was helping to expose serious social problems that would confirm the need for political change, but lately —because of what she considered the misleading nature of the questions asked by the interviewers—she had begun to feel like an apologist for the system.

Aware of the enormous impact the report would have on the public, Coco was scrupulously careful about her editing, wary of altering any meanings, even though she felt as if she were participating in a whitewash. Basically the study reflected Lionel Hearndon's vision-less viewpoint and sought exotic, rather than obvious, causes for ordinary unhappiness. The Social Science Institute's National Infelicity Index ignored the fact that the entire United States' social system was out of order.

"I still haven't correlated this batch against our Be-havioral Measures for Function and Adjustment," David continued unhappily. "But compared to other subjec-tive social indicators on satisfaction and happiness these figures seem way too high. I mean—given the low per capita GNP, the high rate of unemployment, the inflation that's strapping the middle class, and all the other social and political disasters of the past five years—I simply can't believe our national infelicity rate is so low. I mean—this is all post-Watergate and nobody seems very upset about the state of the nation. Besides, the Self-Reports just don't jibe with the Job Satisfaction and Attitudes Toward Violence and Racial Feelings questionnaires we finished correlating before Christ-mas."

Coco nodded again.

"Measures of Perceived Life Quality usually corre-late with Economic Indicators and Class Locators. I just don't understand," David said fretfully. "I'm beginning to wonder if Hearndon's been messing around with the numbers." He shook his head disbelievingly. "I suppose I should have one of the interns run all my stats through the computer once more this afternoon to see if I might have screwed up on the programming."

"But why would Lionel want to make the numbers look good?" Coco asked. "Why would he want the report to show Americans are happier than they really are?"

"Shee-it, I don't know," David shrugged. "I don't understand it either. Maybe somebody bought him off. Maybe Mobil Oil or the National Endowment for the Humanities wanted a High Felicity response for the money they gave us," David said, still speeding sheets of paper through the machine.

"Well, maybe you should mention it to someone on the Board," Coco said. "Diana's inviting everyone over for cocktails after the meeting. Maybe you can talk to John Canada or Jamin Benn or Noah Annan about it."

"Yeah, that's what I was thinking," David said, inserting the last page of his papers into the IBM. "But I'll have one of the interns rerun the stuff so I'll know more by this evening. Anyway, we should get down to the conference room because Lionel wants to talk to us before the Board gets here."

Coco collected her unfinished work and walked beside David back to the woodpaneled conference room where she took a chair at the large round table. Lionel Hearndon was already seated, waiting impatiently for his staff to gather. An upperclass, married but childless, humorless, and ambitious man, Hearndon was a classic careerist—humble with his superiors and haughty toward his inferiors. He looked upon his staff with indelible disdain.

"What I wanted to say," he began, leaning against the table, "is that the objective of this Board meeting is to finesse any potential opposition to our Infelicity Index *before* its publication." He looked around with a patronizing, paternalistic smile that instantly revived all of Coco's ancient adolescent resentments. "The more academic artillery we can defuse in advance, the bet-

ter chance we have of launching the Index successfully." He flashed his private-club profile at his staff
as he turned to assure himself that no outsiders had
entered the room. "Anybody see any reasons why we
shouldn't be able to accomplish that here today?"

No one responded, but that was unsatisfactory.
Hearndon didn't look pleased.

"Are all the Board members going to receive advance
copies of the report?" David finally asked, to fill up the
expectant lull.

"Of course," Hearndon nodded his grey head.

Coco sank back in her chair feeling relieved and
reprieved. Ever since she had been put on the Social
Science Institute staff—to do the same thing she'd done
as a consultant only at twice the pay—she felt obliged
to accommodate and placate Lionel Hearndon who now
represented all the authority figures in her life whom
she'd ever hated.

"I also plant to stress that our Index is accurate
enough to predict as well as measure social infelicity,"
Lionel Hearndon continued. "If we can convince the
Board of that—then we'll have it made."

He sat down.

Coco smoothed her hair in anticipation of John Canada's arrival.

# CHAPTER THREE

When the receptionist opened the door to admit the first Board members, Lionel Hearndon got up to greet them. The ingratiating expression that raced across his face reminded Coco of her gynecologist, Dr. Luis Armando, who went rushing from one examination room to the next trying to meet new feminist demands for personalized pelvics without cutting back on his caseload. Just like Dr. Armando, Lionel Hearndon stretched himself schizophrenically thin, trying to foster an air of favoritism through a political veneer of impartiality.

Both Luis Armando and Lionel Hearndon made Coco feel crazy.

Gradually the fourteen Social Science Institute Board members straggled into the conference room. Most of them were white, middle-aged men with long faces and well-cut hair curving over the collars of their tweed sports jackets. Morosely, Coco looked at the clean-shaven landscape of faces, remembering the hairier sixties when men wore beards and braids and tried to shake off their market-oriented, career-conscious hang-ups. Unfortunately, now during the seventies, as the men reached middle age, they regressed back to their original 1950 adolescent selves so that once again they were leading dull lives with deadly seriousness.

John Canada was the last Board member to arrive. Apart from his current political prominence, his physical height put him head and shoulders above the others. He was a handsomely weathered, outdoor type with wide shoulders, enormous hands, and well-developed forearms which bulged beneath a Navy surplus sweater.

After greeting the other Board members with a marshmallow white smile that sliced through the toasted crust of his tanned face, he looked over at Coco.

Instantly she felt a blush rise to her face.

It was clear that John Canada was sexually interested in Coco Burman. Despite the fact that slim, svelte Diana Whitcomb was sitting nearby, Canada chose to focus on Coco, confirming her recent observation that women of her age offered older men the same sort of attractions as a favorite pair of old blue jeans—a bit faded, stretched-out and baggy in places, but still preferable to brand-new ones which inevitably felt stiff and crept up to irritate the crotch.

Outside the windows a soft flaky snow began to fall and the room felt cozily collegiate as Lionel rose to welcome the Board. First he read the agenda, emphasizing that administrative matters were to be treated perfunctorily so that the entire afternoon session could be devoted to discussion of the Social Science Institute's National Infelicity Index. Then he turned the meeting over to the chairman of his Board.

John Canada rose to his feet causing Coco's heart to flutter. His casual country style evoked instant images of backpacks and mountain trails, bonfires and zippered sleeping bags, private planes and polo ponies. Pushing his sweater sleeves up over his elbows, so that everyone could see the light blue trolleytracks of his veins creeping over the mountains of his muscles,

45

and assuming the classic classroom slouch that was the trademark of a tenured teacher, Canada cupped his huge hairy hands around the microphone.

Coco felt a swarm of sexual feelings.

John Canada had thick blunt fingers that looked like precision instruments designed both for proficiency and pleasure. He was clearly a home-fixer as well as a home-wrecker, a handyman as well as a hand-jobber. As he advanced gracefully through the agenda, it became clear why President Carter had named him chairman of the Council of Economic Advisors. John Canada was a classy conservative with the style of a sexy actor and the authority of a skilled director. Between items of business he rubbed the long aluminum stem of the mike with his rough, calloused hands, casting a spell over Coco.

A soft smile stirred her lips. She really liked John Canada. If anyone could, he would be able to make the trivia of Coco's life recede so that joy would rise up within her like a phoenix once again. Lawrencian feelings would irrigate and enrich her soul as she was subsumed by a reckless, irresponsible affair. Rendezvous would relieve the tedium of her days and passion would obliterate any anxieties about her nearest and dearest. Romance would replace responsibilities and make Coco forget about the messiness of her homelife.

At 12:30 two of the stenographers brought in platters of sandwiches and cans of softdrinks. Everyone remained seated while they ate. After lunch Lionel Hearndon rose to speak again. Pompously promising that the National Infelicity Index would set the tone for social scientific research during the coming decade, he then described in a scholarly way how the interviews had been structured, how various measures had been

46

developed to determine infelicity rates within specific societal sectors, and how the survey had been conducted.

Letting Lionel's words wash over her, Coco looked out the window at the falling snow and wondered whether the storm would create drifts on the roof which might bring down the Burmans' tired drainpipe or ruin the recent repatching job. Then she began to wonder whether the city buses would continue running since everything in Washington stopped at the first flurry of flakes. If the buses stopped, how would the children get home from school? Had all of them been able to find sets of mittens with appropriately opposable thumbs? Would Mike remember to pick up Josh? And what if Nicky forgot his house key? How would he retrieve the extra emergency one, buried beneath the azalea bush in the backyard, if the ground was frozen and covered with snow? How would the storm affect the delicate ecology of their coordinated schedules?

Disheartened, Coco glanced over at John Canada.

He was looking at her, but didn't flinch when their eyes met. His obvious infatuation bloated Coco with an almost forgotten sense of boldness—creating the same effect as some top hit tune from a distant teenage summer that instantly evoked a mindless rush of indiscriminately romantic dreams and desires.

How lovely it would be to be involved again—to feel anxiously inadequate, beautifully demented. How delicious it would be to ache and yearn, long and lech for a lover.

Coco returned her gaze to Lionel Hearndon, but her heart was pounding impractically.

"The Social Science Institute's Infelicity Index, along with Gross National Product figures, could provide a universal instrument for determining how basic human needs are being met across the world," Lionel promised. "This is a megabreakthrough in survey research and will reshape the national welfare priorities of the Carter administration. Our Index will serve as the basic outline for any new federal programs aimed at relieving, or alleviating, areas of national infelicity. And," he concluded after a long momentous pause, "the government, the media, and the prestigious Board gathered around this table will be *amazed* to discover that America's citizens are considerably happier than conventionally believed."

What a crock of shit—Coco thought, as a round of enthusiastic applause erupted around the room. —What a throwback to the fucked-up Fifties.—

Impulsively Lionel extended his arm toward David Macintosh to acknowledge the wonderful job being done by his research director. There was another enthusiastic ovation. Then Lionel pointed at Coco and said that under Ms. Burman's editorial supervision the report would be published before the May first deadline. A slightly softer, although still charitable, wave of applause rippled through the conference room.

And then suddenly John Canada was on his feet, clapping his huge hairy hands with unwarranted enthusiasm. After an embarrassed pause, his clapping ignited another ovation on Coco's behalf and, flattered and flustered, she elevated her buttocks an inch off the chair before sinking back deeper into her seat. There was no longer any doubt about it. John Canada was announcing personal, rather than professional, approval of Coco Burman, and his applause escalated his infatuation into a public event.

Finally the clapping subsided.

48

A moment later Diana Whitcomb stood up to announce her cocktail party and then left after dispatching a meaningful look at Coco to remind her of her promise.

At 5:00 P.M. Coco slipped out of the conference room, stopped to reclaim her jacket from her office and hurried outside into the snowy streets to find a taxi.

Diana opened the door of her co-op-turned-condo apartment.

"Oh, hi, Coco, I'm so glad you came early."

Even from the hallway it was apparent that Diana's entire apartment was done in ultra-hygienic white-on-white. The floors were bare, their bright polyurethane sheen interrupted only by an occasional, expensive, Mexican rug. White burlap cloth covered the chubby, mod-modular couches, and a flock of toss pillows, clothed in an assortment of Marimekko prints, picked up the hot accent colors of the art deco lampshades and pop art posters. Growing from natural-straw baskets fastened to the ceiling, glamourously green ferns offered a silent rebuke to Coco whose own hanging plants remained inside their pots like undescended testicles.

"Take off your coat," Diana suggested.

Coco hung her jacket over a bright enamel hook on the white hall wall and followed Diana through the immaculate living room into the kitchen, which had a stained-glass window, a skylight, and an odorless, smokeless, multicolored-flame chemical log burning in a huge brick fireplace. Everything was in perfect order. Everything was pretty. Everything matched.

The kitchen table was a professionally dipped and stripped industrial spool surrounded by six soda chairs

49

painted a navyblue. The trashcan was a wicker basket painted to match the chairs and the navyblue cookware hanging on a pegboard above the stove. A little postage scale, apparently used for weighing calories, and an interesting British biscuit tin converted into a breadbox had also been painted with a high-gloss, blue enamel to coordinate with everything else. Even the push pins, holding scissors-cut recipes from the *New York Times* and rooms torn out of *Better Homes and Gardens* on the bulletin board, were navy blue.

"I was just finishing this tray," Diana said, standing back to admire the regiments of paper-thin low-caloric Norwegian crackers encircling several huge hunks of nonprocessed natural cheese on a wooden serving board.

Coco looked at the spotless wine glasses waiting on the table alongside gallon jugs of red and white Gallo, unlit candles and large baskets filled with fruits, candy, and expensive nuts.

Of course, Coco thought resentfully. Of course Diana's kitchen would be clean enough to eat out of. It had all the charming karma of any childless home where guests would never find a bite missing from the bottom of a rosy apple, empty peanut shells mixed back in with the uncracked nuts, or small toothprints marring a piece of chocolate candy that had been tasted, rejected, and recklessly replaced in the box. No, Diana would never discover her candle wicks buried beneath a mess of molten wax or watch her tabletop blister beneath big blobs of tallow that bled through dents or holes bored by restless children around the rims of chubby candles.

"What should I do?" Coco asked, trying to sound enthusiastic.

"Why don't you fill up the sugar bowl?" Diana suggested.

Coco opened the appropriate early-American canister and found a pure unmarred mountain of white sugar inside.

Why not?—Coco thought bitterly.

She should have known Diana wouldn't have to stash her staples in the wrong containers because of an imbalance in the familial supply-and-demand cycle that caused a chaotic mislabeling among Coco's canisters. No, Diana wouldn't have to keep her coffee in the FLOUR jar, her flour in the COFFEE or her sugar in the FLOUR, leaving only the tacky Lipton teabags stashed in the correct container. Even Diana's drainboard looked desolate and deserted. Unlike Coco's counters, which always displayed an array of plastic glasses with pouty rims—permanently puckered by overcrowded conditions in the dishwasher—and open Skippy peanut butter and strawberry jelly jars with knife handles jutting out of them, Diana's kitchen surfaces were beautifully barren.

"You could also take out the cream," Diana continued.

Coco opened the refrigerator. It was spotlessly clean and tidy. No half-full bottles of duplicate condiments crowded its shelves, no dabs of jelly stuck to the walls, no yokes oozed out of soggy egg cartons, no packs of pink hamburger bled through cardboard containers to form sour stagnant swamps beneath the vegetable crispers. Even without checking, Coco knew that everything in Diana's freezer would be frozen a #7 solid so that no sludge of chocolate ice cream would be seeping out through the seams of its carton to move like a California mudslide across the hills of TV dinners.

"They should be getting here soon," Diana said, drop-ping puffy parsley around a platter. "If you want to freshen up, there's a bathroom off my bedroom down the hall."

"I guess maybe I should comb my hair," Coco con-ceded.

She walked down the hall to Diana's bedroom which was an open, airy space furnished with a four-poster bed, a few pieces of fine wicker furniture and several sheer ferns fanning out around the window. An exer-cise rope, lassoed around a doorknob, identified the bathroom which was also filled with expensive, expan-sive plants that camouflaged the plumbing fixtures.

Agonizing over the disparity between Diana's home and her own, Coco took the cosmetic kit out of her purse, freshened her makeup, brushed her hair, and breathed into the cup of her hand to test her breath. Her mouth smelled briny. Opening the medicine chest to look for some Listerine, Coco discovered a display of fancy drugs from trendy places.

Diana's medicine chest held no half-full bottles of pediatric-pink penicillin prescriptions innocently left unadministered, or old rectal thermometers ambiva-lently pickled in a glass of alcohol destined to be spilled during some sick insomniacal night. Instead, exotic bot-tles with unfamiliar foreign labels marched across the spotless shelves. The Lomotils came from a fancy phar-macia in Acapulco—proving they'd been bought on lo-cation rather than imported from the States by any anxious, amateur tourist anticipating dysentery—sleep-ing pills from the St. James Royal Pharmacy in SW I, London, headache compounds from a good arrondis-sement near the Champs Elysée, and barbiturates from several sexy-sounding Caribbean islands.

Coco felt simultaneously challenged and conquered.

When the doorbell rang, she flushed the toilet as an alibi for her lengthy stay in the bathroom and hurried back to the kitchen from where she saw Diana walking through the living room, stopping to gently rotate each of her plants as she passed, so the leaves, which turned toward the windows during the day, would face her guests for the duration of the party.

The next moment Coco caught sight of John Canada among the Board members crowding into the entry hall and, suddenly feeling shy, turned to pour herself a large goblet of white wine. She was still standing beside the table when Canada and Lionel Hearndon came into the kitchen. Surprised to see Coco there, Canada moved forward with a smile.

"Hi," he said softly.

"Hi," Coco answered, feeling deliciously and enormously inadequate.

"That was a helluva long meeting, wasn't it?" Canada asked, reaching for a gallon Gallo jug.

"Really," Coco consented sweetly, sipping her wine.

Lionel, however, was still hyped up. "I would say the meeting was long—but highly productive," he said reprovingly. "A drink or two will revive everybody."

Subdued by the strain of their mutual expectations and the presence of Lionel Hearndon, Coco and Canada both fell silent.

"A party is just what we all needed," Lionel Hearndon continued, flushing with pimplike pleasure because he had inadvertently provided the chairman of his Board of Directors with a woman who pleased him.

"That's true," Canada agreed.

Then he somehow began angling Coco out of the kitchen, herding her into the nearest corner of the living room where the bulk of his body segregated them from the people milling about. Coco caught sight of the chubby switchboard operator from the Social Science Institute but pretended not to have seen her.

"So? You're actually going to beat your deadline," Canada grinned, after taking a gulp of wine. "That'll be a first for the wide world of social science."

Coco smiled while trying to decide if she should call him by his first name.

"Did David Macintosh get a chance to talk to you?" she asked.

"No, did he want to?" Canada turned and looked around the room. "I don't think he's gotten here yet."

"He wanted to ask you something about the Infelicity Index," Coco said, finishing her first glass of wine.

"Well, what do you think of the report?" Canada asked, letting his gaze come to rest on Coco's face.

Coco blushed and bent over to raid a bowl of dry roasted peanuts set on the table that put a period at the end of Diana's long white couch.

"Well, to tell you the truth, I do have a few problems with it," Coco confessed, licking the salt off her fingertips. "Of course, I'm just supposed to edit the thing, but . . ."

"But what?" Canada prompted.

"Well, actually, I'm a little worried about creating an index that measures such a personal thing as peoples' 'infelicity,'" Coco said.

"You think it's . . . morally wrong?"

"Oh, I don't know," Coco shrugged and stooped over to scoop up another stockpile of peanuts. "Sometimes I worry because I think that an Infelicity Index might be used by the government to identify and isolate infelicitous groups. You know. They might decide that some groups, with exceptionally high infelicity scores, are potentially subversive and need some surveillance or something."

"Ah, ha!" Canada chuckled. "I think I smell a rad . . ical."

Then, gently removing the empty wineglass from Coco's hand, he disappeared into the kitchen and returned with two full goblets.

"Now. Explain to me exactly what you mean," he said, handing back Coco's glass.

"Well," Coco faltered, uncertain whether her criticism of the National Infelicity Index was turning him on or off. "You know that . . . historically some groups like exploited minorities, for example, have been traditionally infelicitious. And the National Infelicity Index identifies these groups so that the government could . . ." Suddenly remembering Canada's recent presidential appointment, which was still awaiting Senate confirmation, Coco panicked. "I don't mean *this* government," she said, "but some future one might decide that infelicity is synonymous with political dissent." She began dropping peanuts into her mouth through the anuslike exit of her fist more rapidly. "I mean, I think there are political implications to an infelicity index because it can be interpreted politically."

Alcohol and excitement began coalescing to put the room into motion. As if from a great distance, Coco heard Canada chuckle again.

In a politically sterile period, her comments might be considered dangerous by a member of the establishment. Nervously, Coco gulped some more wine.

"I mean, some people might think a certain infelicity rating on the index indicates potential political instability or social unrest."

55

Coco drained her second glass of wine and felt Diana's living room tilt and start to twirl.

"I mean," she began again compulsively, "some politician might consider a felicity drop dangerous to our national security because sometimes it's hard to tell if a felicity shift is a reaction to a national emergency or the recovery from one. I mean, a felicity peak following a crunch like the Cuban missile crisis could look like a legitimatizing act of approval or just relief about escaping a nuclear disaster. Do you see what I mean?"

Coco couldn't tell if Canada was restraining laughter or anger over her drunken critique so she continued eating peanuts with increased speed. Why had she chosen to talk politics with a fiscally conservative, conventionally liberal man in his fifties who would have been over thirty even during the sixties? She really should have known better.

"Are you married?" John Canada inquired.

"Yes."

"Children?"

"Four."

"Happy?"

"Well, we have our problems . . ."

"How about another glass of wine?" he suggested, reaching for her empty glass and disappearing again.

It was happening.

John Canada was ready to make a move. Coco felt a rush of excitement as she watched him return from the kitchen to brace himself in blockade position once again.

But suddenly David Macintosh burst into the apartment, surveyed the living room, and began elbowing his way toward the corner where Coco and Canada were standing.

"I'm really sorry to interrupt," he said with polite determination, "but I have to speak with you, Dr. Canada."

Pressing Coco and Canada into the corner, David turned the three of them into a triangle.

"What's up?" Canada asked, hardly hiding his irritation over the intrusion.

"Well, let me run through the whole thing very quickly," David said.

The serious rather than insolent side of his character was in ascendance. "I spoke to Coco about this earlier today because I've been awfully worried about some of the statistics that have been surfacing in our final computations. I explained to her that the final figures didn't seem to jibe with the individual state-by-state breakdowns we'd received before Christmas. I did most of the programming myself, but the results still didn't look right to me."

David was sweating. His black turtleneck T-shirt clung to his ribs and his slacks seemed permanently creased into V's around the crotch.

"So while we were in the Board meeting today, I asked one of my assistants to run some of the numbers through the computer for me again, and he came up with totally different results. Then, right after the Board meeting broke up, I went back to my office to test them again—which is why I was late getting here—and I compared today's results with the ones Lionel produced as the final figures."

"Maybe we should talk about this later on," John Canada said, looking around uncomfortably.

But David, after locating Lionel on the other side of the room, continued. "It looks to me like Dr. Hearndon has been doctoring the data so we would get lower

57

national infelicity scores. In fact, I even found some of the early raw data from Colorado, Kansas, and Tennessee in my files—xeroxes I'd made from the originals way back when they first came in—and they just don't match at all with the figures Lionel gave me to program. I think what he did was change the raw numbers before giving them to me to computerize. In other words, I think he fixed the results of a federally funded research survey."

"Oh, that's wild," Coco gasped.

"Now those are *very* serious accusations," Canada said sternly. "You're accusing one of the country's leading social scientists of fraud and I think you'd better be absolutely certain of all the facts before you mention this to anyone else."

David fell silent.

Canada finished his glass of wine and assumed a tutorial tone of voice. "First of all, David, I've been in the social science racket for a long time, and the most amazing thing I've learned is that it takes very little to make people happy. Despite what you or I or the media or the government might interpret as bad times, Americans continue to find simple pleasure in simple things."

"Yeah," David said doubtfully, "but our survey covers the Watergate years and these figures show that the people were totally impervious to what was happening. They seem totally unfazed by the inflation and indifferent to Vietnam or any of the Watergate scandals. There just doesn't seem to be any correlation between what happened and what the report claims people felt. Even the disaggregated figures—broken down by race, age, social class, and geographic location—indicate a fairly high level of felicity from 1970 to 1975.

History and the National Infelicity Index seem to be at odds."

Coco looked first at one man and then the other.

"I'd like you to show me everything you've got in the way of evidence that led you to this conclusion," Canada said earnestly. "I know a little bit about computer programming and I could maybe run the stuff through once more." He moved in closer to David. "I'm going to be in town all of this week so why don't you and I get together for lunch—say, tomorrow or the next day—so you can fill me in on all the details? Then we can work it out together at your office one of these nights."

Coco felt a squeamish sensation shiver through her body. Having lived in Washington during Watergate, she could detect a cover-up before it happened. Still—she didn't want to blow her amorous plans by looking suspicious.

"Well, should I telephone you tomorrow?" David asked.

"Sure, I'm staying at the Hay Adams," Canada said. "Why don't you give me a buzz around ten?"

David nodded and walked away.

The fact that Coco hadn't liked much of what Canada said didn't diminish her interest in him at all. Unfortunately her lifelong habit of seeking male approval was totally unrelated to any moral, ethical, or political principles. Coco had to feed flirtations to her insecurity just as she had to keep popping peanuts into her mouth.

Once again Canada situated himself at an angle that completely cordoned off the crowd.

"Listen," he said, cozily renestling into their encounter. "Since you've been editing the National Infelicity report you've probably read it more closely than anyone else. How about us having dinner together tonight so we can talk about it? Lots of times an editor knows the material better than the writers or researchers."

Coco looked up into Canada's face. There was no question about his attractiveness, but his conservatism seemed to interrupt his style like an overdose of obnoxious commercials spoiling a TV movie.

"Can you break loose for . . . a couple hours?" Canada asked.

Coco smiled at his thoughtful acknowledgement of the many possible impediments to her freedom and liberty.

She could feel the wine flushing her face and surging through her system. Confidently drunk, Coco decided she must look quite dramatic standing against the clean white wall in her good black jumpsuit as alcohol alchemized her fatigue into cunning and kindled bright lights in her nutmeg-brown eyes. Indeed, John Canada was looking at her with unadulterated adoration.

"Besides wanting to sound you out about the report, I also have some other things I'd like to discuss with you," Canada pressed. "So how about it? Why don't we have dinner at my hotel?"

"Well," Coco stalled, "I have to pick up my car at a service station near here before nine."

"OK. We'll stop there first and then drive over to the Hay Adams."

In silent agreement, they left the party separately and met downstairs outside Diana's building. Canada hailed a taxi and as soon as they were settled inside, looped his long arm around Coco's shoulders. When the driver made a U-turn and headed toward the Gulf service station on Adams Mill Road near the National Zoo,

Canada began a witty description of some of the Carter Southerners he'd been meeting.

Although Coco tried to pay attention to what he was saying, she felt as if she were walking—dead-drunk —on a high wire without a safety net below. The ancient, rickety Burman marriage certainly could not incorporate any obvious adultery and now that Canada was pressing toward the ultimate conclusion, Coco had to reassess the situation. Busily she began weighing alternative alibis to offer Gavin, realizing why the anticipation of an affair was more satisfying than its actualization. Indeed, since it was already eight o'clock, it was clear to Coco that she had even less time than taste for such an adventure. Gavin would certainly go berserk if she traipsed home around midnight and, undoubtedly, would smell something fishy if he tried to embrace her as usual.

When Canada began to caress her shoulder, Coco looked out the window at the snow still mounting up along Connecticut Avenue and wondered why she was doing what she was doing. She hadn't even called home to check if everyone had gotten back from school safely.

Coco was clearly acting like a father instead of a mother and she felt miserable.

When Canada began describing the testimony he was preparing for his Senate appearance on Wednesday, Coco wondered if Gavin would be able to regulate their temperamental thermostat so the house wouldn't overheat, and whether the basement would flood when the snow started to melt. When Canada withdrew for a moment to light a cigarette, Coco wondered whether Mr. Murdock's mechanic had been able to fix her car so she could pass her District motor vehicle test on Monday morning. After speculating on how much the repair bill would be, she slid her hand inside her purse to check if she had returned her Gulf credit card to her wallet where it belonged.

When Canada rewrapped his arm around her and leaned close enough so that Coco could feel his breath against her cheek, she remembered how often quick sexual encounters ended with a dose of venereal disease, a urinary infection, a tenacious fungus, an unwanted pregnancy or a flurry of malicious rumors. But when Canada gently kissed the side of her face, Coco sighed and decided to stop thinking altogether.

# CHAPTER FOUR

The moment the cab stopped in front of the service station Coco disengaged herself from Canada's arm, scrambled out of the back seat, and ran across the snowcapped sea of cement toward the square building situated, like an island, in the center. Somewhat surprised to see that the overhead door of the body shop had already been rolled down, Coco bent over to twist the handle at the bottom of the garage door.

It was locked.

Pushing back the sleeve of her fur jacket, Coco checked her watch in the dim light cast by the street lamp. It was only 8:15. Then, looking over toward the business office, she realized it was ominously dark. The Gulf station had closed forty-five minutes early!

When the cab driver gunned his engine, Coco whirled around but was too late to stop the taxi from pulling away. Through the lacy curtain of falling snow she could see Canada advancing past the gasoline pumps in front of the business office. Reluctantly Coco started to retrace her footprints, but when she reached the narrow passageway between the body shop and business office she stepped inside to wait for Canada beneath the sheltering roof. Suddenly Coco became aware of muffled voices behind the steel-plated side door of the garage. Pressing her face against the icy surface, she could make out the sounds of men talking.

Flooded with relief, Coco began to knock on the door.

"Hello! Hello in there."

The voices ceased. Coco paused briefly and then began to knock harder.

"Hey. Open up. It's Coco Burman. I've got to get my car out of there. Monday's the deadline for my motor vehicle inspection test."

With her ear against the cold steel surface, Coco was certain she could hear whispering.

"It's not nine o'clock yet," she called out accusingly. "You can't close before the regular time without notifying your customers. Open up. I have to get my car out."

More silence.

Desperate, Coco grabbed a snowshovel that was parked against the brick wall and, gripping the long wooden handle, began to bang on the door. The metallic roar of the aluminum shovel against the steel was wondrous. After a few minutes Coco began to drum more rhythmically. Finally, as Canada walked into the passageway, Coco took a last steely bang before flinging the shovel to the ground and then turned around to complain about the gross injustice of her situation to John Canada. Since she was facing the street when the side door swung open, she didn't see the person who suddenly knotted her arms behind her back and clamped a hot hand across her mouth.

Above a suffocating mountain range of brown knuckles, Coco saw Izzat's two compatriots, still dressed in their Gulf station grease monkey suits, wrestle John Canada to the ground.

Terrified, Coco went limp as she was dragged backward into the body shop. Above the pounding of her heart she could hear the sickening sound of John Canada's head thumping against the cement. Then the door slammed shut and a heavy bolt dropped into place. A moment later the darkness was shattered by overhead fluorescent lights. Coco's captor released her arms and removed the hand from her mouth.

She turned around.

Izzat was standing behind her, pointing a pistol toward the wall where the other two men were holding Canada. A few feet beyond them, slumped on the garage floor, was the handsome Iranian Ambassador dressed, as usual, in his customary tuxedo, ruffled silk shirt, and black cashmere cape. Except for the fact that his long dark hair was rumpled and his hands were tied behind his back, he looked exactly as he did in all his society-page photographs.

"Izzat," Coco wailed. "Izzat, what are you doing?"

Her heart was pumping noise into her ears and fire into her face.

"Stand back against the wall," Izzat shouted impatiently, prancing back and forth so that he splattered rings of wet slush off the floor.

Slowly, Coco inched her way toward the grey cinder block wall and leaned against it. The room had begun to whirl about and Coco fought her fear so that she wouldn't faint. Attempting to anchor her consciousness, she focused on Izzat strutting, with parade marshall precision, back and forth in front of her. He looked totally different than he had early that morning. Now his stocky body was wired for action and he was wielding his revolver like an exhibitionist. His face hardened with concentration as he watched the men tie Canada's arms behind his back. Then Izzat turned and skidded through the slush toward Coco.

The earth moved beneath her as she watched him

pull a coiled rope out of his coat pocket. When he began lacing it around her wrists, reality exposed itself to Coco like a flasher.

—Oh, my God—she thought.—I'm a hostage.—

Immediately her consciousness began rushing down her body like dirty bathwater swirling toward a drain. Without a sound, Coco sank to the floor, unable to stabilize herself against the wall with her hands tied in front of her. The pool of icy water in which she sank quickly seeped through her corduroy pants and sent a chill up her body, shortcircuiting the feeling of faintness.

"OK, OK," Izzat stuttered, waving his revolver threateningly at the three captives. "We didn't want any more hostages. But you," he cast a wrathful look at Coco, "were making such a goddamn racket we had to stop your mouth. Now we're going to use you to get what we want."

From a foreign exchange student with a part-time gig at the Gulf service station, Izzat had changed into a tough revolutionary ready to kill or die for his political goals.

Coco felt weakness flush through her again. Her chin dipped down into the soft furry triangle of her collar as panic pummeled her from within.

A terrible mistake was happening.

Coco and Canada were being homogenized into a hostage package with the aristocratic ambassador from Iran who was obviously an enemy of his people.

—This is all wrong, Coco thought. —In a minute everyone will realize what a mistake this is and let us leave.—

With a great effort of will, she sat up straighter and smiled at Izzat to indicate her secret solidarity with all revolutionary forces fighting oppression around the world.

His black eyes flickered right past her.

"We have been fucked over too long," Izzat continued in a voice fueled by fury. "Now the Shah must release our comrades or," he turned with a cruel smile toward the Ambassador, "we'll kill you. You have oppressed the Iranian people for too long, Mohammed. Now 123 of our comrades will go free or you'll pay with your life. If the Shah doesn't do what we say, we'll kill you right here in this garage."

The Ambassador looked back at Izzat with diplomatic inscrutability.

"And you," Izzat shouted at Coco, suddenly enraged again, "because you blundered in here you must remain our hostages. You will fly with us to Algeria to guarantee our safe passage. You and your friend will be released there if we find our comrades safe in Algeria." He laughed sarcastically. "You should be happy to know you are helping advance the revolution in Iran and the return of Palestine to Aly's brothers in the P.L.O."

Shocked, Coco turned to look at the two men stationed on either side of Canada. She knew that the taller, meaner-looking one was named Abass and that he, like Izzat, was Iranian, but she certainly hadn't known that the plump young student with the straight fringe of bangs capping his brows was a Palestinian.

That frigid fact was terrifying to Coco. How could she ever talk her way out of this mistake? How could she ever convince her captors of her political sympathies when the Jews were the heavies in the Palestinian struggle and there was a PLO person involved in this caper? Why should the terrorists believe Coco

Burman was against Israeli militarism and racism? And what would happen if they found out that John Canada was a recent Carter appointee? How could Coco establish her political independence from the Carter administration when she had been captured with a cabinet-level designee? How could she convince Izzat that she disagreed with Canada's publicly stated support of Carter's energy policy and last year's legislation deregulating natural gas?

How could Coco flash her flag under such compromising conditions?

Another wave of weakness shimmied through her system, leaving her limbs limp and her head light.

Suddenly Coco remembered a conversation she'd had with Izzat shortly after the UN passed its resolution equating Zionism with racism. Izzat had been putting new windshield wipers on Coco's car when he unexpectedly made a mean remark about the affluence of American Jews who, in retaliation for Mexico's affirmative vote on the UN censure, had boycotted Acapulco resorts that winter and almost bankrupted the Mexican government. Although Coco had been surprised that her own ethnic group could afford enough winter vacation reservations to rock a country's economy with their cancellations, she had let the comment pass uncontested. In retrospect, that seemed fortuitous.

"For once we will be treated with justice," Izzat predicted proudly. Then, looking at Aly, he said, "The Arab people have been discriminated against by the American people and the American media for too long. Now we will prove that we can execute a political action right here in the nation's capital."

Coco's head lolled back against the wall. Despite what was happening she felt certain Izzat wouldn't hurt her. Basically she believed he liked her too much to do her any bodily harm. For years now, regardless of conditions in the Middle East, Izzat had always been very friendly.

Coco closed her eyes.

But what made Coco so sure that Izzat really liked her? Couldn't that just be another misconception based on the same kind of false analogizing which, for years, made Coco believe shrimp grew up to be scampi, that mice became rats if they ate enough gargage, and that snorkeling naturally evolved into scuba diving? Just because Izzat smiled flirtatiously while wiggling his dipstick in Coco's oil tank didn't mean he truly liked her.

Now Coco felt the stinging preview of tears behind her eyelids.

When was she ever going to learn that one species of things didn't change into another or that people in servile jobs didn't really like the customers they serviced year after year?

When was she going to stop being so stupid? When was she going to catch on?

Coco opened her eyes and looked over at Canada. Izzat's two comrades were still holding him up against the wall. The privileged Princetonian who had entered the board room of the Social Science Institute earlier that day now seemed totally ineffective—if not effete. Canada's hair, a soft sandy color streaked with grey which turned it beige, dipped despondently down over his eyes, obstructing his vision and preventing Coco from evaluating his condition. But how could a man, who obviously always took great pains to take good care of himself, accept such accidental, gratuitious violence? Obviously it would go against his pale Protestant grain. There was no doubt John Canada was truly being terrorized by the terrorists.

Coco lowered her eyes. Of course it really was incredible how quickly their lives had changed. In just a few minutes they had drifted from the giddy brink of a love affair to the edge of death.

A sudden chill coursed through Coco's body. Was Coco perhaps being punished for having planned to commit adultery? Was all of this happening because she had been trying to escape reality by making moves on Canada? Perhaps she had been kidnapped by Middle Eastern revolutionaries because God thought that intentional, rather than accidental, adultery actually warranted an extra stiff sentence.

An unexpected vision of her four children, neatly lined up in a row, floated into Coco's head but she forcibly ejected the image. Certainly Coco couldn't afford the emotional luxury of thinking about her family right now. That would only weaken her. She had to concentrate on saving her life for them—not luxuriating in sentimental love. How could she survive twenty-four hours in this cold, cavernous, unheated, unfurnished garage where men did mysterious things to machines, if she felt sorry for herself or her family?

With a swell of practicality, Coco looked around the room. Beyond a row of Gulf Company oil drums that served both as trashcans and room dividers, was her Monte Carlo Chevrolet suspended some four feet above the ground on a hydraulic lift. Its twisted chrome trim jutted, like hangnails, away from the fenders and guiltily she glanced over at her captors wondering if they read the chrome as evidence of her indifference to economic sanctions against the repressive racist government of Rhodesia.

Probably.

The crooked clothes hanger that Mike had attached to the tender stump of their amputated antenna rose above the car like a brave flag of surrender that had lost its white banner.

Suddenly Izzat shouted something and his two friends began shoving Canada along the wall toward where Coco was sitting. For some reason Canada started to struggle violently during this episode, so that finally Abass, the mean-looking Iranian, whacked his fist across the side of Canada's head.

The sound of bumping bodies made Coco panic and she screamed as Canada was thrown to the ground beside her. Her shriek startled everyone and the terrorists backed away, but after a moment Izzat came over and propped Canada back up into a sitting position. Looking into his face, Coco decided that Canada was more stunned than hurt, although his glazed eyes seemed to stare sightlessly beyond her.

Seconds later the terrorists moved in on the Ambassador and, without lifting him up, pushed him like a bag of groceries along the floor until he too was closer to Coco. Coco looked at the diplomat's handsome tawny face. He showed no emotion whatsoever. Apparently he had already adjusted to his fate with amazing Islamic ease—possessor of a fatalism completely foreign to Coco's western willfulness.

Coco sighed heavily.

Perhaps the Koran, unlike the Old Testament, enabled Moslems to accept the inevitable. Certainly the Ambassador was facing death with an equanimity Coco couldn't muster up even for a long round-trip plane ride.

It was, of course, possible that beneath the fine facade of his face, fear was disassembling the Ambassador. But on the surface at least, resignation reigned. The Iranian aristocrat seemed to have accepted his capture—and possible death—with the same ease as the sands of the desert shifted into new patterns and formations with the wind. The diplomatic tradition was standing him in good stead; trained to tutor his responsive emotions, he appeared astonishingly impassive.

Having consolidated their captives, Izzat and his friends moved away to engage in a whispered conversation near the rear of the garage where an ancient pay phone was pasted on the wall.

Coco shifted about slightly in the puddle of dirty water in which she sat until she was a bit closer to Canada. Somehow his nearness was reassuring and she felt less alone even though Canada did not seem aware of her presence.

"John, are you OK?" Coco asked in a stage whisper.

After a long while Canada began to shake his head slowly from one side to the other, as if in a state of shock.

"Did they hurt you?" Coco asked again.

"I can't believe this," Canada said, barely moving his mouth and still staring straight ahead like a ventriloquist. This was the same technique Coco's kids used to exchange forbidden obscenities or threats at the dinnertable. Canada's eyes became mere slits in his long thin face as he jerked his shoulders upward in a sign of total disbelief.

"I think we've had it," he whispered grimly. "It's all over for us."

"Oh, no," Coco protested in a whisper. "I know these guys, John. They're not really violent. They're all just exchange students from Howard. They just want us to ride on the plane with them to make sure they get where they want to go and then they'll release us."

The irony of Coco attempting to comfort Canada didn't escape her. Everything was topsy-turvy. Coco Burman, who was afraid to eat alone in a public restaurant (except for the luncheonette counter at the People's Drugstore right near her house) or ride the long steep "down" escalator at the Dupont Circle Metro station, was trying to calm John Canada. Coco Burman, who hyperventilated when she got nervous and who once developed "gulping disease," a sickness common only to thoroughbred racehorses, was actually consoling a six-foot-four-inch, legendarily self-sufficient, intellectual jock nationally known for handling all kinds of challenges—a man of wit as well as nature— a man famous for writing books, advising presidents, shooting rapids, fording rivers, pitching camps, teaching classes, subhosting talkshows, racing cars, running campaigns, sailing boats, and raising barns, children, horses, and occasional hell at Elaine's or Studio 54.

"Jesus, are you putting me on?" Canada exploded with ventriloquist venom after looking up to assure himself the terrorists were still occupied in their own conversation. "Anyway, if these kooks don't kill us, the cops probably will with some wild rescue stunt. We haven't got a chance in hell of getting out of here alive."

"Oh, I'm sure Izzat won't kill us," Coco said weakly. "Even if the Shah refuses to meet his demands, Izzat just wants to use us as hostages for awhile."

"Shut up, you two," Abass suddenly roared from the back of the garage. "Shut your mouths."

Canada flinched and Coco collapsed back against the wall again.

Then she closed her eyes.

Didn't she believe what she had just said to Canada? Wasn't it true that Izzat was just going to use them for a little while? And what was so terrible about being a hostage for a bit, anyway? Indeed, hadn't Coco lived most of her life as a hostage if you defined a hostage as a person who couldn't do what she wanted to do until something over which she had no control occurred? Hadn't Coco been born into captivity and kept there by parental admonitions that if she didn't do such-and-such, something terrible would happen?

So hadn't Coco spent thirty-seven and a half years toeing the line to make sure nothing awful took place? Certainly, ever since becoming a mother twelve years ago, Coco had been held hostage by fate and superstition, believing that if she went out for a cocktail after work one of her kids would get mugged on the way home from school, or if she was too lazy to stop at the store for bread, Mike's wisdom teeth would grow in impacted?

Oh, yes, Coco had always been a prisoner—if not of hate then of love—the captive of a family who demanded the unconditional surrender of her attention and affection. Actually, because of her previous hostage experience, Coco knew exactly how to behave now— Coco was certainly conversant with doing things other people wanted her to do out of fear of the consequences if she did what she wanted. So didn't it stand to reason that John Canada would be frightened to death? How could such a healthy, wealthy Gentile know anything about losing control of his own destiny, about being held as security while other people negotiated their interests? What could Canada know about making deals with God to keep life intact and children out of harm's way?

—Please dear Lord make them take us to Algeria—
Coco prayed from her perch in the puddle—instead of
killing us.—

This was the only kind of deterence Coco understood
—bargaining with Fate to avert some fatal mishap by
negotiating for one of lesser magnitude, begging for
bad—rather than fatal—car accidents, for material—
rather than human—disasters. Weren't trade-offs the
only true deterent against disaster?

Coco looked up as Abass jogged back toward them.
Apparently still angry at Coco and Canada for talking,
he began gesticulating with his gun. He sneered at the
Ambassador. Then he leered at Coco. His eyes seemed
bleary and there were several cold sores on his dark
brown face, one coming out of his nose, like a stream
of frozen snot, and the other traversing his upper lip
like a mustache. An oily strand of hair drooled down
over his forehead, and he looked as if he should be
home in bed somewhere, drinking hot tea with honey,
rather than acting like a commando in an unheated
garage.

"Now we're going to call Pacifica Radio to read them
our demands and I want the three of you to sit right
where you are and keep your mouths shut. If you don't
make trouble, you won't get hurt."

As if to accentuate his promise, Abass walked over
to Ambassador Mohammed and kicked him squarely
in the stomach.

The ambassador grunted and doubled over. Then he
struggled to right himself without the use of his arms.
When he had finally regained his original position
and composure, Mohammed Mohammed leaned back
against the wall. His dark eyes, tracked by laughlines
from happier moments, showed an Islamic intensity

shimmering beneath his burnoose of stoicism. Like a fire still sparking beneath suffocating banks of sand, his faith was sustaining him. Indeed, the Ambassador seemed to have achieved a state of consciousness which elevated him high above the fray. Coco sensed a political rage being deterred by self-restraint and she felt secured by the kind of will which could forestall such fury.

"What's your name?" Abass asked, turning back to Coco.

"Charlotte," Coco managed to whisper, "Charlotte Burman. But if it's about ransoming me, you'd better say Coco. Most people know me as Coco."

Abass looked down at Canada. "You her husband?" he asked contemptuously.

"No. No, I'm not her husband," Canada said quickly. "I'm John Canada."

Surprised, Abass turned around and yelled something to Izzat in a language Coco had never heard before.

Izzat came running over. "Are you the man Carter just named to the Council of Economic Advisors?" he asked excitedly.

Canada confirmed his unconfirmed appointment with a nod.

"Great," Izzat shouted. "That's great! Now Carter will really have to put pressure on the Shah since we've got one of his administration officials in here too. You did us a good deed," he said, grinning at Coco.

A wind of dizziness blew through Coco's body as the two Iranians retreated to the rear of the garage once again. There they engaged in an excited discussion which became more and more animated.

Aly was clearly requesting something that was objectionable to the Iranians and he kept turning around to look at Coco as if she were the cause of the controversy. Coco watched their dispute with growing apprehension. Although the trio of terrorists was terrifying she didn't like them quarreling among themselves and her heart trembled as she studied the scene. There was something about Aly that made him seem more reckless than either of his comrades. He was younger than the Iranians and had an alarmingly adolescent manner that suggested the slightest insult might set him off into a teenage tantrum such as Mike had recently begun to perform. When Izzat reached out for the telephone, Aly grabbed his arm and initiated a fast angry shuffle to stop him.

Nervously Coco bit her bottom lip and looked around the body shop to familiarize herself with the layout in case she had to take cover during some shootout. The place was the length of a football field and the width of several cars. Tires hung like doughnuts from curved hooks on the walls, creating a bunkerish effect, exaggerated by boxes of automotive parts around the room. Except for the floor, which was covered with dirty water that had probably melted off snowy cars brought in for servicing that day, the garage was extraordinarily clean. It was clear that Mr. Murdock ran a tight ship, for even after a mutiny everything looked quite orderly. Farther down the wall against which Coco leaned was a Macke cigarette machine with an out-of-order sign dangling like a necklace from one of its knobs and a squat red Coca Cola dispenser with an invoice taped across the coin deposit slot.

For a moment anger replaced fear in Coco's heart because both vending machines were out of order and eventually she would need cigarettes and would have enjoyed a coke. But of course the machines would be

77

out of order. Why not? Why should they be any different from anything else?

Bitterly she continued surveying the room, finally
focusing on three cardboard shirt-straighteners hung
like paintings on the back wall of the garage.

```
LABOR
$15 per hr.
```

```
BATTERY CHARGE
$2.50
```

```
NO  MECHANIC
ON WEEKENDS
```

Suddenly the soft paunchy face of Mr. Murdock, the
genial Southern gentleman who owned the Gulf service
station, appeared in Coco's mind. What had Izzat and
Abass and Aly done to Mr. Murdock? Had he simply
gone home at the first sight of snow, panicked like
most Washingtonians by the flimsiest flurries, or was he
lying injured and dying next door in the darkened business office, perhaps bayoneted by the long spindle on
which he speared invoices. Had the mideastern revolutionaries been so embittered, after years of working for Mr. Murdock, that they murdered him? Did he
deserve to be murdered? Had he been paying his workers less than the minimum wage—working them too
hard and too long for too little?

There was another loud outburst of angry talk among
the three conspirators and then Izzat turned away from
his comrades and walked back toward Coco. Nervously
Coco twisted about to see if she could possibly excavate
a cigarette from her shoulderbag while her hands were

still tied, but finding even that comfort beyond reach she sighed despairingly and watched Izzat move in so close to her that the tip of his boot touched one of her bent knees.

Involuntarily Coco recoiled at the contact, half-expecting him to kick her.

"You're Jewish, aren't you?" he asked flatly.

Coco strained to see his eyes. "Of course," she said in a surprised whisper. "You know I am."

"Well, since you barged in here the way you did, Aly wants to try exchanging you for three of his friends who are in jail in Jerusalem."

Coco's eyes dilated.

What a crazy idea! Did Aly whateverhislastname-was really think that the militant State of Israel would cough up three Palestinian prisoners in exchange for Coco Burman who hadn't even bought season tickets to the High Holiday services at the Hebrew Congregation Reform Synagogue last year? Did Aly really think that the State of Israel was going to release three dangerous "ragheads," as some militant Jews called Arab rejectionists, for a diaspora princess who, just a month ago, had to skip the last night of Chanukah because she hadn't properly multiplied the incremental number of candles necessary to complete the celebratory cycle? Was Aly really so silly as to think he had snagged a prize when he caught an assimilationist J.A.P. who never gave to U.J.A., who had cashed in all the Israeli war bonds her parents bought her as a child, and didn't even know whether or not she would go through the drill of getting her son tutored for a Bar Mitzvah next year?

The Shah might very well release 123 Iranian dissidents to reclaim his playboy ambassador, but the State of Israel would never ransom Coco Burman who made hummus for cocktail parties and baklavah for birthdays.

"Well I can assure you that the State of Israel won't release any Arabs on my account," Coco said with an air of infinite political wisdom. "I mean, I'm Jewish, but I'm not an Israeli exile."

She paused for a moment to wonder why she automatically prefaced the word "Israel" with the phrase "state of." Certainly there weren't any other countries she would reflexively identify in such a redundant way. Did the application of such a handle unconsciously expose Coco's concern about Israel's supernationalistic hard-line foreign policy?

Izzat looked at Coco glumly. "Then maybe you can try to talk him out of it."

By now Coco's nose, throat, and lips felt totally dehydrated, although the bottom half of her body was completely drenched. Her legs had begun to grow numb from the cold, and hysteria was panting behind her like a posse on horseback. Frantically she looked over at John Canada who carefully avoided meeting her eyes.

"Well, I'll try, Izzat," Coco said mournfully, feeling an enormous surge of longing for Gavin.

A moment later Aly sauntered over to them, whirling his pistol around his forefinger as if it were a yo-yo.

Coco smiled to cover her confusion as she tried to collect her thoughts. How could she—a woman who couldn't even recall the names of all the Arab nations without composing a secret anagram similar to *HOMES* which was how she remembered that Huron, Ontario, Michigan, Erie, and Superior comprised the Great

Lakes (which at least stayed put and didn't keep realigning themselves)—persuade a patriotic P.L.O. partisan that she had some partisan feelings for the Palestinian people.

"Izzat told me what you want to do," Coco said solemnly.

Aly grunted in response. His round cherub-like face revealed no emotion.

"But I really don't think it's a good idea," she continued. "First of all, asking for 123 prisoners in exchange for the Ambassador is pretty steep. Not that he isn't worth it," she added quickly in deference to the diplomat who was obviously listening to the conversation, "but to ask for some more prisoners—from a totally different country—well . . . that seems sort of excessive to me. Because I can really assure you, Aly, Israel won't put out anything for me. You know their policy—they won't even exchange prisoners for real Israelis. And you also know how obstinate Israel can get. There's always the chance they might just try another Entebbe scenario and land some soldiers out there on the runway. I mean, the driveway."

Aly didn't smile. He was beginning to look like a brown rubber doll with a permanent expression painted on his face.

"So I really think you're jeopardizing this whole action by injecting a new angle into the negotiations. I think you should just keep this a simple, single-issue operation so it doesn't get overcomplicated."

Aly continued watching Coco without any change of facial expression.

"And then the next time," Coco said in a positive, promising voice, "I'm sure some of the Iranian prisoners you're helping get released will feel indebted to you and maybe assist in some separate Palestinian action."

Coco couldn't believe she was tendering tactical advice to a terrorist and felt a smile of silly incredulity slide across her face.

"Aren't you a Zionist?" Aly asked coldly.

Coco paused. Now *that* was really putting it to her. *That* was a toughie. Was she a Zionist or wasn't she a Zionist? And what exactly was a Zionist anyway? Wasn't a Zionist simply someone who had a stake in the survival of Israel? Certainly Coco had that. Indeed, if it were true trees propagated every twenty years, Coco probably owned several forests over there by now because she had religiously purchased one sapling after another, year after year, through her Sunday School's Israeli Reforestation Program to stop the erosion of that Promised Land by anchoring it down with real roots. So while Coco did not actually have dual loyalties, she certainly had a stake, if not a forest, in Israel and was totally committed to its existence, even though she was still unclear as to her exact position on the West Bank.

"I'm not sure what you mean by 'Zionist,' " she said, looking Aly straight in the eye to indicate that her equivocation was honest confusion rather than political evasion. "But I always denounced the intransigence of Begin's policies."

"Really?" Aly asked in a suspicious voice.

Coco nodded, but then stopped speaking.

—Oh, I'm not going to get into this now—she thought more militantly—It's all too complicated and even if I do feel bad about Israel's treatment of the Palestinians I don't have to say so to someone from the P.L.O. who kills athletes at Munich and children at Mallot—Coco was clearly being mau-mau-ed and the symbolism of her situation struck her like a fist.

"Do you admit that the Jews stole Palestine from my people?" Aly asked.

"No," Coco answered bravely. "The Jews were *put* there after the Second World War."

"But why were they given our land?" Aly asked. "Why not German land or French land or Japanese or American land?"

"Well, I don't know the answer to that," Coco lied, knowing full well the awful reason. "I suppose they were put there because that's where they came from originally."

"But I came from there, too," Aly objected. "Both originally and lately. My family lived on the same land outside Haifa for hundreds and hundreds of years. How come we got moved off *our* land? Why did *my* family have to become refugees, run to Beirut, so that I don't even know where they are?"

"I don't know," Coco said, stung with guilt, "except that maybe international powers wanted it that way. They do those kinds of things you know."

"Not any more," Aly announced abruptly. "Those days are over. We are going to take back our land."

Coco swallowed with difficulty. "But where should the Jews go?" she asked, with a tremor in her voice. "What should happen to them?"

"They should go back where they came from."

"But they *did* come from there, Aly. They don't have any other place to go back to."

"Well, since I'm risking my life in here, I want to free some of *my* friends too," Aly whined petulantly. "Izzat and Abass seem to place a higher value on the lives of their Iranian brothers than on the Palestinians who are engaged in the same kind of liberation struggle."

Coco didn't know what to say.

"But I'm going to tell you something," Aly whispered, bending down closer to Coco. "If my so-called comrades don't support my demands, I'll . . . I'll start operating unilaterally."

"What do you mean?" Coco whispered, titillated by her own terror.

In response, Aly turned and walked away, contemptuously dismissing her question as irrelevant to his own interests or intentions.

"Aly," Coco called out in a weak wail. "The Israelis won't do it. They really won't."

Then she sank back against the wall again.

Oh, no. There was no way Israel would ransom Coco Burman—no way in the world. And if Israel wouldn't do it, who would? Compared to the Iranian Moslem and the Waspy Brahmin, both of whom had either religious, political, or cultural constituencies, Coco Burman was the living symbol of an isolated, alienated, unaffiliated person—a poor investment opportunity for any established institution. Without money, connections, or recourse to resources, Coco was a loser as well as a loner.

Woefully she wondered if the Institute's Homeowner's floater policy had a kidnapping clause, or if the Social Science Institute's Group Health-plan covered employees who became hostages. Certainly Coco could harbor no hopes of her boss, Lionel Hearndon, Ph.D., LL.D., SSI director, spending any of his matching money, from the National Endowment for the Humanities and the Mobil Oil Company, to ransom an employee. Briefly she thought about Amnesty International and wondered if a free-lance editor, imprisoned for political reasons, might qualify as a potential "adoptee" in their literary category.

Shifting into a squat so as to elevate her bottom off the wet ground, Coco looked toward the rear of the garage. Izzat had begun talking on the telephone, reading what Coco guessed was his laundry list of ultimata from the back of a Gulf station invoice. Unable to decipher the words which he delivered into the mouthpiece, Coco sank back to the floor again and watched Aly pacing and posturing along the rear wall. She could see that he was becoming more and more upset, twirling his gun and grunting to himself as he danced through the slush. Apparently Izzat wasn't relaying Aly's demands for a separate exchange of prisoners and the Palestinian's anger was clearly mounting.

Finally Aly began to yell in English at his two comrades. "Why do you always sell out the Palestinians?" he shouted. "Why are we always left out? Where is your brotherhood? Where is your solidarity?" This time he twirled his gun in the direction of the telephone. "Tell them what I want," he ordered. "Go ahead. Tell them."

Izzat put his hand over the mouthpiece and turned to exchange some Persian words with Abass.

Coco closed her eyes.

She was in big trouble. If Izzat refused to ask for the exchange, Aly was clearly ready to turn on his cohorts. Perhaps Aly would take his own hostage from among the small group already assembled there. Perhaps there would be a takeover within the takeover, wrinkle upon wrinkle of terrorism. Although Coco couldn't quite decide whom Aly might capture, she was certain that her life was doubly jeopardized by this split among the league of Arabs. If Aly took Coco off somewhere else with him in an effort to sabotage the Iranian deal, Coco was clearly going to become an endangered species—a second-class hostage held by a traitorous terrorist.

Suddenly Aly began yelling at Izzat again and Izzat, holding the receiver against his chest to muffle the sound of the argument, said in English that Aly should make his demands directly to the President rather than relay them through the same intermediary carrying the Iranian demands.

The three terrorists discussed this for a while.

Coco felt light-headed.

It was almost 10:30 on the old-fashioned Midas Muffler clock on the back wall. Two-and-a-half hours had passed since Coco had had her last cigarette and she felt withered from wanting one. Realizing she was the only hostage whose arms were tied in front of her, rather than behind her back, Coco lifted one hand to her mouth and began biting her fingernails.

Finally Izzat began talking into the telephone as if the quarrel with Aly had been resolved.

Coco sighed with relief and dropped her hands back into her lap.

She could no longer feel the toes on her feet.

# CHAPTER FIVE

After Izzat's telephone call, the three students sat down on the bench built along the back wall of the garage and began circulating a wine bottle which each of them tilted and sucked. Then they smoked some cigarettes and talked quietly for a while. About half an hour later, Aly walked behind a pile of boxes and returned with a small portable TV which he set atop an oil drum but left unconnected so the cord trailed down, like the curly string of a Tampax, over the edge of the barrel.

Coco stared at the television. It was the same old Sony which Mr. Murdock always kept on his office desk. Undoubtedly he'd watched daytime soap operas while his Third World employees stood outside in the rain and snow, probably earning less than the minimum wage, while pumping the vital fluid of their homeland into high-consumption, American-model cars.

The terrorists must have liberated the television so as to watch the news coverage of their escapade.

Uneasiness gripped Coco. She simply couldn't imagine under what circumstances Mr. Murdock would have voluntarily relinquished his television set to his workers. As she began to feel more queasy and uneasy, the neurodermatological itch inside the crook of her left elbow flared up. Awkwardly, she tried to slide one bound hand inside her jacket sleeve, but finding that impossible, rubbed her arm against the side of her rib cage as an unsatisfactory substitute for scratching.

While Coco was coping with her excema, Aly walked out into the center of the garage. Slowly extracting his revolver from the deep pocket of his monkeysuit, he spread his legs apart, stiffened his arm, and cocked the gun.

Coco heard a shrill, high-pitched cry echo through the silence as she screamed.

Nervously Aly whirled around so that the pistol was pointing at Coco.

Then she heard the quiet click of a gun with a silencer exploding and her head hit against the wall as her body recoiled.

She didn't feel any pain although she thought she had been shot.

Slowly she became aware of a thumping sound to her left and turned to see if the bullet had missed her and hit the ambassador. Mohammed Mohammed had twisted around so Coco couldn't see his face.

Then she heard two more shots and slowly turned to look back at Aly. For a moment she couldn't understand what he was doing, but gradually she realized he was shooting at a huge black rat that was weaving along the bottom of the garage door, leaving a trail of alarming red blood in its path. As the rat reached the far corner of the room, a geyser of black oil suddenly erupted into the air.

One of Aly's bullets had hit an oil drum.

Heavy black fluid began pouring out of the barrel, spreading an inky slick across the floor.

Coco drew her legs closer under her body as she watched the oil advance.

Aly was still shooting.

Coco turned to her left again. The ambassador had resumed his original position and was placidly watching Aly's performance. On Coco's right, John Canada's head had disappeared into the hollow formed by his drawn-up legs. He looked capable of conducting a lewd act Coco had always heard was impossible.

Suddenly Izzat and Abass, who were still sitting on the back bench, began laughing and calling out rude remarks to Aly.

"Shit," Aly cursed, jamming his gun back down into the deep pocket of his coveralls. "I need more target practice."

Shaking her head with incredulity, Coco looked down at the oil tongueing her boots and wondered if rat blood was mixed in with the black slime.

Bile rose up in her mouth.

—It's like television—she thought—When something extraordinary happens its just like television—

—Silencers are television—

—Guns are television—

—Death is television—

The next thing that happened was that Izzat got up, walked over to Coco and without a word, untied her wrists before returning to the bench.

"Oh, thank you, Izzat," Coco said, teary with gratitude and surprised to discover she could still form words into meaningful messages.

Quickly she inserted each hand up the opposite jacket sleeve to scratch her elbows and then, using the back of one fist as discreetly as possible, wiped her nose before affectionately embracing herself to massage her arms and activate the circulation. Next she opened her shoulderbag and began to pick through its contents, seeking the silky cellophane wrapper of her Marlboros. After fondling the familiar shapes of her personal paraphernalia, she reached the bottom of her purse where she could feel all the loose tampons which had lost their paper wrappers and slid out of their cardboard cylinders like furry caterpillars leaving their winter cocoons behind. There was the grungy wad of soiled Kleenex which Coco continually refolded and recycled in a miserly search for virgin surface and all the crumpled up telephone messages from her office. Only her cigarettes were missing.

Coco had obviously left her Marlboros at Diana's apartment.

Impossible.

Unreal.

Unfair.

Having already seen that the cigarette machine was out of order, she felt totally disoriented. Perhaps she could borrow Aly's gun and shoot the vending machine open. Or perhaps she could just borrow a cigarette from someone.

Unhappily, Coco turned toward Canada. "I'm going to ask Izzat for a cigarette," she whispered nervously.

"Oh, I wouldn't do that if I were you." Canada projected his protest without moving his mouth.

"Why not?" Coco asked with sudden defiance. "I also have to go to the bathroom. Hostages have human rights too, you know."

Impulsively she stood up and walked toward the three students sitting on the bench. When Izzat rose and drew his gun, Coco's eyes spliced the scene so that for a moment she thought she saw an erect penis extending from his torso. Revulsion, as well as fear, spilled through her until she realized she was hallucinating.

"Hi," she said, averting her eyes from the grey revolver at his groin.

Izzat moved a few steps closer to Coco and looked down at her suspiciously. "What do you want?"

"Oh, nothing important," Coco shrugged. "I was just sort of wondering . . . how things are going. I mean—I'm kind of nervous because I've never been kidnapped before," Coco confessed with a giggle. "I mean, I've sort of felt . . . like . . . a . . . hostage lots of times . . ." she spaced her words so they would have political reverberations, "but I've never actually been . . . captured like this."

Izzat turned so that his back was to his comrades. "Look. Don't worry too much," he said softly. "I'm pretty sure the Shah will accept our deal."

"Oh," Coco breathed, "that's good." Then she too lowered both her head and her voice. "You know, since we never really had a chance to talk about politics, I didn't know you belonged to any Arab activist group."

"Iranians aren't Arabs," Izzat snapped angrily.

Coco gasped. Iranians weren't Arabs? Then what were they? To what race did Izzat belong that he should be so insulted at being called an Arab? What other races were there?

"Well . . ." Coco laughed nervously, "I just thought that since you were working with Aly, you might be involved in some P.L.O. activities, too." She smiled apologetically. "That's what I *meant* to say."

"Aly is working with *us*," Izzat corrected her coldly.

Coco gnawed at her lower lip which had formed some shingles of chapped skin, and slid her right hand up her left jacket sleeve to scratch the itch inside her elbow.

"Oh, I see," she said humbly, "I didn't understand that."

"My two brothers were thrown in jail last month," Izzat continued, obviously trying to control his rage. "Neither of them had a trial. I don't even know if they're still alive. What I'm doing now is trying to save their lives."

Coco felt her eyes dilate with horror. Izzat's two brothers had been imprisoned without a trial in Tehran where they could be tortured and executed at the drop of a hat? Wasn't *that* reason enough for Izzat to pull such a stunt?

"Well," Coco murmured. "I guess . . . you're just doing what you have to do."

Izzat looked at her intently.

"I mean, I'd want my son Mike to do something to get my two little boys out of jail, if they were illegally imprisoned and . . . I think you're handling the whole thing . . . very well. I mean, as much as I know about these sorts of things from watching the news. I suppose you contacted Max Winthrop over at WTOP, didn't you? I think you're supposed to. I mean, I think he's the best media middleman to deal with." From the corner of her eye, Coco could see the Ambassador straining to hear her conversation. "You should always find some good media people to hang around outside to keep an eye on the police. Also, I think you should ask to have some pizzas sent over from Eddie Leonard's. That always cools out the cops because they figure if you're hungry you're human."

"You think so?"

"Yes. And I also think Algeria is a very good country to go to," Coco continued. Then she paused for several seconds. "By the way, what ever happened to Mr. Murdock?"

Izzat gave Coco a hard look. "He went home early today because of the snow."

"Oh, good." Coco flushed because she didn't believe him.

"So tell me something," Izzat said, moving in a little closer to her. "Do you think Carter would try to double-cross us about safe transport out of here?"

"Gee, I don't know," Coco said uncertainly. Coco's suspicions about Carter stemmed from the fact that he had talked like a populist while campaigning and then, right after the election, appointed and anointed a cabinet composed mainly of corporate executives, banking officials, multinational moguls and military leaders. Since some of Carter's cabinet appointees were executives of corporations whose defective products Coco owned, she felt somewhat cynical about the quality of government service they would provide. Coco did not like the track records of Bendix, Coca Cola, or IBM, and even though Michael Blumenthal had seemed sweet on "Meet the Press," he did, after all, produce a washing machine that couldn't remove all the spots from Nicky's Batman sweatshirt.

"Well, Carter does come on pretty strong about human rights," Coco said judiciously. "And since it would obviously be inhumane to turn you over to the Shah, I don't really think he'd do it."

"I just don't understand him," Izzat said uneasily. "I heard he was real cool when Pacifica called the White House to relay our demands. They said he just thanked them for calling and said he'd check out the situation."

"Well, he is a complicated guy," Coco agreed. Desperate to extricate herself from the conversation before becoming responsible for Carter's behavior, she looked

93

furtively toward the half-opened door of the toilet. "Do you think I could use the ladies' room, Izzat?"

"Leave your purse outside on the floor," Izzat answered irritably.

Coco set down her purse, walked into the bathroom, and turned on the light.

Just as she'd suspected, the cubicle was dirty and smelly. The one small window set close to the ceiling had been boarded up and squares of toilet paper were disintegrating in pools of muddy water on the floor. Coco locked the door, looked at the toilet seat with various colored smears streaked across it, gagged and then recovered.

Quickly she pulled off her fur jacket and hooked it over the doorknob from where one of the sleeves drooled down into a nasty puddle on the floor. After shaking the water off the fur, Coco unzipped and stepped out of her corduroy jumpsuit, awkwardly elevating each leg high above the ground so the cuffs wouldn't get wet. Then, naked except for her bikini underpants, Coco began drawing sheets of paper out of the metallic mailbox dispenser and daintily arranged them around the toilet seat as if coupling toy metal boxcars on an electric train track.

Sitting down carefully so as not to create a draft that would send the papers drifting onto the floor, Coco balanced herself on the edge of one thigh to avoid direct contact with any syphilitic germs on the soiled toilet seat that might penetrate the paper and send an infection spiraling up into her private parts.

Then, holding her breath to inhibit inhalation of any objectionable odors, Coco looked into the sink. It was worse than she had anticipated. A green-colored mold floated atop the shallow reservoir of dirty water in which a regatta of debris was sailing. Hair of various ethnic origins raced around with a cellophane cigarette wrapper that had filled up with water like a loaded condom. Beached on the sink ledge was a soiled bar of melting soap with several hairs stuck to it and a rubber drain stopper trailing its metal chain toward the floor.

Morosely Coco looked around the cubicle wondering whether the Burman's bathroom would end up in the same condition if Coco never returned home again. Would Gavin ever think of tidying up the toilet in order to maintain some minimal sanitation and safety standards? Would he ever remember to deposit his double-edged Schick Injector blades in the smiling slash marked "For Used Razors," inside the medicine chest? Would he be aware of the fact that someday even that repository might back up and release its lethal reserves onto the floor? Would he remember to navigate the bathroom scale into its proper longitudinal and latitudinal dock between the third and fourth aisles of tiles so the marker wouldn't wiggle when a person stepped on board and leaned forward to study the ////s between the numbers? Would he check to see if the spindly tub drain was in open position every night so no dripping faucet could flood the house? Would he remember to turn off the dishwasher to conserve the hot water whenever someone took a bath and ban all toilet flushings when someone was in the shower so there would be no sudden cutoff of cold water which could cause a child to get scalded by an all-hot spray? Would Gavin get out of bed in the middle of the night to jiggle the toilet handle and stop the nerve-wracking noise of running water which sometimes made Josh wet his bed in his sleep?

The thought of running water made Coco's bladder start to function.

Crumbling up a handful of toilet paper, she automatically wiped herself with the front-to-back motion recommended by her mother who believed all vaginal infections were caused by women recklessly wiping themselves back-to-front and thus introducing rectal matter into their vaginitis—vulnerable vaginas.

For one brief moment after getting redressed, Coco considered cleaning up the bathroom but then—remembering she was a hostage, not a hostess—opened the door and walked outside to retrieve her purse. Chilled from sitting naked on the toilet, she hugged her fur jacket close to her body as she approached Izzat again.

"Would you happen to have an extra cigarette?" she asked, trying to sound casual and comradely. "I think I lost my pack."

Impatiently Izzat reached into his pocket and pulled out a crumpled package of Winstons.

"Here. You can keep these. I have plenty."

"Oh, thank you, Izzat," Coco said emotionally, stuffing the package into her jacket pocket. But after she returned to her place on the floor and smoked two cigarettes, Coco felt Izzat's warm reassurances begin to fade and the possibility of never leaving the Gulf station alive became more real to her again. Visions of her four beautiful children filled her head, and Coco felt an unbearable yearning to see and be near her family once more. Now—after all her complaints about physical, mental, emotional, sexual, organizational, domestic, and professional exhaustion—all Coco felt was an aching desire to return to her husband and children. Now that the responsibilities that harassed her were threatened with termination, they all suddenly seemed desperately dear. Fear-for-her-life had melted away all her resentments like a warm spring breeze shrinking a lumpy old snowman in the backyard.

It was perfectly clear to Coco that Gavin would be unable to run the house without her. With Coco gone, who would pick up the dirty socks from the living room floor each morning where they lay crumbled up like some successfully exterminated mice who had eaten the poisonous pink pellets planted in the pantry by Meyer's Exterminating Company? Who would fingerpleat the Sarah Lee cake covers back into their original tinfoil dents so the Danish coffeeroll wouldn't dry out, or warn the kids that the spice bottle behind the minced onion was filled with marijuana, not oregano? With Coco gone, who would recap the whiskey bottles after each party so the alcohol wouldn't evaporate, or carry home tasty treats in doggie bags from overpriced restaurants to use for the children's brown-bag lunches the next morning? If Coco were killed, who would rescue the sofa pillows from the dogs who, frenzied by the inexplicable behavior of the mailman approaching the house and then retreating without attempting entry, savagely shook the pillows until they shimmied out of their covers like snakes shedding their skins to expose archaeological layers of the previous prints in which Coco had recovered them? If Coco didn't return home again, who would, in a brief three or four years, explain to Jessica about menstruation and break her first Midol in half so she could swallow it down?

Coco felt self-pity welling up inside her until she noticed Abass get up off the bench and walk over to the Ambassador.

Then panic pinched her and she cowered back

97

against the wall. This time, however, instead of a kick, Abass delivered Mohammed a long lecture in Persian before untying his hands.

Immediately the Ambassador stood up, flipped back his cape with a debonair shrug, and began searching through the pockets of his tuxedo jacket.

"I'm afraid I don't have a dime," he said in English, turning to Coco.

Coco felt a rush of irritation irrigate her nervous system. She had always been resentful of the foreign diplomats who lived easy elitist lives in Washington, impervious to parking restrictions and immune to prosecution when they ran down pedestrians. The Ambassador was obviously so insulated from real life that he didn't even know the price of a public telephone call in the District of Columbia.

"You need fifteen cents," Coco said coolly, extracting a nickel and a dime from her purse.

"Thank you very much." The Ambassador took the coins and then began patting his slim buttocks fretfully. "But now it appears that I have left my address book home."

"Why don't you call information?" Coco suggested. But then, perceiving the depth of his privileged helplessness, she stood up and accompanied him to the telephone. "It's 411."

Mohammed nodded, lifted the receiver, deposited the money and adjusted the mouthpiece an antiseptic distance away from his face as he dialed. The receiver was so far from his ear that Coco could hear a recording repeat *Please check with your directory first. If you still need help just stay on the line* before an operator interrupted the message.

"Hello. This is Ambassador Mohammed Mohammed

of Iran. We have an emergency situation in progress here and I need President Carter's private telephone number immediately."

"One moment, please."

Several seconds passed before the operator spoke again. "I'm sorry, sir, but your party has requested that their number not be given out."

"But this is an emergency, operator."

"I'm sorry, sir. But the Carters have an unlisted number."

"Everyone in Washington has an unlisted number," Coco said bitterly. "It's just a big status stick. Why don't you ask for the White House switchboard?"

The operator could apparently hear Coco as well as Coco could hear her.

"That number is 462–1414," she said immediately.

The Ambassador depressed the receiver hook and waited for the coins to return.

Nothing happened.

Delicately Coco thumped her fist against the side of the telephone box several times. She was about to start thrashing it when the Ambassador grabbed her hand.

"I don't think we can afford to break the telephone right now," he said with a gentle, apologetic smile.

Coco shrugged, opened her purse, and found another fifteen cents. The Ambassador deposited the money, dialed the number and, still obviously repelled by an oral receptacle intended for the general public, adjusted the receiver away from his face again. When the White House operator answered, the Ambassador identified himself and asked to be connected with the President. A moment later, the media-familiar, porridge-thick drawl drooled out of the receiver.

"Is that you, Mr. Ambassador?"

"Yes sir, Mr. President."

"Are you all right?" Jimmy Carter inquired anxiously.

"Yes, sir. Pretty good, sir."

"I only heard about your situation from a radio station manager about an hour ago," the President said. "Since then, we've verified everything your captors said. Police Chief Callahan has already set up his position outside the gasoline station there and we have a situation control room going here in the East Wing. I've got Ham Jordan contacting all your embassy and UN people and our technicians are setting up a hotline to Tehran right now."

"Well, I certainly appreciate all you're doing, Mr. President, but there's been a new development since our captors sent their first message to you. One of the terrorists is a Palestinian chap who's a member of the P.L.O. and he's demanding the release of three prisoners from a Jerusalem jail in exchange for our Jewish hostage. As you know, Dr. Canada was captured in the company of a Mrs. Charlotte—or Coco—Burman whose car was being serviced here at the station," the Ambassador explained. "That's why I was asked to telephone you."

"Oh, no," the President groaned unhappily. His sugar-smooth syllables kept sliding out through the space between the Ambassador's ear and the receiver. "This muddies up the waters considerably. I wonder—would it be possible for me to speak with John Canada?"

"Of course, sir." Ambassador Mohammed looked over at Abass. "I mean, I'll inquire, sir." Unhappily Mohammed turned toward his captors. "The President would like to speak with Mr. Canada," he announced.

Abass shrugged his consent and Canada instantly

rose to his feet. His unbuttoned trenchcoat, gaping open like an unzipped fly, flared out around him as he ran to the telephone.

"Good evening, Mr. President. John Canada here," he said, wedging the receiver between his cheek and his shoulder.

There was a long pause and Canada's facial expressions flickered from strain to shame as he listened to Jimmy Carter. Coco could no longer hear the President because the receiver was lodged tightly against Canada's face.

"Well, it's a somewhat complicated story, Mr. President," Canada said, his face reddening with embarrassment. "It was actually a combination of coincidences."

Abass began retying the rope around Ambassador Mohammed's wrists.

"Yes, sir, Mr. President," Canada said, after a lengthy pause. "I certainly understand how this might look to the media, sir. But Mrs. Burman and I were at a Board meeting earlier today and she was simply going to drop me back at my hotel."

The Ambassador, the three terrorists, and Coco were listening with astonishment. Apparently the President was more upset about the incriminating circumstances of Canada's capture than the kidnapping itself.

"I'm really awfully sorry, sir, but I can assure you that it was absolutely innocent," Canada said before the President interrupted him with another long tirade. Clearly, the boyish Baptist President was scolding Canada for not keeping his lust locked in his heart where it belonged.

"Yes sir, I certainly understand your feelings, Mr. President. I know there's been a lot of weird scandals lately, and I'll certainly read the *Guidelines for Presidential Staff Members* as soon as I'm released, sir. Yes, sir. Thank you, sir."

Coco stepped forward to hang up the receiver.

Visibly upset by his presidential reprimand, Canada looked at each of the grave faces watching him before focusing on Aly. "The President is going to call the Israeli ambassador," he said.

Then, without another word, Canada returned to his place on the floor and sat down, burying his face in his arms.

Suddenly, with no forewarning, Coco started to cry.

She wanted to talk to Gavin. She wanted to tell him where she was, so her life would be secured by his knowledge of her whereabouts.

Tears ran down her face and sobs shook her shoulders as she ran toward Izzat.

"Izzat," she cried, almost sliding into him because of the slush underfoot, "please let me call my husband and tell him where I am. He was expecting me home hours ago and he's going to freak out when I don't show up. He can't even go look for me because there's no one else there to take care of the kids."

"He'll know where you are," Izzat said, nodding toward the television set. "It's probably been on the news already."

"Oh, please, Izzat," she sobbed. "If it's public already, please just let me talk to him for one minute. I can't say anything you haven't announced already."

Izzat looked at Abass and Aly. Although he spoke in Persian, Coco sensed he was pleading her case. Finally, Abass grunted his approval.

"Go ahead," Izzat said.

"Oh, thank you," Coco wept. Opening her purse, she

dug through the coins in her wallet and dropped two dimes into the telephone.

"Hello?"

"Gavin? It's me. Coco. I've been captured, Gavin. I'm a hostage at the Gulf service station on 18th and Columbia Road."

"Coco! I know. Someone from the White House just called me. Are you OK, honey? Are you hurt?"

"No. I'm OK, Gavin. Just a little shook up. Are the kids OK?"

"Yeah, they went to bed about eight so they don't know yet and I'm not going to tell them until the morning. It's incredible, Coco. I can't believe it. What did they do to you, honey?"

"Oh, nothing really, Gavin. It's just Izzat and those two friends of his. You know them." She turned her face toward the wall and lowered her voice a little. "Except the short guy is a Palestinian, Gavin, and now he wants the Israelis to release some Arabs in exchange for me. They're holding the Iranian Ambassador until the Shah releases 123 political prisoners. Two of them are Izzat's brothers."

"I know, Coco. The guy from the White House told me that."

"Oh. And did he tell you that John Canada is in here too?"

"Yeah. How did that happen?"

"Well, he was over at Diana's and I invited him to come home with me after the party so you could meet him and we took a taxi over here to pick up the car first and that's when they caught us."

Silence.

"Gavin?"

More silence.

"Are you there?" Coco asked.

"Bullshit," Gavin said.

"What do you mean, bullshit?" Coco squeaked.

"Did you have a date with John Canada, Coco?"

"Oh, Gavin!" The blade of injustice that sliced through Coco's breast was retroactively authentic. Since her affair with Canada had been aborted, she felt she had regained her honor.

"First you leave for work at six in the morning and then you announce you have to go to a party right after work and then at eight o'clock you're out on the street with some Romeo . . ."

"Oh, I can't believe you're talking like this," Coco sobbed, genuinely aggrieved. "I can't believe you'd suspect me of something like that at a time like this. For God's sake, Gavin. I'm a hostage. I might get killed in here. I might die and all you can think about is your damn . . ."

"Coco . . ." Gavin tried to interrupt.

"You've gotten so goddamn *jealous* since your problem started," Coco complained. "You never used to be this way, Gavin. You're so obsessed with sex that's all you think anyone else ever thinks about. Can't you imagine how I'm feeling right now?"

She looked around the body shop. Although no one was looking at her, she felt that everyone was listening.

There was another long pause from Gavin's end of the line.

"OK, honey," he said finally. "I'm sorry. Forget what I said. I love you, Coco. I've been out of my mind ever since I got the telephone call. I don't know what I'm doing or saying."

"That's OK, Gavin. I understand." Coco sobbed louder. "I love you, too."

"I'm going to call the police and the White House and the UN and everyone else I can find, Coco. I'll get you out of there honey. I promise. Don't worry. Don't be afraid."

"I'm not."

"I love you so much, Coco. I need you so much."

Coco rested her cheek against the cold wall. That, at least, was true. Poor Gavin did need her. Gavin, who believed life was perfectible, like a tennis game, so that if you practiced hard, paid attention, and kept your left foot in front of the right everything would be okay, was really going to have his philosophy tested by Coco's capture.

With Coco a prisoner, Gavin would have to take care of the kids and the house and his own time-consuming psychogenic aspermia all alone. Guiltily Coco pictured Gavin masturbating vainly upon his pillow, gradually growing desperate as he awaited his delayed ejaculation. But then, again, it was perfectly possible that Gavin might take care of the whole job more efficiently, effectively, and affectionately alone. Perhaps he would discover that Coco offered no special advantages in terms of his sex problem and would opt for solitude on a permanent basis.

"Gavin, honey," Coco said, "please be very careful how you tell the kids. Don't scare them too much. Explain to them it's just Izzat and a couple of his friends trying to get some free publicity—that they really need. Don't let them get traumatized or anything."

"OK, Coco. Give me the telephone number in there, will you, honey?"

"It's . . ." Coco peered down at the faded figures in the center wheel of the telephone, "232–7865."

"OK. I'll call you back as soon as I find out what's

happening. Be careful, Coco, and call me if you hear anything or if you can think of something I should do."

"Sure, Gavin. I love you."

She was still sobbing as she hung up the receiver. Hurrying back to her same place on the floor, Coco sat down and built her arms into a rectangular frame atop her knees. Then she lowered her face inside the hollow cave for some privacy to continue crying, quietly but steadily, for a while. Basically, she was angry at herself for not having known something awful was going to happen.

Actually Coco had been subliminally registering ominous omens for several weeks now. Sometime earlier in the month the Burman's middle-of-the-line-model small and major electrical appliances had begun going on the blink—breaking down, burning out, shorting, sticking, and jamming. Since Coco had always known mechanical breakdowns were premonitions of human ones, she should have realized that when one of Nicky's socks spun up and over the inner guard railing of her Bendix washing machine to travel like a fatal aneurism up the major artery of rubber hose which expelled dirty washwater into her ancient scrub-tub, (the drain trap of which she religiously harvested for lint, clotted kleenex balls, and disintegrated unused bus transfers after each load of laundry) something awful was about to happen.

Perversely, Coco had resisted reading any pessimistic prophecies into the fact that all her electrical appliances were breaking down and told herself they were simply responding to carefully engineered obsolescence agendas rather than any heavenly dictates. But the fact that the onions and potatoes, which escaped from their sacks in the darkest corners of Coco's kitchen cabinets, had started growing long leafy vines that curled around her canned goods while all the store-bought houseplants began drying up and dying off beneath their expensive incandescent pro-gro lights, should not have been ignored. Despite all the fertilizer and plant food and carefully measured and mystified water with which Coco administered first aid, the sweet-and-sour-pork pink chopsticks from the Yenching Palace no longer supported perky philodendron, and all that remained of her once-thick avocado plant was the split pit sticking out of the damp dirt. Even the cuttings, which she had clipped off ailing plants, leaned limp and listless—like seasick sailors—over the sides of jelly jars docked on windowsills around the house—rotting rather than rerooting in their water.

Oh, Coco should have known! She should have trusted her instincts instead of dismissing them. She should have been guided by her own code of criminal justice so she wouldn't now be sitting and shivering, on the floor of the Gulf service station. Just as Coco subtly punished Gavin when he bought the wrong-sized vacuum cleaner bags or coffee filters, God was now punishing Coco for something.

Racing back through time, Coco tried to remember any sins serious enough to have singled her out for such martyrdom, but this was difficult because Coco always assiduously avoided tempting fate in any way. Indeed, for years she had vetoed a vasectomy for Gavin, since she feared God would construe such a ballsy act as a sign of satisfaction with the status quo and thus a challenge that could create a clear and present danger to the health and safety of Coco's extant children.

Still there were lots of possible reasons. Perhaps this was all happening not because Coco had illicit designs on John Canada but because she had filled her own gas tank at the self-service island last week to save seven cents on the gallon. Perhaps this was the appropriate punishment for jeopardizing the jobs of three hard-pressed foreign students. Or perhaps Coco had provoked God by not bothering to vote in the last local school board election and had almost overlooked the date of the deadline for her Motor Vehicle Department inspection. It was also possible that the Lord was punishing her for no longer bothering to slice bananas into the strawberry Jell-O she made for the children before it solidified or because she had lied when she received her jury duty summons and said she was pregnant so as to receive an automatic postponement. Perhaps God was pissed off because Coco never took any adult education courses or hadn't joined her neighborhood fresh-produce-buying co-op in order to get organically grown tomatoes. Maybe He was doing her, according to His own secret celestial payback equivalency scale, because Coco didn't use a low phosphorous, ecologically sound laundry detergent, or because she didn't have an aggressive vitamin health program for the kids.

Maybe getting kidnapped was the righteous repayment for not cooking in a wok or for stealing stationery supplies from the Social Science Institute and storing them in the trunk of her car, so that if she got rescued the police would find the loot right there in the Gulf garage and charge her with petty larceny. Or perhaps Coco had been kidnapped because she'd pillaged the rich residue in the kids' school's Lost and Found box last week, feigning a search for some specific scarf or sweater while she hastily matched up pairs of unfamiliar mittens and gloves to replenish the Burman's lost reserves.

Oh, yes. The truth of the matter was that Coco had committed a covey of sins which could warrant her capture by a trio of terrorists and a premature death in the Rock Creek Park Gulf gasoline station.

It was perfectly obvious that Coco deserved what she was getting.

# CHAPTER SIX

When Aly finally plugged in the TV set, Coco hurried across the garage to watch her experience over television. CBS had just released a report on the background of the three terrorists. With information obviously obtained from the dean of students at Howard University, Channel 9 had established that Aly—the P.L.O. guerrilla—was only nineteen years old and the youngest member of a family of eleven children, most of whom now lived in Lebanon. When a picture of Aly's large family appeared on the screen, Coco heard the young Palestinian cry out with pain and rage. Coco assumed the photograph had been taken from possessions Aly had left somewhere, probably in his dormitory room, and his anguished outcry echoed through the garage.

The next photograph showed Izzat and Abass, arms around each other's shoulders, standing in front of the Rock Creek Gulf service station. The anchorman said that Abass was an acknowledged leader of the Iranian students in the Washington area and that he had been known to advocate the violent overthrow of the Shah's regime. There was less information available about Izzat so the newscaster could only announce that several students from Howard claimed that Izzat was a hard-working honor student in the engineering department and well liked by his peers.

Next followed a pictorial review of Ambassador Mohammed's career. His life story was voiced over a series of society function photographs of the Ambassador cavorting about with various women, including Elizabeth Taylor. There was also a pictorial tour of the Iranian Embassy on Massachusetts Avenue and a rundown on the most recent parties held there. An official portrait of Mohammed and the Shah of Iran elicited excited hisses from the terrorists, followed by an obscene-sounding Persian jeer.

Next the anchorman read a biographical sketch of John Canada while showing a photograph taken of him with President Carter in Plains, Georgia, shortly after Carter's election. This was followed by a scenic view of a secluded country estate outside Princeton, New Jersey, where the current Mrs. Canada and various of their respective and mutual children were waiting out the ordeal. When the announcer noted the irony of an internationally famous development economist being kidnapped by Third World revolutionaries, Aly laughed out loud and made another ribald-sounding remark, this time in Arabic.

Meanwhile, Coco was experiencing a creeping concern about what picture Gavin would produce in response to media requests. Since the only recent, decent snapshot of Coco was in the bottom drawer of her desk, where Gavin would never think to look, he would probably produce some dreary, bleary photograph taken at the beach which would remain, like an eidetic trauma, on the eyes of the viewing public. Briefly Coco wondered whether a well-organized person like Diana Whitcomb would keep flattering 8″ × 10″ professional glossies at home alongside her fourteen-page single-spaced resumé in some conspicuous place so any good investigative reporter would find it if she were killed in a car crash.

But the next scene, instead of featuring Coco Burman, panned the Gulf service station and showed various vehicles, including armored tanks, lumbering into line behind the gasoline pumps. United States military, National Guard, and Metropolitan police vans were forming a solid wall at the end of the driveway where another several inches of snow had accumulated since Coco crossed it several hours ago. TV camera crews were perched on scaffolds set on the sidewalk where policemen, plain-clothes security agents, and soldiers held back spectators, media people, and crisis freaks who had already convened there.

Watching the TV screen, Coco became aware, for the first time, of vibrations inside the garage caused by the heavy equipment rumbling around in front of the station. The retread tires, hung on the walls, shook occasionally, and Coco could feel the cinder-block walls shimmy slightly when a truck rolled to a stop outside the garage door.

A damp sensation of anxiety washed through her body.

"There's a great deal of tension building up outside this small gasoline station near the National Zoo," the announcer announced in a terse, terrorist-attack tone of voice. "Foreign officials have begun to congregate outside the station along with friends of the hostages and diplomatic representatives from Embassy Row.

"Police Chief Callahan is supervising the situation. A cracker-jack seige negotiator, who has never lost a hostage in his long career, Chief Callahan in 1976 managed the release of the Hanafi hostages at which time, ironically, the Iranian Ambassador, now being held prisoner inside the garage, helped with negotiations. Meanwhile, the White House is making arrangements to fly the terrorists to Algeria if the Shah agrees to release the 123 Iranian dissidents being held in prison in Tehran. The students originally asked for a Concord jet, but since the Concord can't land at National, ground transportation is being arranged to take the group to Dulles. Rumors have also begun to circulate that one of the terrorists—a Palestinian member of the P.L.O.—is requesting the release of three P.L.O. prisoners from an Israeli jail in exchange for the third hostage."

Coco wondered how she got to be third.

"Mrs. Charlotte Burman, thirty-seven, an attractive, active wife, and mother of four young children, lives in the neighborhood near the service station. She and John Canada were apparently captured when they tried to pick up her car which was being serviced at the shop."

Coco leaned forward nervously expecting to see herself on the screen. But it was her house rather than her face that suddenly appeared on television.

Photographed from the street, the Burman's quarrelsomely crooked rowhouse suddenly looked stately and expensive. Self-consciously Coco glanced at her captors, afraid they would perceive her home as a mansion since the camera successfully camouflaged the drastic state of its decay.

From such a soft, flattering angle, no one could tell that the electrical system in the house was defective, the heating system erratic, and the plumbing so rusty that the third floor toilet often presented an aquatic ballet of dancing turds when the seat cover was lifted. From a distance no one could see that the gorgeous green English ivy frosting the front wall was perniciously eating away the cement between the bricks. No one could tell that the corroded drain pipe hugging the corner of the house was wired in place or that most of the windows were outlined with white surgical tape which Coco had applied when she painted the inside frames but forgot to remove before the first frost of winter froze the tape to the glass. Certainly TV viewers couldn't see the mailbox, which had fallen off the front wall because the bricks needed pointing, parked on the top stair.

Coco, however, could tell that Gavin had forgotten to let the dogs out since there were no paw prints on the stairs, no dark piles of dog-do on the hill, or any crusty yellow-rimmed pee-holes in the fresh-fallen snow.

Nevertheless, to a Middle-Eastern exile, Coco's private abode might well look like a palace. Nervously she gnawed at the ruffled skin of her bottom lip again.

As the TV camera shifted slightly, Coco caught sight of a police car parked in front of the Burman house and for the first time since her capture, Coco smiled happily.

All right!

At least now she wouldn't have to worry about her family's safety. Apparently, while she was in captivity, sentries would provide twenty-four-hour protection so Coco wouldn't have to worry about robbers, muggers, rapists, killers, vandals, or thieves entering her home. Indeed, tonight even the family Monte Carlo Chevrolet was safe inside a ring of armed military vehicles so no one could remove the battery or break the front window to steal Coco's D.C. motor vehicle sticker which was about to expire anyway.

Coco sighed as a sweet sense of security seeped through her. At least now that Channel 9 had shown her house under police surveillance, no one would dare steal her chubby garbage cans with B U R M A N printed in bright red paint around the top and the bottom. Now no one would test the little stickers saying THESE PREMISES PROTECTED BY AN ARMED CITIZEN that Coco had bought and stuck on her windows. Now no one would dare steal her *Washington Post* in the morning en route to the No. 40 bus stop. Now local criminals would assume the police had recorded the registration numbers of all the Burmans' removable possessions, making them too hot to fence and thus not worth stealing.

"More news will be brought to you as the situation develops. Regular coverage will continue at 7:00 tomorrow morning."

Coco looked up at the Midas Muffler clock. It was 11:30. Slowly she left the terrorists still standing around the television set and walked back to sit down beside Canada.

"Are you cold?" she asked.

He nodded mutely.

"Did the President upset you?" She leaned over to button his dirty-blond trenchcoat for him.

"What do you think?" Canada growled.

"What did he say?" Coco asked gently, feeling the chill left by Canada's cancelled affection.

"He was pissed off because I stumbled into this deathtrap with a woman who isn't my wife," Canada said, still suffering the sting of his presidential scolding. "And he's sore because the fucking press corps is already hot on that angle. I'll tell you one thing. Jimmy Carter didn't need any adultery rumors after all the other bum raps he's gotten stuck with—Bourne's prescription caper and Jordon's Amaretto fling. So if the papers try to blow our relationship up into something big, that'll blow my Senate confirmation."

"And you're mad at me?" Coco inquired increduously, feeling hurt hurtle through her body and indignant tears swim across her eyes.

"Well what the hell do you think I am?" Canada asked. "Even if we get out of here alive, my life is going to be ruined. My wife will divorce me and roll me for every penny that isn't already assigned to my other wives. She'll bankrupt me."

Coco felt her feelings for Canada turn off like the lights in her house when she plugged the 120-W air conditioner into the 220-W line.

There.

Over and out.

She could never care about him ever again. Never. Indeed, now that he had alerted her to the gossip problem, she began to wonder how to erase the suspicious stains off her own reputation if she lived through the ordeal. Would Coco ever be able to convince Gavin she'd been taken hostage in a state of sexual innocence? Another eruption of eczema in her elbow answered the question.

"You know, it was only 8:15 when they caught us," Coco said defensively, as she scratched her way up her coat sleeve. "That's not very late. I don't think the press can make too much out of that. And anyway, we can just say you were coming over to my house for a drink and that we stopped here to get my car first. That's a perfectly legitimate story. In fact, I think it's a good one."

Canada ignored her comment. "Well, this experience is going to prove very educational for me if I live through it," he said more to himself than to Coco. "The fact that this kind of thing can happen right here in Washington D.C. shows that our government hasn't

116

any political self-respect anymore and that any radical or revolutionary group of kooks can walk all over us. We're so cowed by world opinion and so afraid that communism sounds better than capitalism, we don't even defend ourselves anymore. And it's people like you who make anti-Americanism so trendy."

"I can't believe I heard you say that," Coco gasped. "Marxism is hardly America's major problem. Our problem is that Americans are miserably unhappy and don't like the way our country runs anymore. It's out of desperation everyone's looking for alternative ideas."

"Who's unhappy?" Canada asked belligerently. "You?"

"*Who's unhappy?*" Coco echoed. "Well, needless to say, who's unhappy doesn't show up in the NII, but everybody *I* know is unhappy. People spend their lives trying to make enough disposable income to buy a few crappy products that don't last longer than their warranties do. There's no political spirit or camaraderie left in the country anymore. Did you know that the number of state chapters of the Society of Survivors of Suicides is growing by leaps and bounds?"

"God, you're flaky," Canada said, shaking his head.

"Well," said Coco in retaliation, "I think the NII sucks—because it doesn't deal with any of the basic reasons for America's discontent. In fact, it avoids the fundamental cause for all the social and political problems we're having."

"And what are those?" Canada inquired sarcastically.

"Built-in obsolescence," Coco responded promptly. "I think the reason our traditional values are breaking down is because all our consumer goods conk out on us. I think broken appliances are like broken promises between America's corporations and American consumers. Automobiles and appliances are symbols of the American dream so when those things fall apart people lose confidence in the system. They feel betrayed because they can't believe in corporate integrity any more and that causes political apathy and psychological alienation."

John Canada looked at Coco as if her social analysis were the warm-up spritz of a stand-up comic.

"No, I'm really serious," Coco insisted. "It's the up-keep and maintenance of our appliances that's freaking everybody out. No one knows how to fix stuff anymore and that's why repair work is one of the few growth industries left in the country today, plus the how-to-do-it-yourself book publishing business. I mean, I always believed in small and large electrical appliances until I found out that couples blame each other for nonfunctioning equipment. Faulty technology and obsolescent items create human conflict. Women think men should be able to fix everything and men feel sexually inadequate if they can't."

"You're nuts," John Canada said coldly.

Coco's pulse began to race. "Well it's perfectly clear that you're so *into* the establishment you can't see the truth." Her voice quivered. "You'd do anything to stay on the inside. You even want to engineer a cover-up of the NII project so it won't reflect badly on your damn SSI Board or endanger your damn Senate confirmation."

"What the hell are you talking about?" Canada thundered.

Shaking with rage, Coco stood up. For a moment she looked over at the Ambassador whose deep craggy face had darkened as he listened to the quarrel, but then she looked away again quickly.

Now, feeling totally alone, Coco walked over to Izzat with the slow, aching motions of a marionette.

"Would it be all right if I sat in my car?" she asked. "It's awfully cold on the floor."

Thoughtfully, Izzat looked over at the hydraulic lift where the Monte Carlo, blemished by powder-blue primer paint stains which spread like acne across the front fenders, was parked above the ground.

"OK," he grunted, "you can warm up in there for a while, but I have the keys here in my pocket, so don't try anything."

"Thanks."

Coco walked across the garage to the car and looked up at the door handle. It was about a foot out of reach. Seeing some boxes stacked against the far wall, she went around to inspect them.

The first bunch of boxes were full of disassembled motor parts, melted-down sparkplugs, and miscellaneous metal pieces clumped together like forgotten Tinker Toys in a trunk. Portions of pipes, disconnected joints, and an infinite variety of castoff car parts rose in chaotic heaps inside misshapen boxes. For a moment Coco wondered if any of the blunt metal pieces might become weapons, but then dismissed the idea.

Coco had never really understood what a retread was and vaguely wondered whether one of her captors might find her a good one for a spare while they were all just sitting around doing nothing. Perhaps tomorrow she might even ask Izzat to teach her how to use one of those mysterious tread-measuring tools which could predict and prevent tragic highway blowouts so she might learn some popular mechanics while she was locked up in the garage.

That, at least, would be worthwhile because for

years, Coco had felt technologically incompetent, a gadget-greenhorn who suffered extensively from her ignorance of chemistry, physics, math, and electrical engineering.

Coco looked at the rows of tools in graduated sizes that were mounted on the wall. They looked like an old-fashioned family growing up. Perhaps as real families shrunk and shattered, only tribes of tools would remain intact, spanning the spectrum from infancy to adulthood in traditional Norman Rockwell fashion. Looking at the littlest pliers—a perfect miniature of the monstrous model at the top of the line—Coco thought of Joshie, predictably progressing toward larger-scale standardized proportions.

A sharp intake of air in her lungs tasted of grief.

Coco continued to scan the regiments of auto mechanic tools. Except for the bowlegged womanly wrenches, most of the tools were clearly of a masculine nature. The screwdrivers hung in an erect row on a pegboard, triggerless guns like the pistols the terrorists toyed with as jovially as a gang of little boys on the Burman's back porch preparing for a pissing contest in which to aim and arch their discharge into the distance.

Perhaps technology was only a modern metaphor for previously poetic male/female symbols. Perhaps all the tools around the garage were just industrialized expressions of sexual dualism—the fanbelts, rubber inner tubes, and retread tires only contemporary casings for perpetual penetrating tools. Perhaps guns were only the logical extension of nails and screws waiting to be inserted into empty orbs. Maybe all the various lubricants cased in the Quaker and Halveston oil cartons on the floor were the commercial juices needed to grease the dry mechanical intercourse of modern industrial times.

Remembering her mission she returned to her search for a box sufficiently intact to support her weight.

A carton of something stamped Cruisemaster Belted Bias looked tall enough to stand on but too heavy for her to push. The Safety Vision Products for Safe Driving box was a little too flat, but Coco finally found a squarish Gulf Anco carton that looked right and shoved it around to the front of the car. Then, standing on top of the box, she stretched up to reach the handle. After several tries she got the door open and, stepping on the vestigial remains of a running board, pulled herself up into the front seat. Instinctively she settled behind the steering wheel, instantly noticing that the front seat had been shoved way back and that both the inside and outside rearview mirrors had been shifted. Whoever had driven her car into the body shop had readjusted every movable part for his ten-second stint at the wheel. Coco firmly believed that sadistic mechanics and parking-lot jocks made many needless adjustments just to harass women drivers.

Deciding to leave the seat where it was since she didn't have to reach the pedals, Coco extracted the unnervingly slim package of cigarettes from her purse and, without counting the contents, lit one of them and absorbed a stream of nicotine into her system. The smoke felt terrific. Now all Coco's anguish about smoking or not smoking—about quitting or dying young—was moot. She was obviously going to die young regardless of her health habits or any of the live-forever fads she had contemplated undertaking. Health was no longer a determining factor in her survival.

Cuddled up inside the cloistered car, Coco felt the outside world beginning to recede. Now the contours of the Gulf service station were providing the perimeters of her universe as she looked around the garage from her new heightened perspective, with renewed interest. In front of her car was a collection of tin highway signs someone had nailed to the wall and she became instantly immersed in studying them. The top two read FLAMMABLE and INFLAMMABLE. That contradiction fascinated her. How could two words that looked like antonyms mean exactly the same thing? How could the English language be so careless about such serious words? She thought about that for a long time before moving on to the next sign which said MAINTAIN SPEED. (What if you were afraid to keep driving as fast as you had been?) BRIDGES FREEZE BEFORE ROADS. (How long before and how could you tell if a bridge was really frozen?) WATCH OUT FOR FALLING ROCK. (Were you supposed to look sideways instead of straight ahead?)

THINK METRIC. Somehow the THINK METRIC sign seemed fraught with meaning for Coco who had not yet learned the metric system despite the fact that Riggs Bank—along with her November statement—had sent her a small plastic card called "Approximate Conversion from Metric Measures" as a Christmas gift. Perhaps the metric system was really a metapolitical model —an international code or a Third World cipher which, decoded, would give Coco a clue as to what was really happening. Perhaps metric was a mode of thought like Aristotlean logic and a person was supposed to THINK METRIC all the time—about everything—now during the Modern Period. She tried to decide who had collected, selected, and mounted those directives on the wall. Certainly not Mr. Murdock who had no sense of humor whatsoever. Had Abass or Aly or Izzat put them up? Was there a political message to be learned if Coco could master the metric system?

Sighing, she rolled down the side window and adjusted the outside mirror so she could see herself. Considering the circumstances, she didn't look too bad because she had applied more than her usual amount of makeup in Diana's bathroom in anticipation of a possible rendezvous with John Canada. Still, Coco knew from experience that in a few more hours her makeup would start to fade, like ink on an envelope left too long outdoors, and that then she would appear pale and tired, worn and weary. The parenthetical impressions beneath her eyes would become more pronounced and wrinkles, like the markings of a copy editor italicizing important phrases, would underline her fatigue.

Coco would look *exactly* her age.

She rolled the window back up. It was mirrors such as this and the full-length ones in the fitting room out at Loehman's in Tyson's Corner, Virginia, which occasionally made Coco wonder whether she was, perhaps, going to commence her "change" earlier than normal and start to wither up before she was forty, begin to crinkle and crepe, pleat and pucker, like a basketload of laundry left to lie too long unfolded so that the wrinkles wormed their way into the fabric and become impossible to press away. And, unfortunately, she was particularly vulnerable to aging anxieties at the present time because of the recent—albeit tardy—FDA advisories linking estrogen to uterine cancer.

The loss of the estrogen option had caused Coco great distress, because despite her consumer cynicism, she had desperately wanted to believe in a drug-induced alternative to old age (for what indeed was old age anyway except for all those age-old symptoms commonly associated with it which estrogen was supposed to suppress?) So she had been personally and politically outraged when she heard that the federal government had reluctantly decided to protect her uterus—an organ she had no intention of ever using again—by tightening up FDA controls over the only age-retardant agent available, at a time Coco still felt compelled to look as if she were on her way to a cocktail party from the moment she awoke in the morning until she went to bed at night.

Of course it was perfectly possible that God had arranged to have Coco kidnapped as a punishment for her vain fight against the aging process. Perhaps the perfect punishment for someone afraid of aging was the total deprivation of any old age whatsoever. Perhaps God was going to see to it that Coco would never be transformed into a wizened old woman on Medicaid, too nearsighted to align the invisible plastic arrows on top of one of the newfangled childproof pill bottles dispensed to senior citizens by sadistic pharmaceutical companies.

Indeed, it was perfectly possible that Coco might die this weekend.

Perhaps the police would storm the garage like they hit that small bungalow out in California which burned down with most of the Symbionese Liberation Army inside.

What if something like that happened?

Oh, no!

Impossible. Coco looked back across the length of the garage to where the five men, captors and captives, sat lined up along the side and rear walls. The terrorists

had wrapped blankets around themselves so they resembled pictures of their ancestors resting in the desert.
Canada, too, had something thrown over his shoulders
—a small canvas cover of some sort. Only the Ambassador still remained huddled beneath his frivolously inadequate cape, without any other protection. He looked
miserably cold.

Coco turned around to peer into the back seat. Usually the kids forgot sweaters or gym clothes or mittens
back there. But tonight there was no clothing of any
kind. Even the top of the dashboard was clear, except
for several crumpled envelopes from letters Coco had
read in the car on the way to work, a few wrinkled-up
grocery lists, and several Christmas party invitations
with driving directions scribbled across them.

Coco closed her eyes.

She tried to think of herself as being dead.

She was absolutely unable to envision it.

She could, however, picture the aftermath and she
began to wonder if Gavin would arrange for an open-
coffin funeral. Why had Coco never once, during all the
long years of marriage, bothered to tell Gavin about her
preference for closed coffins? How could he be expected
to know such a thing? And now, under such frantic
circumstances, Gavin would obviously be much too upset to investigate various parlors' policies. Gavin would
simply rent the first convenient mortuary available and,
when the slow motion D.C. bureaucracy completed its
homicide investigation, Coco's corpse would be put on
public display looking like a mess.

Was it really true that human hair kept growing after
death? By the time the funeral arrangements were
made, would those two maverick hairs that occasionally

edged like ivy out of Coco's nose be dangling down? Would that wily, wiry whisker under her chin have reared its ugly head for her last public appearance? Would she look the way she did when she ran out to the grocery store early in the morning without any eye makeup but, at least, a pair of sunglasses hiding the fact?

Coco lit another cigarette, opened her shoulderbag, and probed through the interior again.

"Oh, no," she moaned, before frantically upending her purse onto the car seat. There was her wallet, with an unpaid parking ticket sticking out of it, her calendar, her notebook, her hairbrush, and dozens of writing implements.

But where was her tulip-patterned, plastic cosmetic case?

It wasn't there.

With an audible gasp of horror, she remembered.

Coco had left her cosmetic kit on the sink in Diana's bathroom after putting on her makeup.

The sudden realization that she was going to be caught dead without tweezers made Coco feel exquisitely sorry for herself.

Her treasured collection of Natural Wonder cosmetics, with which she had faced life, was gone now as she confronted death. Diana Whitcomb would find and sneer at Coco's second-class, drugstore cosmetic kit when she found it, because Diana used Estée Lauder products and her purse was handsomely outfitted with a set of matching accessories—beige leather wallet, cosmetic bag, checkbook holder, see-through credit-card carrier, oversize sunglasses case, key chain, coin purse, and cigarette lighter.

The image of Diana's purse pained Coco enormously.

Miserable, she cursed herself for her carelessness in not returning the makeup kit to its rightful place at the bottom of her purse. Oh, why hadn't she dropped it back in? And why couldn't she have kept her medium-firm double-bristle soft-contour toothbrush, with its pretty pink nipple that purged plaque from her teeth, in her purse so at least she could have massaged her gums during her imprisonment? With just a little fore-thought Coco could have alleviated any worries about her breath growing furry, although in her present situation she was prepared to concede that bad breath was better than no breath at all. And why hadn't she just spent a few seconds applying some Jolene hair lightener to her mustache so she wouldn't have to worry about people peering into her coffin and seeing that faint line of peach fuzz above her upper lip to which Tolstoy had drawn worldwide attention.

Coco slumped down deeper in the driver's seat.

And what about all the strangers—the public personnel—who, presumably, would view her corpse? What would the D.C. forensic medical team make of that hairy arrow on Coco's navel—that navigational marker pointing out her erogenous zone which had appeared during her first pregnancy and grown more lush with each subsequent conception until it ran, straight as a highway divider, down the middle of her belly, certainly serviceable as a surgical guideline if any cesarean-style dissection was required for Washington autopsies.

And, now that she thought of it, what would the city coroner make of Coco's legs? Would he waste precious forensic time, at great public expense, trying to figure out why Coco's thighs had a normal amount of hair while everything below her knees was bald? How could any non-Jewish coroner comprehend the religious significance of New Year's Eve or understand why Jewish women of the fifties felt a holy obligation to shave their legs on that holiday—even if only partially—so as to set a certain standard for the coming year?

Tearfully, Coco began returning her possessions to her purse but then paused and plucked the unpaid parking ticket out of her wallet. Ever since Coco had noticed that the number of her driving permit 473–34–0472 was the same as her Social Security, she had become paranoid about possible data-sharing arrangements between separate government agencies. Now, facing death with an unpaid No Parking 4–6:30 ticket in her purse, she began to wonder whether some D.C. Motor Vehicle Department computer would automatically notify the Social Security Administration that Coco Burman had died owing Central Violations $25.00 and request payment of that amount deducted from her old age benefits—money automatically taken from her paychecks without her consent—when she was alive and well and needed it.

Of course Coco had never thought to inquire if Gavin and the kids would receive the Social Security payments to which she was entitled if she expired before she retired. Of course she had never thought to ask about such an important thing. Assuming that the Social Security Administration would subtract the $25.00 from her old age benefits to pay Central Violations (hopefully before the ticket tucked inside her wallet doubled, after fifteen days, into an inflated $50.00 fine), would they send the balance to Coco's survivors to help pay for all her unexpected funeral expenses?

Impulsively Coco reached for her Pilot Razor-Point pen, opened her small notebook and wrote:

Friday night, 12:45 A.M.
"Dear Gavin, I don't want to sound ghoulish or anything, but in case I don't make it out of here, please look inside my wallet for a $25.00 parking ticket I got Tuesday that will double unless you pay it within 15 days. Although I might write the Social Security Administration a letter (which will also be in my purse and which I'd like you to mail if it's there) requesting they pay the ticket out of my unused old age benefits, you must make sure they do it or, if they won't, do it yourself before it doubles. Don't forget to look for both the ticket and the letter. A thousand kisses, Coco."

She recapped her pen, curled her legs beneath her bottom and then opened the notebook again. After pausing to think a moment she wrote: "It really feels funny writing possibly posthumous letters, but I'm hoping this little notebook will help you a little if I don't get out of here alive. Also, honey, now that this has happened, I think you should make a will. Ask the kids who'd they like for their guardian and then ask their first, second, and third choices if they'd be willing to take all four of them together."

Somehow the act of writing to Gavin suddenly made Coco so desperate to talk with him again that she impulsively opened the car door and began to back out of her Monte Carlo as if climbing down a ladder. Hanging onto the front seat, her feet almost touched the Gulf Anco box so when she released her grip, she landed easily on top of it. Then she walked over to Izzat.

"Would you let me talk to my husband just one more

time tonight, Izzat? I promise I won't ask again. I feel
so . . ."

"OK," he grunted, looking at Coco somewhat sympathetically. "Go ahead. One more time. But make it
quick."

"Thanks a million, Izzat. Really."

Coco had to restrain herself from blowing him a kiss.

# CHAPTER SEVEN

Coco dialed her home number and waited anxiously for Gavin to answer.

"Hello?"

It was Diana Whitcomb's voice. For a moment Coco thought she had accidentally dialed the number of the Social Science Institute.

"Diana?"

"Yes. Is that you, Coco?"

"Yes. Where are you, Diana?"

"I'm at your house, Coco. The minute I heard you and John had been kidnapped I just jumped in a cab and came right over here to help your husband any way I could. I mean, with the kids and everything. Really! I simply couldn't believe it when I heard the eleven o'clock news. Of course I felt sort of responsible because you and John had been at my house right before it happened," Diana continued. "I mean if I hadn't given a cocktail party you wouldn't have been captured. Really, the whole thing is ab-so-lute-ly in-cred-i-ble, Coco. And I didn't even know you had *left together*."

Stricken, Coco leaned her head against the wall.

Diana Whitcomb had gone to Coco's house "to help?"

Diana Whitcomb had appended herself to Gavin Burman during a highly charged situation which could only encourage treachery.

Oh, yes. It was perfectly clear that even if Coco somehow got home again—even if she survived a round-trip flight to Algeria—by the time she returned to Washington, Diana Whitcomb would have become the new resident manager of the Burman establishment and the indispensable nocturnal therapist treating Gavin's psychogenic aspermia.

Of course. There was no doubt about it. That was exactly what a young single like Diana would want— a home, a husband, and a herd of half-grown children. It was an obvious singles-swindle and Diana was exactly the sort of Wasp woman who would consider excessive sex with a Jewish lawyer transcendentally "interesting." Now Diana would assume Coco's identity, simulate the sentimentality of motherhood—without any of its anxieties—and confidently pursue her career while rooming with a wonderful family.

Diana Whitcomb would no longer have to worry about being an old maid; she would become a young one.

"Where's Gavin?" Coco asked weakly, rubbing her cheek against the cold cinder block.

"He went up to Seven-Eleven to buy some cigarettes," Diana said.

"But he doesn't smoke."

"I ran out," Diana explained.

Coco felt as if she might faint.

Oh yes. The handwriting on the wall was quite visible now. Coco Burman was going to die and Gavin was going to marry Diana Whitcomb right after the funeral. Diana would become a beautiful young stepmother and —as the memory of Coco faded away—Coco's children would learn to love Diana much more than their real mother.

"If you hadn't hurried off from my party so early maybe this wouldn't have happened," Diana said plaintively. "I mean—just a few minutes one way or the other might have made all the difference." Gradually Diana's voice softened into a whisper, slightly spiked with malice. "Where were you and John going, anyway?"

"Just . . . over to my house," Coco answered, closing her eyes.

Diana didn't care what happened to Coco. Diana was only interested in the gossip and opportunities offered by Coco's kidnapping.

"And what about Ambassador Mohammed?" Diana asked. "What's he really like? I mean, it was a lousy break getting captured, but at least you're in there with two of the most attractive men in Washington."

Tears began to collect in the dams of Coco's eyes. Diana's questions were clearly a ploy to distract attention from her designs on Gavin.

Coco could picture Diana, still dressed in her expensive salmon-colored suede skirt and vest, good silk blouse, and gorgeous wine-colored leather boots, holding the sticky receiver of Coco's kitchen telephone.

At this very moment Diana was probably surveying Coco's bulletin board, snickering at the six unsynchronized orthodontic, periodontic, and regular Dental Appointment Reminder cards or the messy list of telephone numbers for the Poison Center, Children's Hospital and Police Department. Perhaps she was revolted by the pictorial Red Cross First Aid Instruction chart, which everyone could see during meals, demonstrating how to dislodge stuck food from someone's trachea. Yes, Diana might even be reading the form letter from the Washington Gas Light Company:

WHAT TO DO IF YOU SMELL GAS. NATURAL GAS IS ODORLESS IN ITS NATURAL STATE. WE

ADD A DISAGREEABLE SMELL AS A MEANS OF
ALERTING PEOPLE IN CASE ANY GAS SHOULD
ESCAPE

or the *How to Save Energy and Money on Your Heat
Bill Hints* pamphlet from Griffith Consumers that covered the entire left corner of the bulletin board.

"Is the Ambassador . . . nice?" Diana asked.

"Oh, very," Coco answered, suddenly inspired by the
excruciating jealously that was now steaming through
her system. "He's quite attractive. In fact, he's much
handsomer than John is and promises he's going to invite me to all his la-de-da embassy parties after we get
out of here."

"Really?" Now Diana's voice was gelatinous with jealousy.

"Yes. In fact, well, you know how crisis situations
push people together. Actually John and Mo are sort
of involved in a struggle because they both . . . want to
. . . take care of me. You know?"

"You call the Ambassador Mo?" Diana asked incred-
ulously.

"Well . . . sometimes."

"God." Diana sounded overwhelmed.

There was a long silence.

Unhappily, Coco wondered if she was inciting Diana
by suggesting so many sexual possibilities.

"Well, listen, Coco, you just call me up and tell me
if there's *anything* you want me to do. I'll do anything
I can to help."

—I want you to go home—Coco thought, as the tears
splashed out of her eyes—Just go home, Diana, go
home.—

"I mean—if you want me to run out and get anything

134

special for the kids' breakfast tomorrow or anything like that."

"If I think of anything, I'll certainly call you," Coco said, letting sarcasm curdle her words as she digested Diana's announced intention of spending the night at the Burmans'.

Under the veil of a vigil, Diana would seduce Gavin and, being the egotist she was, believe herself responsible for Gavin's extraordinary responsiveness. Not knowing Gavin had psychogenic aspermia, Diana would undoubtedly think she had rejuvenated a wearily married, middle-aged man.

"Just tell Gavin I called," Coco said vaguely. Then, after waiting a few seconds, she replaced the receiver.

So. It was happening. On top of being kidnapped, Coco was being co-opted at the same time.

She remained where she was, leaning against the rear wall of the garage, inwardly railing against Diana.

OK—she thought bitterly—You want it, you get it. Just wait. Just wait until tomorrow morning. Saturday's a dilly, Diana. You'll love it. You really will. But you better try to get some sleep tonight because around seven o'clock in the morning the doorbell's going to ring and a Jehovah's Witness lady is going to be outside waiting to convert you while the heat seeps out through the front door. After that you can make five different kinds of eggs for breakfast, help Jessica with her fractions so she doesn't fail math, fill out all the Blue-Cross Blue-Shield Major Medical forms on my desk and walk your little fingers through the Yellow Pages to see if you can find some heterosexual hair stylist because all the boys need haircuts and they won't go back to Charles the First. Then you'd better order some whiskey and ask Mr. Finkelstein if you can write a check

135

for ten dollars above the exact amount of the bill when the deliveryman comes so there'll be some cash in the house over the weekend. Also you can run our traditional Saturday safari looking for Josh's hamster that escaped from its cage about a month ago (in territory presumably controlled by the Theodore Meyer Exterminating Company) and if you're lucky and don't find it—either dead or alive—you can take Josh up on Wisconsin Avenue to buy a substitute specimen of the same species which, for some reason, is somehow superior to the sort we pay $12.50 a month to exterminate simply because it's introduced into the environment in a ventilated cardboard carrier marked Friendly Beasties.

But then, Diana, you really must start cleaning the house because Saturday *is* cleaning day, you know. Please see if you can get that orange stain off the kitchen linoleum where Josh broke the bottle of Tabasco sauce and be sure to clean out the dogs' dish because old Alpo meatballs tend to get stuck to the sides and start growing a greenish mold that looks like some culture created in a science lab assigned to discover the source of Legionnaire's disease. Also don't forget to take out the garbage, Diana. There's a whole week's worth of large green bags out on the back porch. The bags may split open along the bottom seams letting all the stuff drool out when you drag them down to the alley so just take along an extra, extra-thick green bag. As for all those old newspapers on the porch, just carry them out to the trunk of your car and stack them inside so you can drop them off at the Recycling Collection Center in Rock Creek Park the next time you drive through there because Gavin feels very strongly about recycling old papers.

Really, Diana. Just try it. You'll love it.

And it will all be worthwhile because you'll have a wonderful husband. Mine. And all you have to do to keep him happy is make sure the house functions smoothly and that his balled-up socks match when one disgorges the other and that the tops and bottoms of his pajamas stay together in pairs, wherever they may be, and that his athletic supporter ends up in the same drawer as his tennis shorts. That's all. He's really no trouble whatsoever. Now he may ask you to look for some missing keys while you're cleaning—like the one that came off the piano and the one to his typewriter case and the one that opens up the radiators—but if you just keep your wits about you, I know you can handle it.

Good luck, Diana—

Quite overwrought and fraught with jealousy, Coco stumbled away from the telephone and walked past Mohammed Mohammed. He was still shuddering and shaking inside his flimsy cape and he looked up at Coco with such a pitiful expression that a wave of empathy edged through her.

She paused.

Although she held the Ambassador totally responsible for her plight—for being a *have* who lived so high on the hog that he provoked *have nots* into terrorism—he was, after all, just a man and probably more frightened than either Coco or Canada, since he was both the cause and object of the terrorists' wrath and actually had a death sentence hanging over his head. Remembering the Air France flight crew who chose to remain with the Jews at Entebbe, Coco decided to intervene on the Ambassador's behalf and impulsively turned around to walk back toward Izzat.

"What's the matter now?" Izzat asked impatiently.

"Listen, Izzat," Coco said in her well-practiced, practical-parent voice. "If your Ambassador catches pneumonia in here, he might die before you get what you want for him. And even if he only gets sick, the Shah might change his mind or use that as an excuse not to make the exchange. I really don't think you can just leave him sitting on that wet floor all night. Why don't you let him get in the car for a while to warm up?"

Irritated, Izzat shrugged so that the blanket over his shoulders fell open, exposing one hand holding a gun and the other gripping a bottle of whiskey. When he suddenly thrust his arm forward, Coco reeled back expecting to be shot. It took her several seconds to realize that Izzat was only offering her a drink. Although she hated bourbon, Coco accepted the still-warm fifth, uncapped it, and drank directly from the bottle so Izzat wouldn't think she didn't want to put her mouth where his had been. He, however, wiped off the top on his jacket sleeve before taking another swig.

"Well, what do you say, Izzat?" Coco asked, slightly nauseated from the nasty-tasting bourbon, but warmed by the reassuring act of sharing. "The Ambassador's really less of a threat up there than down here on the floor with you guys. Let him sit with me for a while."

Izzat turned to translate and transmit Coco's request to Abass. After some salacious laughter, apparently directed at Coco's interest in the Ambassador, Abass apparently agreed, for he shouted something at the diplomat.

"Here, you can probably use this," Izzat said, handing Coco the bottle of bourbon. "Keep it in the car with you. We've got plenty."

"Thank you." Coco smiled and gripped the fifth as she watched the Ambassador stand up and walk stiffly toward her.

"They say I can sit in the car with you for a while to warm up, if you don't mind," Ambassador Mohammed said politely.

Coco nodded and led the way across the garage. Anticipating that the front seat, crowded by the steering wheel, would be too cramped, Coco decided to shove her boosting box beneath the back door.

Suddenly the bourbon she'd drunk rushed to her head with dizzying speed. Straightening up, Coco stood motionless for a moment, waiting for the whirling to subside before she was able to mount the box and, with a chinning motion, hoist herself into the back seat. A moment later the Ambassador somehow swung himself halfway into the car and Coco grabbed his bound hands to pull him inside.

Shimmying over toward the far window, Coco realized she had never been in the back seat of her own car before.

The Ambassador, however, was clearly accustomed to riding in the rear of automobiles because he casually crossed his legs and made himself comfortable before turning toward her.

"Thank you for assisting me," he said gravely.

"Oh, that's OK."

"Is this actually . . . your car?" the Ambassador asked Coco, looking at the tattered paw-ploughed upholstery along the rim of the front seat.

"Yes, it is," Coco admitted, bending over to set the bourbon bottle down on the floor. "My dogs did that once when I had to leave them alone for a minute. Anyway, they sometimes do it just because they get overexcited about going for a ride."

The sudden flash of a white smile relieved the dark brooding of the Ambassador's black eyes. Shifting slightly, his wet shoe slid on some Highway Bingo cards strewn across the floor and without the use of his hands to steady himself, he suddenly tilted over on top of Coco.

There was a flurry of apologies, disclaimers, and adjustments as Coco helped push the Ambassador back into an upright position. Then, while both of them attempted to recover from the closeness of their physical encounter, the Ambassador looked down at the floor covered with discarded soda cans, crumpled lunch bags, junk-food wrappers, shells, seeds, rinds, crusts, skins, cores, empty matchbooks, and hatless Magic Markers that would never write again.

Coco felt so embarrassed about the untidiness that for a moment she considered suggesting that after she'd left her car at the garage for servicing, some vandals might have broken in, eaten a picnic lunch, and left their litter behind.

But when Mohammed spoke again it was of weightier matters.

"If you will let me—I want to say something so as to reassure you, a little, if I can. The Shah and I have been close friends for many years. He loves me like a brother. Although I would happily die rather than have him release those prisoners, I'm sure he will meet the terrorists' demands. If I were alone in here, I would try to do something to avert his having to make such a decision." He looked out the window. "I would try to confront them in some way—perhaps even make them shoot me—so as to prevent this awful exchange. But now, with you and Dr. Canada here," he shrugged helplessly and hopelessly, "I believe the exchange should be made."

Coco very daintily drank a bit of bourbon. Mohammed Mohammed certainly looked more like the hero of a wet-dream than a self-sacrificing soldier. However, it was possible that the current crisis was causing his real character to peek through his personality just as John Canada's had done with such disappointing results.

"Believe me," the Ambassador continued, "much to my shame, the Shah will do whatever is necessary to arrange our release."

Coco was beginning to feel more confident and relaxed now. She had never really let herself believe she would be carried off to the ends of the earth, but hearing the worldly diplomat explain the reasons for her conviction was reassuring. The combination of Izzat's bourbon and Mohammed's charm made her heady with optimism.

"Where did they . . . catch you?" she asked with friendly curiosity.

Now it was Mohammed's turn to flush.

"Well, I was on my way to a dinner party and, for indiscreet reasons, recklessly left my chauffeur and bodyguard at home."

"Uhmmm." Coco made a critical cluck about such careless security and looked at the Ambassador more closely.

He had a very slight, but fascinating, overbite which impeded the pronunciation of certain syllables and interfered with the total closure of his sensuous lips. Indeed, Mohammed had some of the qualities of a Camus-like character and the sense of adventure that Coco had hoped to share with John Canada suddenly seemed possible with the enemy Ambassador. Although it was politically embarrassing, Coco felt personally needy enough to compromise her principles.

And why shouldn't she seek some solace from such

a voluptuous villain since Gavin hadn't bothered to return her call? Really, had Coco done anything so awful as to deserve getting kidnapped and betrayed simultaneously? Wasn't that a bit much? Was it really so awful to have planned a brief reprieve from reality in the form of an affair with John Canada? Did God really have to sock it to her so self-righteously—demanding an immediate pay-back—rushing His revenge just as He did when Coco avoided using her backhand and raced against time and the tennis ball to return an awkward forehand shot which God immediately smashed into the net as an instant show of retribution for such cowardice?

"I am, however, very sorry that Dr. Canada revealed his true identity," the Ambassador said sorrowfully, clearly eager to initiate a new subject. "Having another influential celebrity only strengthens the bargaining position of our captors."

Instantly angered by the Ambassador's unconscious class snobbery, Coco felt a sting of emotion which, after a moment, she recognized as a surge of international solidarity with the students who had kidnapped them.

"Well," she said sarcastically, "I hope they don't find out *my* true identity."

Ambassador Mohammed looked up expectantly, his caressive eyes searching Coco's face. "Who are you?" he whispered.

Coco leaned toward him. "I'm a Jewish American Princess."

The Ambassador's eyes dilated as he digested the information and, after several seconds of linguistic joggling, he burst into laughter.

But Coco was angry, and she turned away to look out her window toward the east wall of the garage.

After a while she began wondering what Gavin and Diana were doing.

Since the kids were asleep, Diana wouldn't have any chores to handle at the moment and would still be ignorant of what lay ahead of her.

Coco smiled to herself.

Soon enough, however, Diana Whitcomb would discover what family life was really like. Soon enough she would have to learn how to stop the Burman's nonself-defrosting refrigerator from defrosting spontaneously. Necessity would become Diana's mother and teach her how to lie on her belly on the kitchen floor and stick her hand underneath the GE to try cleaning the dirt and dust and dog hairs out of the air vents. Eventually she would learn how to use the time, while being left on *hold* by the GE Emergency Repair Service dispatcher, to stash dirty cups in the dishwasher by pulling the long, kinky cord of the telephone receiver across the kitchen without getting it tangled around any chair legs, which would shorten her leash and temper while waiting to lodge her complaint.

Over time, Diana would gradually learn how to hunt through the can of souvenir coins from foreign countries to find something resembling American money for the kids to toss into the Metro bus token box when they couldn't find tokens or forty cents in change per person. Soon Diana would learn how to write appealing letters to insurance company adjusters, how to postdate all her checks, and how to really confuse creditors by enclosing the wrong statements in the envelopes along with her payments. Eventually Diana would train herself to remember to have the furnace overhauled in July and to instantly replace any bathroom wall tiles that came loose, so they wouldn't start any domino-type disaster which could make all the other tiles tilt, shift and come unglued like Southeast Asian nations after the liberation of Saigon.

Yes, eventually Diana would automatically run down to the basement and inspect the Bendix to see if Mike's missing Levis were stuck to the inside of the drier like a fibroid cyst on a uterine wall. She would learn how to consolidate condiment bottles to make more space in the refrigerator, when to slosh half-full bottles of Scotch into half-empty ones and when to move the pencil sharpener up or down the inside of the pantry closet door as different height people needed or learned how to sharpen pencils. Of course she'd also have to learn how to unbend a clothes hanger to stick up the Eureka vacuum hose if something stopped the suction and locate the supply house in Wheaton, Maryland, where broken blender bowls could be replaced at half-price.

Diana also would have to learn how to deal with the summer-camp syndrome. She would have to find and keep carbon copies of the kids' Prospective Camper's Personality Profiles on file so as to avoid rewriting four new ones each season. She would have to learn how to sew, laundry-pencil-mark, or iron labels on everyone's summer clothing and remember to ship out the kids' trunks two weeks before camp started. At the end of August she would simply *have* to remember to check the dogs for ticks and the children for lice—or all of them for both.

Was it possible?

Would Diana Whitcomb ever be able to do everything—keep the house clean, the clothes laundered, the larder full, and the meals on time? Would she truly learn to love Coco's children and would they learn to love her, too?

Would Diana learn to love Gavin?

Coco's pulse began to race her heart.

And would Gavin learn to love Diana?

No. Coco couldn't handle that. Coco did not want Gavin to love anyone else but her. She had gradually, over the years, come to realize that she adored having a tall, thin, tyrannically tidy husband around the house and that she enjoyed going to the movies with someone who had the same blood type as the children they left behind with a babysitter of questionable character. She found it sexy having dinner at a restaurant with a man who had named her the main beneficiary of his life insurance policy, his firm's mutual investment fund, and his retirement program. She enjoyed going to parties with a man who carried, at her request, a nongovernmental high-option hospitalization plan with major medical benefits including psychiatric care, and she had even come to see a glimmer of glamour in cohabiting with the cosigner of her house and car loans.

"Please excuse me," the Ambassador said politely, as he interrupted Coco's reverie. "I want to apologize for my gaucherie."

"Oh, that's OK, just forget it," Coco said absently.

"Do you suppose . . ." Mohammed Mohammed hesitated briefly. "Do you suppose you could get the Gaulois out of my jacket pocket?"

Suddenly feeling shy, Coco opened the Ambassador's cape and pulled the tuxedo jacket away from his body so as not to touch his torso as she gingerly removed the powder-blue package from his pocket. Then she took out a cigarette, put it between his lips, and struck a match. The Ambassador puffed contentedly several times while Coco waited for a signal to remove the cigarette from his mouth when he was ready. She watched him closely as he studied her in an old-fashioned speculative way, as if she were an undeveloped country awaiting exploration and exploitation.

There was certainly something distinctively totalitarian about his style, but under the circumstances, Coco could almost overlook the fact that he was the deputy of a despicable despot.

"Did you know," the Ambassador said, his sexy lisp accentuated by the dangling cigarette, "that in ancient Greek the word 'hostage' meant both 'guest' and 'enemy'? That's a rather interesting etymological fact, isn't it?"

"Hmmm." Coco didn't know what to say and unconsciously reached down for the bottle of bourbon. Her jealousy over Gavin and Diana had begun to activate other negative feelings, and she decided to sooth herself—if possible—with another drop of the burning bourbon.

"Have you ever been to the Middle East?" the Ambassador inquired.

Coco shook her head as she delicately raised the fifth and swallowed several mouthfuls.

"Well then, when this situation is safely resolved and we are all released, I want you and your family to be my guests in Iran. We'll have you flown to Tehran and installed in one of our official guest houses as partial repayment for this unforgiveable experience."

Coco smiled politely and thought about Iran for a moment.

Wasn't it, like Mexico, a land of contrasts? Wasn't it a country where beggars worked both sides of the wide white boulevards, where the rich drove Mercedes and the poor walked in camel dung? Wasn't it a land of caviar and beriberi, of fairy-tale riches and human horrors? Wasn't it a land whose leaders had built a city in the middle of the desert to throw a national birthday party while peasants were dying nearby in their burnt-out villages?

Wasn't Iran more than a land of contrasts? Wasn't it a land of catastrophic contradictions? Wasn't it a nation that had hired Marion Javits as its United States public relations representative at the same time that OPEC was boycotting any American companies that employed Jews? How could she possibly consider accepting any invitation from the Iranian Ambassador to visit his country? Certainly it would be more moral to go to a Club Med island.

"I shall look forward to being as kind a host to you —and your family—as you have been a brave and charming companion to me during this outrageous ordeal," Mohammed continued. "You shall stay in Iran as long as you like and, of course, there will be a full staff of servants ready, upon your arrival, to wait upon you."

The bourbon bubbled through Coco's brain crowding it with cliches as she tried to envision the house in Tehran with its large staff of handsome young Iranians waiting to serve and service her—as back in the days of the Arabian nights. Would the house come equipped with a yacht, a jet, a private island in the Aegean, a chalet in Gsaadt, a townhouse in London, a membership at the Clermont gambling club, and a pass to the *haute couture* houses of Paris?

"Well, that certainly sounds . . . nice," Coco said, in an uncomfortable, inconclusive way.

—What's happening now?— she wondered, taking another swig of bourbon.

—Was this it?—

Was this the Heavenly offer Coco couldn't refuse—a Faustian temptation concocted by a teasing, testing God? Certainly Mohammed Mohammed was only a messenger sent to deliver a celestial invitation to test Coco's political character and principles. How could Coco possibly accept the tawdry tainted hospitality of a fascist government which tortured dissenters and persecuted prisoners? But perhaps Mohammed Mohammed was really Lucifer in disguise—laying a trip on Coco so as to accumulate more ammunition and evidence against her? Perhaps he was the devil trying to cut a deal with Coco—offering her a liaison with the dashing diplomat in exchange for her freedom—her body for her life?

—On the other hand— Coco thought, trying to be judicious, despite the bourbon—maybe God, in all His ambivalence, was gifting Coco with a multimillionaire lover like Mohammed Mohammed so she could finally have everything she ever thought she wanted.

The cigarette began to dangle from the Ambassador's bottom lip and Coco quickly plucked it from his mouth.

Perhaps Coco really did need someone who could afford to afford her a few luxuries during her middle years. Perhaps God thought Coco deserved to be indulged by a lover who would send her anemones anonymously every once in a while and buy her a new set of tires for her car or a heavy-duty, industrial vacuum for her home. Perhaps Coco really did need an intoxicatingly indolent, international playboy who would introduce her to the jetset progeny of rich potentates so she could sail the southern seas with lots of sheiks and shiksas who would dock only to dance at discotheques in hidden harbors, safe from the persistent pursuit of *paparazzi* and *Time* photographers hunting "People."

"Well it might be nice to travel a *little*," Coco said cautiously. "Would you like a swig of this bourbon Izzat gave me?"

"Very much," the Ambassador nodded.

Coco held the bottle to Mohammed's mouth while he drank.

Then, somewhat seductively, she took a drag off his cigarette before fitting it back very tenderly between his lips.

"Now tell me," the Ambassador said. "What do you do? What kind of life do you live?"

Coco flushed. "Oh, we're just your basic middle-class American family," she confessed. "My husband's a lawyer and we have four children and I'm working as an editor at the Social Science Institute where they're writing a report on Infelicity in America."

The Ambassador broke into laughter. "Oh! So that's what you were discussing with Dr. Canada. I do find it hard to believe there is much infelicity in this marvelous country of yours."

Quickly Coco composed an icy expression to show she wasn't going to discuss such a subject with anyone who said something like that.

"Well—forgetting the rest of the country, I have trouble running my own little establishment," she said as gayly and giddily as if she were still at Diana's cocktail party. "It's hard for me to work all day and still coordinate the kids' activities and attend their school events and do all the marketing and the cleaning and also try to entertain nicely once in a while."

Abruptly she fell into a guilty silence. What was

wrong with her? Why, even in captivity, did Coco feel compelled to act charming? Why, even while imprisoned, did she have to prostitute her political feelings in order to entertain the enemy?

"What you obviously need is a staff," the Ambassador said.

Coco giggled. "We don't even have enough money anymore for a cleaning lady once a week. I've been doing the house by myself for over two years."

"Then what you need is a couple more husbands to help around the house or a rich lover who could afford to staff you."

Coco blushed at the way Mohammed said "staff you."

"Do you have many employees at your embassy?" she asked, stalling for time.

"Apart from the professional diplomatic staff, I have a personal secretary—who's really my administrative assistant—a social secretary, a bodyguard, a butler, a valet, a gardener, two cooks, one pastry chef, a chauffeur, and a car-mechanic handyman type."

Coco leaned back against the seat and closed her eyes.

Had Coco's luck changed right when she hit the skids? Had Fate intervened to snatch her away from an unappreciative husband and an unreliable lover to install her as the mistress of an amorous Iranian aristocrat who was one of the leading playboys of the Eastern world?

"Actually, if you ever need some extra help for a special party, I can lend you my social secretary, Lila Nihemi, who's a professional party-giver," the Ambassador said graciously.

—What's happening— Coco wondered wildly.

Was she drunk from the bourbon or had Mohammed fallen in love with her at first sight? Shyly she looked over at him, smiling from what she considered to be her most attractive angle. Was the Ambassador implying he'd send over some of his staff to manage the Burman household while Coco spent long afternoons making love with him in his lush embassy? Could Coco command a few days of professional domestic services in exchange for visiting some sultry sultan-style boudoir, draped in rich oriental rugs and tapestries, where she would engage in imaginative acts of rapture?

Could Mohammed send over a personal maid to organize Coco's clothes so the long legs of her pantyhose would no longer tangle together like the languid limbs of lazy lovers inside her dresser drawers? Would a personal maid be able to bring order into chaos—harmonize Coco's antagonistic accessories and alchemize her uncooperative separates into coordinates? Would the Ambassador actually dispatch a maid to help Coco dress for parties and to transfer all the essentials from Coco's shoulderbag into her gold lamé evening clutch so Coco would no longer have to drop her entire daytime purse into her slightly larger, more presentable, black nighttime tote—like a bank robber driving his getaway car into the rear of a semitrailer waiting at some prearranged pickup spot out on a highway? Would a personal maid rescue Coco's clothes from the closet floor and hook the belts on appropriate hangers with the proper dresses? Would a personal maid take Coco's clothes into—and out of—the cleaners and purchase reasonably priced but attractive garment and shoe bags to unclutter Coco's closet? Would she do all Coco's packing—in some new set of matching luggage which the Ambassador would probably provide—placing things in alphabetical order or according to color, style, or usage so that priority items would self-sort and surface first? Would she tie sets or pairs of things together with satin ribbons and paste a paper diagram, portraying the layout of the suitcase, on the top lid like a map inside a box of Whitman's chocolates?

How delicious!

"Well," Coco murmured demurely, "I could certainly use some professional party assistance once in a while. Anyone who works full time always needs a little help."

"Lila is certainly a pro and I'd be happy to lend her to you any time."

Coco waited for the hook.

It didn't come.

Then, seeing that the Ambassador's cigarette had become a stub, she took it from his mouth and mashed it inside the armrest ashtray.

"Are you sure you wouldn't like to lie down back here?" Mohammed Mohammed asked.

Ah ha!—Coco thought.

"I'm not really tired," she protested.

"Because now that I've warmed up a bit, I could sit outside again."

"Really—I'm fine," Coco insisted, unconsciously comparing Mohammed's solicitude with John Canada's insensitivity.

It was certainly ironic that this curlyhaired *café-au-lait* Iranian—whom Coco's mother would definitely have mistaken for a Jewish C.P.A.—was comforting Coco while the American Wasp heartlessly abandoned her. Here was an Arab—or whatever Iranians were—taking care of Coco during a crisis and, perhaps, even after-ward—on an illicit but permanent basis.

Coco leaned back against the seat. It was almost two A.M. and the bourbon was making her sleepy. She turned to look at her companion again.

"Do you think Izzat would let me get a blanket out of the car trunk, Mr. Ambassador? I'm really getting cold now."

"My dear! Please. Please call me Mohammed."

Uncertain whether he meant his first Mohammed or the second, Coco decided not to call him anything at all.

"OK," she said.

Suddenly, without a word, Mohammed Mohammed hooked his bound hands around the door handle, pressed down, and, without hesitating, leaped out of the car like a parachute jumper. He landed on his feet.

Within seconds, Izzat and Aly were running toward him with their guns drawn.

There was a long loud argument during which Coco cringed in the back seat. Eventually, however, Aly walked away and Izzat made a big production of push-ing several boxes toward the rear of the car. A few min-utes later he reappeared below Coco's window.

"Hey," he yelled. "I can't get your damn trunk door open."

With a superior smile at Izzat's mechanical failure, Coco shimmied out of the car and climbed atop the boxes stacked beneath the trunk. With the confidence of a safecracker, she inserted the key three quarters of the way into the lock, wiggled it once, rotated it twice, and very gently applied some elbow pressure to the curved rump of the trunk.

When the door sprang open, Coco's heart reared up inside her breast. The jumbled interior looked as familiar and welcoming as her own living room. There was the red-and-black plaid blanket the Burman's always used for picnics. There was the box of office supplies Coco had stolen from the Social Science Institute. There was the pile of overdue library books Coco intended to drop into a Night-Hours-Only depository box so as to avoid any angry encounters over fines with the cranky Cleveland Park librarian. There was the large collection of broken electrical appliances Coco always kept in the trunk in case she passed an appropriate repair shop on her way to somewhere else. There were Joshie's cowboy boots, destined for the shoemaker, and a bulging ball of Gavin's dirty shirts stuffed inside the inner rim of the spare tire like vanilla custard filling a doughnut hole.

Suddenly inspired, Coco surveyed the library book titles. Oh, yes!

There was the *Quotations from Chairman Mao Tse-Tung* which Gavin had finished reading last week. What a plus! What a coup! Wouldn't Coco's captors be impressed that she had Mao Tse-Tung's Little Red Book in her car trunk? Certainly a copy of the *Quotations* would corroborate Coco's claim to a progressive political position if she were compelled to present some proof of her ideological integrity. Quickly she reached out to confiscate the book.

"Hurry up," Izzat ordered angrily.

Untangling the plaid blanket from a badminton net which was twisted around the tire jack, Coco jumped off the boxes and scurried back up into the car where she settled down cozily in one corner with the Little

Red Book and the bottle of bourbon clasped in her arms beneath the slightly mildewed woolen blanket.

When the Ambassador struggled up into the car again, he sat in the opposite corner of the back seat, leaving a safe amount of space between them.

Coco made herself comfortable.

# CHAPTER EIGHT

"Why don't you try to sleep?" Ambassador Mohammed suggested again. "You don't have to be afraid. I'll stay awake and guard you."

Coco looked at him.

What in the world made Mohammed think she was in any danger of sexual assault?

It didn't seem to Coco that any of the men in the garage were lusting after her body. Indeed, cuddled up safely inside her Monte Carlo, it occurred to Coco that if she hadn't been worried about losing her life, she would have been worried about losing her looks. In any other situation she would have been obsessing about her size or her smell—wondering if her body was too saggy or soiled to touch, her unwashed face too unfresh to kiss or her breath too briny to provoke passion.

If Coco hadn't been so worried about dying, she would have been worried about aging, wondering if the insidious grey in her hair and incipient sag in her skin, the slump of her breasts and girth of her hips foreclosed any future moves being made upon her. Of course it was ridiculous to feel defensive simply because no one wanted to rape her, but the image of herself as nonentity neuterized by age into an object instead of an objective was intolerable to Coco.

Indeed, hadn't John Canada turned against her the moment he received a presidential reprimand for his aborted intentions? Didn't the three young terrorists view Coco only as a prisoner rather than as a person?

Hadn't Gavin forgotten and forsaken Coco the moment Diana appeared to replace her? And why was the Ambassador so certain he could resist temptation that he dared offer to become Coco's sentry? Why wasn't he aroused by their proximity in the back seat of a car after midnight on a weekend?

Apparently, Coco's sexual conditioning during high school had been strong enough to survive twenty years after graduation so that she still responded to the stimuli of slightly odoriferous car-seat covers and the suggestive protrusion of handles on the doors. Indeed, if Coco Burman were to be perfectly honest, she would probably have to admit she still preferred stinky-finger back-seat sex to any other variety and enjoyed necking more than intercourse since, by definition, it was inconclusive rather than delineated and thus—like chewing gum that never lost its flavor—kept its texture, taste, and interest longer.

"I'm really not sleepy," Coco finally responded. "But tell me something . . . Mohammed. What does your handyman do?"

Mohammed Mohammed shrugged his shoulders in a continental way. "Oh, you know. Odd jobs—yard work and a little carpentry or some cabinet-making when necessary."

Coco nodded solemnly and then closed her eyes. In her exhausted, half-drunken state she thought again of the services the Ambassador might provide if she ever became his mistress.

Now, from the depths of her apolitical id, Coco summoned up a handsome young Iranian handyman who could repair TVs, adjust audio components, change camera film, ceiling lightbulbs, phonograph needles, and tape top tunes off the radio so that kids wouldn't want money to buy records. She saw a young man who enjoyed enclosing ugly radiators, replacing mailboxes, building bookcases, planting organic vegetable gardens, mending broken sports equipment, reinforcing fences, recovering stolen yard furniture and gardening implements, restringing tennis rackets, sharpening ice skates, waxing skiis, patching bicycle tires, replacing bent spokes, hand-pumping inner tubes and footballs, mending badminton nets, sharpening kitchen knives, tightening pot handles and teaching women or children how to load a Minolta as well as coordinate the speed, light, and distance adjusters.

Would Mohammed's handyman perhaps be able to open up a section of the cellar wall to see if a rodent was stuck in there, defecating or dying so as to cause a stench in the basement? Could he find out why the roof still leaked even after it had been retarred? Could he sand down the wooden kitchen chairs which kept ejecting an endless crop of slivers into the children's thighs and buttocks necessitating removal by the pediatrician at inflated office visit fees not covered by the Burman's insurance?

Could he take down the screens and put up the storm windows—washing, before installing, them and possibly even writing the proper location at the top of each frame with an indelible pen so someone else could tell where they belonged next year? Could he replace torn screens and straighten warped frames?

Given enough time, could Mohammed's handyman fix Coco's erratic front doorbell, flash the roof gutter, point the bricks and make the DRIEST cycle on her Bendix work so Coco could dial the fastest heat? If she had an affair with the Ambassador would it last long enough for his handyman to screen in the second-floor back porch so Coco could work outside on nice summer nights without killing pretty little moths drawn to the red ON button of her electric portable where they were struck down by the deadly weight of the automatic carriage-return, leaving Coco with a graveyard of mangled corpses to extract from beneath her roller? Would he have time to box in all the water pipes in the basement so a college student might live down there rent-free in exchange for domestic help? Could Mohammed's jack-of-all-trades build a separate basement entrance so that, in their later years, Coco and Gavin might rent out that space as income property? Could he convert the Burmans' third-floor porch into a greenhouse and the butler's pantry off the kitchen into a cozy home office which Coco could decorate and use for paying bills and managing household accounts?

If Coco were to have an affair with Ambassador Mohammed Mohammed, might he reciprocate by lending her his valet? Might an expert wardrobe-maintenance man appear some morning to offer his services so Coco could get all her frayed clothes resewn with double seams that could be released with a quick tug of the runner thread if she ever gained a pound or two? Would Mohammed's valet have the talent to sew a breast pocket inside Coco's bathrobe so she'd have a place to stash student bus tokens, prewritten notes giving permission for one of her kids to skip gym, letters written late at night that the kids could mail on their way to school, and a small note pad for jotting down grocery items discovered missing while she made lunches at breakfast time? Would a personal valet be able to turn all the collars on Gavin's shirts, replace missing buttons, wash everyone's sweaters, by hand, in Woolite, and iron patches on the kids' jeans, each of whom had four pairs which meant thirty-two knees to be recovered or reinforced?

Perhaps, with a little luck, Mohammed's valet would have a sewing team in reserve, some turn-of-the-century-type sweatshop crew of Semitic seamstresses who would huddle downstairs in the Burman's basement beneath the low-hanging low-wattage bulb, slavishly safety-pinning pairs of dirty socks together—or, at least, matching up and mating clean ones—unjamming stuck jacket zippers so the kids wouldn't have to step into their coats, and happily mending, sewing, darning, hemming, reweaving, reinforcing, reinserting, altering, lengthening, shortening, patching, tacking, knitting, crocheting, needlepointing, quilting, taking in, letting out, turning back, and making Halloween costumes when necessary?

And what about the chauffeur? Couldn't he help Coco out just once in a while? Couldn't he drive the Tuesday or Thursday morning car pools and do a few big monthly grocery shopping expeditions so Coco wouldn't have to rush through the Safeway after work with her four children dangling like participles behind her, thoughtlessly grabbing extravagant items she didn't need? Couldn't Mohammed's chauffeur tend her engine, clean her spark plugs, replace her shocks, change her oil, adjust her carburetor, water her radiator, align her wheels, adjust her headlights, charge her battery, change her snowtires, check her antifreeze and install a tapedeck with speakers? Couldn't he take her car through inspection each year, paste the new 1979 validation stickers on her plates, pay her parking tickets in person down at the Central Violations Bureau on Indiana Avenue, and remove all the old parking lot receipts from under the windshield wiper to file away, along with parking tickets incurred during professional working hours, to be used as business deductions on the Burmans' income tax? Couldn't he vacuum the interior of the car, regionally rubber-band road maps together inside the glove compartment, empty the ashtray, and straighten out the trunk? Was that so much to ask from a lover's chauffeur?

And what would Mohammed's bodyguard be doing while Coco and Mohammed were closeted away making love? Since Mohammed's body would be safe couldn't the guard go over to the Burmans' house and help out a little? Couldn't he shift from bodyguarding to detective work and try to locate lost wallets, sweaters, earrings, cufflinks, lawn chairs, baseball mitts, rakes, garbage-can covers, school books, the rubber plant someone had stolen off their back porch or the WELCOME mat missing from the front stoop? Couldn't he launch a full-scale investigation to see if someone was sneaking into Coco's house to make long-distance telephone calls to unrecognizable numbers with unfamiliar area codes? Couldn't he find out if someone was trying to drive her crazy by stealing her silverware or stuffing it down the garbage disposal? Couldn't he find out why the Motor Vehicle Department claimed there were still outstanding parking tickets on Coco's record, even though she was certain she'd paid all of her fines except for the one still stuck in her wallet? Couldn't Mohammed's bodyguard check the stacks of the Martin Luther King public library to see if some of the books reportedly still outstanding had been reshelved without being recorded?

Couldn't he do *SOMETHING?*

—This is absolutely ridiculous—Coco said to herself. —This is no way to spend what might be the last night of my life.—

There were many other things she could do.

Since it was becoming increasingly clear Gavin wasn't going to return her call—that either Diana hadn't relayed Coco's message or Gavin was too sexually entranced to interrupt his reverie for a five-minute chat with his kidnapped wife—Coco could simply dictate her desires onto paper. Opening her purse again, she extracted her notebook and turned to the page with her letter-in-progress to Gavin.

"While looking in the trunk for our blanket, I found your dirty shirts and Joshie's cowboy boots. If I am taken to Algeria, please get the car out of the garage and drop off all that stuff at the cleaner's. Josh just needs ½ cleats on his heels. Also, return the books to the library and—if I'm killed—look for any claim checks for various things in my wallet."

Coco paused to sip some more bourbon from the bottle. Hospitably she turned to offer the Ambassador another swig, but he was leaning back against the car seat with his eyes closed. Somewhat relieved about not having to share her diminished supply, Coco recapped the bottle, tucked it beneath the blanket, and returned to her writing.

"Please remind the kids not to eat anything with #2 red food dye in it. This means no more maraschino cherries or jimmies on their ice cream cones. Also: tell them not to put their personal cereal spoons into the sugar bowl but to use a "center" spoon for serving.

"I believe that once a year you should hire an industrial cleaning crew to do the house. They wash walls, furniture, and everything all at one time. Check the

Yellow Pages and do some comparative pricing. The front-hall closet must be cleaned seasonally, and all sports equipment should be clearly marked with the name of the owner or user.

"Gavin, please arrange with the Circulation Department at the *Post* and the *Star* to pay our subscription fees by mail so the paperboys won't come to collect when the kids might be home alone with no money. Also, if some credit company calls you on the telephone, ask them to hold the line for a minute. Then get back on and say you've just turned on your tape recorder and that you're going to record the conversation because it's illegal for credit companies to harass debtors over the phone.

"All of the tablecloths are in the top drawer of that bureau in the pantry. Some of them are round, some square, and some oblong. Please try to determine which is which before you unfold them because it's very hard to re-create the same creases again.

"Please do not push the kitchen chairs back against the wall as they leave marks on the paint.

"*More reminders:* We need a new dipstick. The name of the service department manager at Williams Chevrolet is Bill. Bill" (Coco paused to decide whether to put the verb in the past or present tense and then decided not to be maudlin) "likes me a lot, so just say you're my family when you take the car in. I also think you should consider changing gasoline stations, since I'm not sure Mr. Murdock paid his helpers the minimum wage. Also: the last time I went to the drugstore I started to leaf through a *Playgirl* sitting on a pile by the cash register and found that its pages had been Scotch-taped together so no one could flip through it. I thought this was revolting and suggest you change drugstores too. Also: Since you're not home much during the day, you probably don't know that La Fonda restaurant has a telephone number only one digit different from ours. Late in the afternoon people start calling up our house to make dinner reservations. Either tell them that La Fonda's last number is 8 not 9, or take their reservations so they won't keep calling back and bothering you.

"Darlings: Since you like spaghetti so much I'll tell you how to make it so they don't stick together. Pour a few drops of olive oil into the boiling water before you add the spaghetti. That will keep them slippery and stop them from sticking. Also, if you rinse hot pasta in cold water you can get the starch off. I don't think you should test the consistency of spaghetti by tossing a few strands up at the ceiling to see if they'll stick anymore, because even though it's a good test for doneness, they're very hard to get down. Also, although I seriously doubt that you'll ever cook cabbage, if you do, just drop a walnut into the boiling water. It will absorb the smell and leave the house odor-free.

"The best cookbook for you kids to use is Peg Bracken's *I Hate to Cook Book*. One thing she advises, which I think is a very good idea, is to keep some parsley on hand at all times to make plain dishes look fancy. Parsley's that curly stuff you see at restaurants that looks like the top of a carrot. However, parsley *DOES WILT*, so keep it in the fridg in an empty jelly jar with a cover and it will stay fresh almost indefinitely.

"Children: it is important to remember appointments and the best way to do that is to WRITE THEM DOWN ON OUR NEW 1979 SCHOOL CALENDAR. Jot down everyone's birthday, school events, anniversaries, (she crossed out anniversaries) dental and medical appointments, holidays—national, school, or Jewish (ask Granny when those are)—and any social events you're invited to. Do not sharpen the kitchen knives on the back of the can opener because it's broken. Also, when trying to insert a screw into the wall, first make a hole by pounding in a nail.

"Read the 7 DANGER SIGNS OF CANCER pasted on the pantry wall at least once a month.

"Do not let the dogs eat any chicken bones because you *KNOW* what happens. You can tell if they got some out of the garbage because their stool turns whitish.

"*A Few More Household Hints:* Always drain off the watery yellow juice excreted by hamburger. You can pour it on top of the dogs' Solo since they like that flavor.

"When cutting an onion, slice off the bottom to create a flat chopping surface. This makes dicing much easier, but remember, Jessica can't stand onions in anything.

"You must all remember to flush the toilet after each use. If you don't forget there are many underdeveloped countries which have no indoor plumbing, you will feel grateful about having a toilet and remember to flush."

Suddenly Coco paused, stung by an ancient memory of kneeling before the toilet bowl, up to her elbows in water, as she rinsed out the residue from dirty diapers. An intense longing for her children as babies overwhelmed her and she was crying silently as she began to write again:

"I have also noticed matches floating around in the toilet. I know some people think it's polite, if the bathroom smells after they use it, to light a match so the sulphur will absorb the bad odor before the next person arrives. However, this is only OK to do if you are over 8 yrs. old.

"Also: When you tear off a piece of wrapping paper —like tinfoil or Saran Wrap—only tear it along the perforated edge of the box or else the next person can't find the end of the roll since it's usually invisible. This also goes for Scotch tape, because it's even harder to see than masking, adhesive, or electrical tape ends.

"Do not take telephone messages on my personalized stationery."

Coco nibbled on the tip of her pen.

What weirdness! What did it really matter if the kids used her cheap, department store, offset stationary if she were dead? What else should they do with that paper? Actually, it was probably economical to use it up as a message pad.

Coco was crossing out the last line when she heard the pay phone start to ring. As if from a balcony in a theatre, she watched Izzat answer the call and then turn to motion that it was for her.

Quickly Coco wiggled her way across the Ambassador's lap and opened his door. Forgetting that the car was hydraulically hoisted high above the ground, Coco began to fall and broke her plunge only at the last moment by grabbing the door handle. She bumped hard against the front fender of the car as she landed but, visibly favoring her left leg, was able to limp toward the telephone.

"Hello?"

"Coco! It's Gavin. How are you now?"

"Great," Coco answered hysterically. "Are you having a good time with Diana?"

"Well, she's right here next to me," Gavin said in

verbal italics. "And like all your friends, she's terribly worried about you."

"I can just imagine," Coco said.

"In fact, she wants me to ask if there's something we could do for you while we're waiting."

Coco tried to clear her head so she could think. She had been internally jarred by her fall and still felt somewhat drunk from the bourbon. But she was determined to punish Gavin in some way which would be meaningful.

"Well, I suppose you could run some errands tomorrow so if I get out of here I won't be all backed up, and if I don't get out of here, things will be in better order before you have to start making all the funeral arrangements."

"Oh, Coco, honey. Please don't talk like that. Just tell me what needs doing. Tell me what I should do."

It was a heartfelt plea of reformation for his domestic dereliction—the only gift Gavin could give under the circumstances.

"Well, you *could* go to the grocery store tomorrow," Coco said. "I don't think there's any milk or vegetables or bread left. In fact, you might as well do the whole week's marketing. Just take my food list off the bulletin board." Coco's malice was mounting. "And I suppose you'd better buy some bird food and dog food and fish food and plant food, too. Also, get three seed bells for the green parakeet."

"Jesus, Coco," Gavin grumbled. "The only place they have those bells is out at that drugstore in Chevy Chase. It takes almost half an hour to drive there."

"Well, that's the only kind she'll eat," Coco said.

"Then she should fly out to Chevy Chase and get them herself," Gavin said in a suddenly stubborn voice.

"I always drive out there to get them," Coco countered.

"Yeah? Well just because you got her hooked on those bells, doesn't mean I should supply her habit at a time like this."

Coc shrugged. "OK, but if you decide to send the birds, have them pick up a package of gravel paper for the cage and some perch covers, too, would you?"

Gavin laughed. "OK, what else do you want us to do?"

"Well, if you happen to be near a dimestore or a drugstore, everyone needs new shoelaces," she said coldly, trying to envision each of her childrens' scruffy shoes. "Buy yourself some twenty-six-inch dress blacks, some thirty-inch leather thongs for Mike's desert boots, a pair of twenty-four inch browns for Josh, and a pair of twenty-eight-inch heavy-duty athletic whites for Nicky's Adidas."

"Now how the hell do you know what size everybody's shoelaces should be?" Gavin challenged her, although apparently bracing himself for another barrage.

"All you have to know is the number of holes in the shoes," Coco said, watching Abass and Izzat escorting Canada toward the toilet. "The second digit on the shoelace wrapper should correspond to the number of holes that have to be threaded. So if your shoes have six holes you have to get size twenty-six. Or if they have four holes you get twenty-fours."

"Gotcha," Gavin said.

"Good. And Gavin, please cross off the things you buy and bring back the list showing the stuff you couldn't get, so the next person will know what's still missing. Then those leftover items can be the beginning of next week's list. And, listen, Gavin, you *can't* make substitutions. I mean, there are lots of different ways to make coffee but we happen to use the drip method, which means if they're out of drip you can't substitute regular or perk. You know what I mean? Just don't get any, if they've only got the wrong kind or size."

"Okay, Coco, honey, we'll do it. Don't worry. I wrote everything down. And it'll be good for the kids to get out of the house for a while."

Suddenly Coco burst into sobs.

"Coco. What's the matter? What's happening? Say something."

Coco tried to speak, but her words were indistinguishable.

"Coco! What is it? Tell me!"

"Forget everything I said," she gasped, as the tears tracked down her cheeks.

"Why? What's wrong?"

"You can't go," she sputtered. "I've got the car."

Gavin waited patiently while she wept. Then, in a megabreakthrough, Coco smashed down thirty-seven-and-a-half years of fiscal conservatism. It was suddenly perfectly clear to her that if a group of young university students could control international affairs by telephone, Coco could conduct her household business in the same way.

"Gavin, listen. Why don't you just call up Larimers, read them our grocery order, and have it delivered? It can't cost more than five or ten dollars extra and we've never ever ordered by phone before. Given the circumstances—I think we should do it. Just this once. That would really make me feel good.

"OK, honey. I will, but why don't you just forget all this stuff now and try to get some sleep. It's almost three o'clock. I'll call you first thing in the *morning*."

He said "morning" so significantly that Coco knew he meant "alone."

"OK, Gav," she said. Then she replaced the receiver and returned to the car.

Wearily she climbed up on the box and waited as Mohammed opened the door for her.

"Anything wrong?" he asked, helping pull her inside.

"No. It was just my husband," Coco said, scrambling over Mohammed's knees.

She was unaware of the tears rolling down her face until she noticed the Ambassador looking at her sympathetically as she curled up in her corner again.

"What is it?" he asked gently.

"Oh, it's everything," Coco hiccupped. "My husband can't do anything around the house and I didn't do the laundry this week and there's no groceries and our motor vehicle permit expires on Monday . . ."

"Ah, my dear, you must try to be a bit more philosophical," the Ambassador said. "You must view this experience as an opportunity. There is, after all, much that can be learned during such an ordeal. You must look at this experience in larger terms. Is there really any difference between the time spent here in the garage and a lengthy stay at some ashram?"

"How would I know?" Coco wailed. "I've never been to an *ashram*." She pronounced the word with religious belligerence.

Mohammed Mohammed smiled. "What I'm suggesting is that any period of withdrawal from the world can be fruitful in terms of contemplation and meditation. Certainly you can achieve a state of altered consciousness in a prison cell as well as in a monastery. It's all a question of attitude—whether you *do* time or *use* time."

"Oh, Mohammed," Coco objected irritably.

"A person can be free anywhere," he continued.

Coco pulled the blanket up to her chin.

Why was Mohammed passing her little Zen messages like Gavin handed her Milk Duds at the movies?

"It is not a sin to find something of value in adversity," Mohammed insisted gently. "Here you are in a terrifying situation—facing possible death—and you're fretting about your laundry and your groceries and your inspection permit. Isn't it possible you are trying to avoid the truth by focusing on trivia? Isn't it possible that you have avoided thinking about your inner life— all your life—by immersing yourself in such details? Can't you attempt a broader perspective and acquire a more global view? I would consider that a very creative use of your captivity. You could actually gain some freedom during your imprisonment. You could destroy your old order and create a new one."

Coco turned, in a way which clearly concluded the conversation, and looked out her window at the THINK METRIC sign.

What did that sign really mean? Was metric a mode of thought combining Marxism and Zen Buddhism? Was it a new form of existentialism? Was what the Ambassador said actually true? Could Coco possibly put her life in order during the next hours by thinking differently, perhaps metrically, so that by midnight— when she would be released from the garage in one form or another—things at home would be better? Perhaps Coco should reconsider the standard arguments against rearranging deckchairs on the *Titanic* while it was sinking.

Again she looked at the THINK METRIC sign. If people thought metrically could they transcend reality?

Could Coco perhaps reorder her life and her values while *doing time* in a garage? If facing death alleviated aging anxieties by making old age seem preferable to its alternative, could Coco find freedom in captivity? Maybe she should view her capture as a liberation and being a hostage as a hiatus. Perhaps Coco should let circumstances lull her for awhile like a double feature on a 747 transatlantic flight.

Certainly she had more freedom in this situation than she did on a Caribbean island holiday where Gavin always held her hostage with the threat of his displeasure —constantly demanding she be cheerful, sexually passionate, and overtly enthusiastic about chartered trips in glass-bottomed boats or multilingual tours through old Spanish fortresses—in exchange for which she would win her release and a return plane ticket back home.

Perhaps this was the chance Coco needed to get her head and her house in order. If people could order *out* pizzas and order *in* groceries, why couldn't they order *events*? If people could give and take orders, shouldn't they be able to wrench some meaning out of an order that they imposed? Momentarily, Coco felt herself on the verge of some profound discovery, but the meaning eluded her the more anxiously she pursued it. After half an hour she felt exhausted, and the idea she had pursued in all its exquisite forms had escaped her. Unhappily she looked over at the Ambassador but he had fallen asleep with his head against the window.

Anxious and disoriented, Coco reached down to recover the *Quotations from Chairman Mao Tse-Tung* which had fallen on the floor.

Although the overhead garage lights were still on full force, the corner of the car created a shadow so that Coco had to hold one arm extended straight in front of her to keep the book within the arc of light. Aware of her enormous ignorance about the Chinese Revolution, she read through the introduction before beginning to skim the book. Gradually, as time passed, some of the short aphorisms began to capture her attention because they seemed to echo her earlier musings.

> Everything reactionary is the same; if you don't hit it, it won't fall. This is also like sweeping the floor; as a rule where the broom does not reach, the dust will not vanish of itself.

Coco thought of the dirt beneath her bathroom radiator, dirt that always looked suspiciously like the decomposed corpse of a dead mouse, and nodded thoughtfully. Yes, it was true. Coco should sweep away whatever dirt or dust she saw beneath or between the rungs of all the rusty radiators, stationed like sentries around her house, collecting soot in their ornately scrolled surfaces. Despite the fact that Coco's radiators disobeyed the dictates of her Honeywell thermostat, and often heated the house to a temperature that caused the self-adhesive picture hooks to shrivel up and slide off the walls—catapulting cheap prints in expensive frames to the floor—Coco still had an obligation to dust her radiators regularly.

Excitedly, her eyes skimmed across the pages, pausing over particularly pertinent passages.

> In order to speed up this restoration and development, we must do our utmost, in the course of our struggle for the abolition of the feudal system, to preserve all useful means of production and of livelihood, take resolute measures against anyone's destroying or wasting them, oppose extravagant eating and drinking and pay attention to thrift and economy.

Coco stopped reading and pictured the cluttered countertops in her kitchen, crowded with all the terminally tired appliances she'd acquired at suburban Gift Redemption Centers with Top Value or S&H trading stamps. Throughout the sixties, Coco had saved and redeemed her bonus trading coupons for small electrical gadgets colorfully featured in the glossy gift catalogues that she studied with great and greedy concentration.

But now, a decade later, the Salton hot tray she'd selected for dinner parties she never gave was missing its cord, and the shark-toothed waffle iron she'd chosen for eternally postponed Sunday morning brunches had sprung its hinge so its yawning jaws would no longer close. The whip, puree, and chop cycles of her twenty-two-speed blender were broken, while her can opener was too corroded to any longer decapitate anything. One beater from the Hamilton hand mixer was lost and the electric popcorn popper, deep-fry skillet, sandwich grill, and twelve-cup coffee pot were all in the final stages of an expertly engineered evolution toward obsolescence.

Coco skimmed several more pages:

We should support whatever the enemy opposes and oppose whatever the enemy supports.

This too was true. It was clear that Coco's enemies were the corrupt corporate capitalists of America who kept her occupied and preoccupied servicing bad goods and transporting partially paralyzed appliances to repair centers. Oh, yes. It was clear that Coco lived in custodial bondage to her electric blankets, steam irons, shavers, toothbrushes, FM clock-radios, hair curlers, rollers, blowers, misters, dryers, and GE sun lamp, as well as the larger skeletons in her broom closet such as electric waxers, buffers, sanders, vacuums, and rotisseries.

Oh, yes. It *was* true. Lulled by those long yellow streamers of sticky trading stamps offering quick kickbacks, Coco had been numbed by the opiate of affluence so that she was totally unprepared for the day when she found herself pounding, hysterically, on the door of the locked-up Bethesda Trading Stamp Redemption Center—as panicked as any person beating on a boarded-up bank back during the Depression.

Now a prisoner, sitting three feet off the ground in the back seat of her Monte Carlo reading the *Quotations from Chairman Mao Tse-Tung*, Coco started to see very clearly the road that ran from consumerism to skepticism, from skepticism to cynicism, and from cynicism to socialism.

> In the West imperialism is still oppressing the people at home.

Mao was right! Capitalism was a gyp at home and a hype abroad.

Not only were U.S. multinationals raping the resources of the planet and using Third World people as cheap labor to manufacture crap for American consumers, but the bad goods being produced were perverting the human values of the customers who slaved to buy them.

Yes, imperialism was spoiling everything—threatening Coco's marriage, corrupting her children, decreasing her creativity, dissipating her energies, and paralyzing, or at least inhibiting, Gavin's ejaculatory powers by upsetting him with consumer concerns.

For years Coco had been oppressed by her country's disastrous domestic policies and suicidal foreign ones.

Nonessentials were given priority positions while human values and lives were neglected. American technology, the trump card of her culture, focused on improving the taste of toothpaste and the smell of deodorants rather than housing or teaching its people.

The most highly industrialized society in the world had sold out its principles for a batch of 12,000 BTU blow dryers.

It was true. For a long time Coco had known that 60 percent of her tax dollars went to military and defense-related industries. Out of her miserly salary she supported a vast, imperialistic, militaristic system that protected racist, reactionary governments and used the world's wealth and resources for inhumane purposes. For too long Coco had passively acquiesced to the status quo, never questioning the fundamental profit motive of monopoly capitalism or confronting the inherent inequities of a free-enterprise system.

After reading Mao's Maoist maxims for several hours, her incipient doubts about democratic capitalism came into focus like a message from some foreign agent written in invisible ink which emerged only after sufficient rubbing. Krushchev was wrong; Western civilization would bury itself under a mountain of defective and obsolete products, while the best minds of its people were discombobulated by worthless information about useless technological items.

It wasn't Coco's fault that her house was disintegrating, her car deteriorating, and her kid's teeth decaying. Domestic turmoil was designed by the social engineers of her culture. Her very own government supported and subsidized industries that produced trouble-making, labor-saving devices to divert her attention and energy away from worthwhile human pursuits.

A revolution is not a dinner party, or writing an essay or painting a picture or doing embroidery, it cannot be so refined, so leisurely and gentle, so temperate, kind, courteous, restrained or magnanimous.

How could Coco have been so stupid?

Buoyed by a vision of herself emancipated from her household appliances, Coco fell asleep.

# CHAPTER NINE

Izzat was pounding on the car window with the end of a broomstick.

Coco woke up and looked around. The Ambassador was gone. The Midas Muffler clock on the wall read eight-thirty.

"What do you want to eat?" Izzat yelled.

Coco rolled down the window.

"Are you ordering out?"

Izzat looked up at her impatiently. "You're the one who suggested we should," he said wearily. "Remember?"

"Oh, right. Well, where we going to get it from?"

"From the U.S. government, baby."

"No. I mean which restaurant?"

"MacDonald's."

Coco dampened her lips which were dry and chapped. The roof of her mouth felt scratchy, as if she were catching a cold. Still, she was hungry and there was nothing she liked better than hamburgers for breakfast.

"Well, I guess I'll have some Big Macs," she said.

"How many?"

Coco opened the door, looked down, and then jumped. She landed on her feet only a few inches away from Izzat.

"Three," she said finally, pushing her hair away from her face. Although she was confronting death and thus no longer compelled to count calories, Coco felt a twinge of embarrassment as she gave up any semblance of feminine respectability.

"Can you really eat three?" Izzat asked impressed.

Coco nodded nonchalantly. "Also, I'd like a large light coffee and an apple turnover."

Izzat was scribbling down her order in something that looked like Arabic.

"And don't forget cigarettes," she called back over her shoulder, as she started across the garage toward the toilet. "Ask them to get me three packs of Marlboros, please."

Coco used the bathroom and then returned to sit down on the bench along the back wall. She was suddenly suffused with memories of her family on cozy Saturday mornings. She thought of Joshie who had only recently been weaned by intense sibling teasing from his stuffed teddy bear but had taken to carrying a small magnetic panda in his pants pocket as a metallic, metaphorical reminder of babyhood. Joshie was only four and a half. He still needed Coco. A lot. And Jessica . . . Jessica's eighth birthday was only two weeks off and Coco still hadn't addressed or mailed the drugstore package of pink party invitations. If Coco didn't get back home, who would make the party for Jessica?

If Coco died, would her children remember how hard she had always worked on their birthdays, patiently planning all the petty, pretty details which made each event so special? Certainly they would remember how she always found Charlie Brown or Batman paper tablecloths with matching napkins at Murphy's dimestore and finger-pinched color-coordinated crepe paper, inch by inch, into curly streamers that they draped over the dining room chandelier. Oh, yes, certainly they would remember that Coco had never skimped on anything—that she had always gone all the way for every one of them, factoring in each celebrant's age, sex, season, sign, special interests and eccentricities annually for each of the—was it only twenty-eight?—idyllic birthday parties she had produced—eleven for Mike, seven for Jessica, six for Nicky and four for Josh? No. Coco had never shortchanged any of her children on their birthdays, so for that reason alone they would certainly remember her with loving tenderness.

Attempting to avoid tears, Coco opened her purse and took out her little notebook again.

"*Special reminders for some very special people:* Jessica darling: Look through our kitchen telephone book and pick out the names of your eight best friends to whom you want to send birthday party invitations. Daddy will help you mail them. Mike darling: On Tuesday, Thursday, and Sunday nights when you don't have to wear your retainer to bed, please do not leave it in the bathroom drinking cup because in the middle of the night someone might take a drink of water and either choke on your retainer or swallow it.

"Joshie: Lately I've noticed you've gotten a little careless about carrying scissors. Remember when you walk and carry scissors at the same time, you have to point the scissors downward so if you fall it will go into the floor instead of into your chest or your face or your EYES. This is especially true when running up or down stairs.

"Jessica: I've noticed lately that you've been reading with the lamp light pointing TOWARD your eyes instead of letting it come from *behind* you. Remember that your eyes are your most precious possession and you should read only with the lamp BEHIND you.

"Nicky: I don't know if I told you this before, but if there's a hurricane go down the basement; if there's a tornado, open all the windows in the house so it can blow right through, and if there's an electrical storm, stay in the car instead of outside in an open field. Everyone: If any of you must open a can of Drano or turpentine, remember to point it away from your face as you uncap it, so if it explodes, it won't go in your eyes. Also, if you get scratched on a nail sticking up out of the floor, remember to put a little Mercurochrome on your scratch because those nails are pretty rusty, and check with Dr. Goldberg as to when you last had your tetanus shots.

"Another thing: You know those Mexican bowls which I like so much with the red flowers painted on them? Well, it's okay to use them for cereal in the morning, but never use them for hot soups or oatmeal because Granny says the colored glaze on Mexican pottery has carcinogenic chemicals in it. Also, when using tacos from a box, just hang them over the rungs of the oven rack (like shirts over a clothesline) at 225 degrees, before serving, so they'll taste better."

Coco continued writing memos until the food was delivered and left outside the garage. Shotgun in hand, Abass opened the side door just wide enough to pull the fragrant package inside. Then he sat down on the floor with Aly and Izzat. Hesitantly, John Canada joined them, but Ambassador Mohammed remained seated against the wall.

Hungry, Coco joined the group even though, like all Jewish women, she felt inhibited about eating in front of strange men and would have preferred being alone in the car with her Big Macs. However, for political reasons, Coco thought it best to lunch with her captors even though that demanded she nibble, rather than greedily devour, the tasty hamburgers bought at city expense.

For a long while no one spoke.

"I don't know why they can't give Heinz catsup," Coco complained after finishing her first Big Mac.

"It's too expensive," Aly answered immediately. "They wouldn't make enough profit if they used Heinz's catsup."

Coco glanced at Aly to see if he was being sarcastic, but then realized he was simply explaining a basic fact of capitalism to her. Embarrassed, she smiled and then turned to look at the television set which was running without its sound in deference to the meal.

ABC was showing the slow line of traffic moving past the Gulf service station. Drivers were straining to see the carnival-like scene through their car windows before being rerouted away from the garage by policemen. By now there was a lot of snow piled along the curbs and some kids were playing in the drifts. The camera panned the crowd corralled behind the police barricades running along Adams Mill Road to the corner of 18th street. Coco sipped her coffee while searching to see someone she knew.

She saw only strangers.

Life was going on without her.

People had already accepted the fact that she lived as a prisoner in the Gulf garage.

When the channel returned to its regular programming it picked up an old "Gilligan's Island" rerun which Coco had once watched with her children. Homesickness was hounding her now, constantly producing fresh images to make her ache.

Unhappily, she helped herself to some more communal french fries.

"Don't you think we should invite the Ambassador to join us?" Canada asked unexpectedly.

"He's murdered members of my family," Abass answered, lifting the lid of his Half-Pounder to inspect the insides.

"Oh, I doubt that Ambassador Mohammed ever did anything like that," Canada said with a congenial smile that chased the concern for protocol off his face. "That's why it's important to talk with him . . . to find out where he's really coming from."

"Are you kidding?" Izzat's brows met like drawbridges over his nose. "He doesn't want to know us. He looks on us as vermin."

"I'm sure that's not true," Canada protested, carefully dissecting his Big Mac in half. "Of course he's a member of the government, but you have to accept his class constraints in the same way we all have to accept each other's. Otherwise, there can't be any meaningful communication between various political groups."

Coco groaned to herself. Canada was on such a power-trip that he was now going to try making peace in the Middle East to deflect the President's anger about the compromising circumstances of Canada's capture.

"We don't want to communicate with him," Izzat said calmly, dunking a french fry into the puddle of catsup and mustard he'd mixed together in his plastic hamburger box. "Our government wants to exterminate us. They arrest everyone in Iran who disagrees with them. Savak watches all of us all the time and offers money to anyone who will inform on their friends."

Izzat ate several more french fries in quick succession. "I can't even communicate with *you*," he concluded impatiently, "so why the hell do you think I'd want to talk to *him*?"

"Mohammed is too highly placed not to know what was going on," Abass appended. "He has always condoned the torture and execution of political prisoners."

"He's a killer," Izzat snarled, as if translating Abass's comment.

Coco drained the coffee from her container. It was clear that all the publicity photos of Mohammed at his embassy throwing petro-dollar parties where he served imported champagne, caviar, and bellydancers to Euro-dollar diplomats had enraged his compatriots studying at Howard.

Indeed, now Coco could understand that the quick kick in the belly Abass had delivered his Ambassador the night before was a blow against Mohammed's greedy, gluttonous lifestyle.

"Your Ambassador is probably as ignorant of what goes on inside the government as any uneducated peasant," Canada persisted simplistically. "Powerful men are often as isolated as the powerless."

Coco looked at Canada. His showboat diplomacy was like a red flag to the terrorists, but he was oblivious to the effect of his liberal attempt to conciliate blood enemies. His blindness to revolutionary rage, which made him a U.S. national treasure, also made him an international hazard. Coco could hardly believe that just twenty-four hours ago she had been lecherously plotting to sleep with him. Now that she was forced to see Canada as a human being—instead of a male sex object—she felt ashamed.

"We're one of the richest countries in the world," Abass continued, "But the Shah does nothing for our people. Our leaders are unable to spend all our national income, but they let people die in the streets from starvation. What Mohammed spends on booze at his embassy every year could feed most of our country's children."

Now Abass looked at Coco, who slowly returned her third, uneaten Big Mac to its container.

"Being an exile is like a living death," Aly said suddenly. "You're not part of any world. You spend your time in limbo, instead of living."

"One of my brothers was trying to find a way to kill himself in prison," Izzat said. "I don't know if he succeeded or not."

Coco looked at Izzat and felt her heart twist into a fist and the muscle of her soul knot in a spasm. Izzat was one of the wretched of the earth, one of those destined by birth to a brutal life and an early death, eternally excluded from any comfort or careless pleasures. He was one of the tortured and tormented, the despised and disdained, the frightened and forgotten.

Although Coco, as a Jewish mother, couldn't condone terrorist tactics, she certainly had to concede the educational expediency of political blackmail in alerting the public to Third World causes. Basically, she believed the use and abuse of innocent people was counterrevolutionary and that progressives should restrict their actions to relevant public officials who actually had the power to make politically appropriate amends. But, of course, she knew revolutionaries were as careless as everybody else and would capture innocent people just as governments did.

Coco closed her eyes for a moment to think about the isolationist hands-off-me policy she had just thought about.

"Well, I don't know why I'm here," she said solemnly, looking at each of her captors. "But I can certainly understand why you are—and why you're doing what you're doing."

Canada threw Coco a withering look of contempt before he stood up to slide through the slush toward the Ambassador, bearing several Big Macs in his hand.

"Ambassador, you might not remember," he said loudly enough for everyone to hear, "but I attended a dinner in your honor when you came to Princeton last June to receive your honorary doctorate."

"Oh, of course," the Ambassador responded with easy elegance. "At the Guggenheim's."

"That's right," Canada said.

Coco looked at the two men. Vaguely she could recall the incriminating sequence of events recorded in the *Washington Post*—increased educational grants from the government of Iran to Princeton University, an increased number of Iranian students admitted to the school, and finally an honorary doctorate conferred upon the Iranian Ambassador. Indeed, it suddenly occurred to Coco that the Shah might be willing to ransom John Canada, as well as Mohammed Mohammed, if Princeton would further increase its quota of Iranian engineering students.

"How many students do you have at Princeton now?" Canada asked cordially.

The Ambassador flushed. "Well, I'm not sure. I know we have about 20,000 students studying in the United States, but I don't know how it breaks down by universities."

"Savak could answer your question for you," Abass called out to Canada. "However, I can tell you that more than 40 percent of the student body at Howard are foreigners."

Suddenly Coco experienced an oceanic surge of humanistic love for some amorphous entity known as the Third World. Political passion poured through her. Hadn't Coco willingly and willfully joined a system that was a moral morass of injustice and apathy, betraying her own principles?

Oh, yes, wasn't there really a need for a new world order? Didn't Coco really want to see the earth's wealth distributed more equitably? What did Coco have in common with the slim, svelte, sophisticated Ambassador from Iran or the prim, prissy Princeton professor? Wasn't it the gasoline attendants with whom she really identified?

The telephone rang and Izzat walked over to answer it. "Come to the phone, Coco," he called. "It's the Israeli Embassy."

Coco's heart tumbled.

She tried to stand up, but her legs buckled and Abass reached out to steady her.

Humiliated, Coco pulled her hand away from him and lurched toward the telephone.

"Hello," she said inaudibly, so that she had to repeat herself.

"Is this Mrs. Charlotte Burman?"

"Yes, it is."

"Shalom. This is Aveiri Cardozo, Second Secretary of the Israeli Consulate. We were contacted last night by President Carter who informed us that one of your captors is a member of the P.L.O. who wants to make special arrangements for your release in exchange for some Arab prisoners in Jerusalem. We have spent a great deal of time considering the particulars of this situation, but it is our government's policy never to exchange any prisoners for any hostages. It is our policy never to ransom any Jews—even Israelis."

"Yes, I know," Coco said quietly. "That's what I told Aly . . . I mean, our P.L.O. representative in here."

She felt the tickle of a trickle of liquid motion stir her inner organs.

"I'm sorry," the Second Secretary said.

"Well, so am I," Coco whispered. "But thanks just the same."

"Our prayers are with you, Mrs. Burman. Shalom."

"Shalom," Coco answered.

It was the first time she had ever used the word.

So. That was it. Even if the Shah agreed to release the Iranian prisoners, Aly might kill Coco to prove he wasn't a slouch.

Slowly Coco replaced the receiver anticipating a wave of terror that would inundate her, but instead she envisioned the two laundry baskets full of dirty clothes parked at the top of her basement stairs.

Oh, why hadn't she done the wash Thursday night as she had planned? Why hadn't she done any of the things that needed doing?

Emboldened by desperation, Coco ransacked her purse for the last of her coins, picked up the receiver, and dialed her home number without asking permission.

After an alarming number of unanswered rings, Gavin finally said hello.

"Gavin! Honey. It's Coco. How are you? Did you tell the kids?"

"Yeah," Gavin answered. "I told them as soon as they

woke up this morning. Josh cried so hard he got the hiccups and I had to call Dr. Goldberg to come over to give him a sedative or something and the President called while the doctor was here . . ."

"What President?"

"The President of the fucking United States, Coco. *That* president."

"Well, you don't have to yell, Gavin."

"And then your parents called for the tenth time and Jessica vomited and Mike went out without saying where he was going and he's still not back. I suppose he's outside over there."

"Over *where?*"

"At the Gulf station, Coco."

"Oh."

Coco fell silent as she digested the idea of Mike standing a few feet away from her on the other side of the heavy overhead door, mingling with a crowd of overexcited strangers.

"Did he wear his boots?" she asked.

"How the hell should I know?" Gavin roared. "I didn't even see him leave."

Coco tried to modulate her voice. "Well, isn't Diana there, Gavin?"

"Yes."

"Can't she help out?"

No response.

From Gavin's silence Coco concluded Diana was close enough to overhear the conversation. Why the hell wasn't she playing Go Fish or Blackjack with the children? Why was she hanging around Gavin?

"Well, maybe you wouldn't mind telling me what *you're* pissed off about?" Coco asked in a ruthlessly cold voice.

"I'm not mad," Gavin said.

"Bullshit," Coco stormed, as incredulity wrapped itself around her. "You're so upset you can hardly talk. Or maybe you just don't want Diana to hear you bawling me out. What are you trying to do—put on a good-guy show for her?"

"Okay, Coco. Do you want to hear? Do you really want to know why I'm pissed?" Gavin asked. "You want it straight? Then I'll tell you. I'm pissed off because none of this would have happened if you hadn't been out alley-catting all over town. If you hadn't been putting the make on John Canada, none of this would have happened. And now the kids are berserk and . . ."

"Let me talk to them," Coco interrupted.

"It's not a good time right now, Coco. They're all too upset. When they calm down a little we'll call you back."

Gavin had adopted a maternal manner that made Coco feel like an irresponsible father.

"I can't believe this," she protested, starting to cry.

"Well, you better believe it," Gavin said coldly. "And you better own up to the fact that you were out looking for trouble when you found it."

"Oh, Gavin, I wasn't!" Coco turned toward the wall so no one could hear her. "I just thought maybe I could get a job from Canada on the Council of Economic Advisors. I didn't say anything to you about it before because I wanted to see if I could pull it off first."

"Pull what off?"

Coco cried harder. "I can't believe you're talking to me like this now," she said. "Here I am in a life-or-death situation and you're blaming *me*." She sputtered and sniffled. "But I should have known you would because anytime *anything* goes wrong you *always* blame me.

If the bacon grease plugs up the sink or the ice cube trays get twisted in the dishwasher—you *always* blame me."

"But you're not supposed to put plastic stuff in the dishwasher, Coco."

"Oh, Gavin! You might never *see* me again! The children won't have a mother," she wailed.

"Well, if you were so worried about the kids why the hell were you out galivanting around town with John Canada?"

"Gavin! You've *flipped out.* Did you know that the Israeli embassy just called to say they wouldn't ransom me? Do you know what that means? That means I'm really in big trouble now. I mean, John Canada knows Jimmy Carter and Ambassador Mohammed is tight with the Pahlavi family, but who have I got? Just you. And the kids. And my folks. And a few *real* friends. And now you're picking a fight with me. Right when I'm about to die."

"Listen, do you think I'm crazy about what's happening?" Gavin demanded. "But I keep thinking none of it really *had* to happen."

"I'm hanging up," Coco announced.

Furious, she slammed down the receiver and, seething with rage, ran back to her original place against the wall. Her captors had obviously overheard one or both of her conversations because none of them looked at her. Aly was busy cleaning his fingernails with the corner of a matchbook, while Izzat examined his gun and Abass sat impassively staring straight ahead.

John Canada had hidden his head inside his arms again.

Only Mohammed Mohammed was looking at Coco from his location on the floor several feet away.

"I gather the Israelis said no," he remarked after a while.

"Yes, they did."

"I'm really surprised. They are a very progressive and enlightened nation."

Coco didn't answer. Approval of the State of Israel from a reactionary diplomat was something she didn't need at the moment. She did not want to hear any Iranian rhapsodies of praise that could only contaminate a country she cared for—even if it didn't care for her.

"That's the last time I'm going to call my husband," she said to change the subject. Tears were still pressing through the locks of her eyelids. "He makes me feel worse than I already do."

"Well, at least they let you use the telephone," the Ambassador said bitterly. "They won't even let me talk to my embassy. I can't understand why they're treating me so shabbily. I don't think I've been unreasonable since my capture. In fact, I think I've been quite co-operative. I simply can't understand why they're so unpleasant to me."

"Oh, Mohammed," Coco said impatiently, trying to check her tears, "you know you represent . . . something they hate."

"But I refuse to be seen as a *symbol*. I am a man. Granted, I represent the Shah, but I am also an individual. It is precisely for these reasons that civilized people fear these lunatic leftists. They simply refuse to make distinctions. They refuse to see people as individuals."

"Well, you see all of them as lunatic leftists," Coco countered.

"But I am *NOT* a symbol," Mohammed insisted

again, more emotionally. "I do not simply represent a regime. I am a *man*."

"Of course, you're an individual," Coco said reassuringly, "but you're *ALSO* a symbol."

"How can you say that?" Mohammed demanded hotly.

"Well . . ." Coco took a deep breath, hovering between honest hostility and dishonest diplomacy. "An ambassador represents his country just like a flag does, Mohammed. And I also think they're angry about your . . . personal lifestyle. You do live rather . . . lavishly, you know."

"That," he said dismissively, "is a matter of my government's policy and preference."

Guiltily, Coco remembered her own drunken fantasy of sharing Mohammed's staff.

"Look," she said, eager to return to her own private thoughts. "You have to face facts. All three of these students have had horrible lives. If you saw a documentary about them you'd probably be horrified. You know what kind of government you have and how the Shah uses his army and police."

"But that's not *me*," Mohammed moaned. "I am a religious man, an indulgent uncle to my nephews and nieces, a good friend. I am putting the son of my laundrywoman through college at this very minute."

"Well, if you don't want those young men to see you as a symbol, why don't you tell them all of that?" Coco suggested, nodding toward the terrorists and adopting a tone of voice which indicated she was not going to talk politics with any Islamic millionaire member of a ruling class which suppressed dissent and suffocated freedom.

Then, to punctuate their conversation, Coco got up

and walked back to her car. Settled inside, she took out her notebook again.

Organization was clearly the answer to her household problems and, with a little imagination, she could see that she too had a staff of her own. Even if some of them were very short, she had only to train them. Excitedly, Coco turned to a fresh page and wrote:

DAILY SCHEDULE FOR GAVIN

6:30 A.M.: Wake up. Start getting kids ready for school. Try not to lose temper. Think of interesting new sandwiches to make once in a while. Leave housecleaning until evening when everyone can do it together.

7:30 A.M.: If you went to work earlier, could you come home earlier?

Estimated Times of Arrival Home from School:

Mike—ETA 5:00, exc. Wed. when he goes to orthodontist to have his braces tightened.

Jessica—ETA 4:15, exc. Tues. when she goes to dance class.

Nicky—ETA 4:15, exc. Tues. when he waits for Jessica to bring him home.

Josh—ETA 3:30 M–F

6:00 P.M.: Collectively cook supper. Talk about day's events while working in kitchen.

8:00 P.M.: Help kids with homework. Josh and Nicky to bed.

9:30 P.M.: Jessica and Mike to bed.

WEEKLY SCHEDULE FOR GAVIN

Monday–Friday: See above.

Saturday: Do marketing, clean house, yard, car, etc. Do something educational *and* recreational with kids.

Saturday night: ?????

(Coco left a large blank space to fill in comments which might occur to her as the midnight deadline approached. She did not intend to give Gavin any specific advice about a second wife, but she thought she might warn him about Diana's anal compulsive tendencies.)

Sundays:  Relax. Everyone has to bathe, shampoo their hair, and start the laundry (procedure will be explained later on).

"A *Few Random Comments:* Gavin: The burners on the stove are terrifically dirty. They are also not set into their proper slots so they sometimes tilt rather dangerously. Can you straighten them out so they're level, since the kids might be cooking more often? Also, the tinfoil underneath the burners—to stop grease or crumbs from dropping down into the interior of stove—must be changed. The left front burner has some carmelized graham-cracker crumbs on it which, I'm afraid, you will have to scrape off so they won't catch on fire. Always keep some Arm & Hammer baking soda above the stove in case of a grease or electrical fire.

"Gavin: Can you think of some way to organize the canned goods (in alphabetical order, maybe?) so the kids can find the stuff they need? Maybe you could put them away according to some organic principle like fruit, soup, vegetables, etc. Maybe the spice rack could be rearranged according to geographic origins such as the West Indies, etc., etc., which would be educational as well as simplifying. (Remember about the jar of oregano, Gavin!)

"Gavin: As you probably know, Frigidaire shelves can be shifted up or down to render different cubic heights and spaces. (Is this THINKING METRIC, Coco wondered, pausing to chew the tip of her pen.) If Shelf I is lowered, so the gallon milk containers fit, Shelf II suffers a serious height loss. It is questionable whether

195

there are enough short things, or stuff that can lie down horizontally, to make such a shift reasonable. The butter dish would fit, but what else? Is it better to have the oversized bottles stand erect on Shelf I or lie down on Shelf II—which could possibly lead to a lot of dripping. Please see if you can work this out.

"Also, it might be a good idea to insert zip codes into our kitchen telephone-number book. Make sure you keep it roped to the radiator so it doesn't get lost.

"Gavin: Re: the oven. The spots on the broiler pan that match the pattern on the oven walls *CAN* be cleaned off, but it takes elbow grease to eliminate cooking grease. Also, please wipe off that little light bulb at the rear of the oven because it might get overheated from being greasy and explode!

"Don't take the bandages with our name written on them off the bottoms of the serving bowls, because the kids always take them to school around Christmastime and those adhesive tapes are our only chance of ever getting the right bowls back.

"Please remind the kids that if they get a breather on the telephone, they shouldn't say anything but just hang up.

"Any or All of You: Because of my carelessness (not spreading newspapers in the tub when I painted the bathroom ceiling) we have those hard paint lumps on the bottom. If each of you devoted a few minutes to picking at just *one* of those paint spots while in the tub, eventually all of them will disappear. Also, there are lots of other things you can do while sitting on the toilet which would help keep the bathroom tidy. If you notice that the paper roller is empty, just reach under the sink, get a fresh roll and snap it in. That only takes a minute or so. You can also wipe off the sink while you're sitting on the toilet if you sit sideways. Also, if you are ever constipated, take the tube of tile caulk off the window sill, squeeze a little on your fingertip and rub it between the tiles that hold the toilet-paper roller to the wall because that section of tile is getting loose. Please don't let any caulk get on the front of the tiles as it's very hard to get off.

"The city will pick up large, unwieldy items such as old mattresses or defunct freezers or Frigidaires, but be sure the doors have been forcibly removed so no children can crawl inside and suffocate. Also, hose down the kitchen windows from outside once in a while so some sunlight can get in because the plants need it to make chlorophyll.

"Don't bother measuring air conditioners for new refill filters, just brush off the old ones and take them with you to the hardware.

"There are certain books that might be helpful to you, Gavin: *How-to-do-it-yourself Book About Plumbing, Appliances and Cars, The Liberated Lady's Guide to Home Repairs, Decorating Ideas under $100, The Mother's Almanac,* the last *Last Whole Earth Catalogue,* and Peggy Bracken's *I Hate to Cook Book.*

"Honey, also, please clean out that little drawer in our bedside table."

Coco stopped writing. She really couldn't elaborate on that suggestion. The police might read her notebook and rush off to the Burman house to examine the bondage boutique beside her bed full of dildoes, vibrators, porny paperbacks, cowboy belts studded with ruby glass stones, penile elongators, edible panties, imported aphrodisiacs, amyl nitrate inhalators, small jars of hashish oil to paint Marlboros, and the tiny teaspoon in which they occasionally treated themselves to some overpriced coke.

Coco certainly didn't want Gavin getting busted on a drug rap at a time like this.

Looking out the window, Coco saw Aly approaching the car. He yelled up at her that they were ordering pizzas from Eddie Leonard's for lunch, but Coco said she wasn't hungry. A few minutes later the Ambassador approached and asked if he could warm up inside the car again for a while. Reluctantly Coco opened the door and helped pull him inside. This time Mohammed squeezed himself behind the steering wheel, while Coco slid over toward the window. Then she closed her notebook and shoved it back into her purse.

# CHAPTER TEN

At that precise moment, the lights went out in the Gulf garage and for the first time it was night.

Instantly, Aly began shouting. "No one move! I will shoot at any sound I hear. Don't be foolish. Stay where you are."

Coco slumped down in the seat, paralyzed by panic. Had the lights blown or had the police cut off the electricity? Were the cops ready to stage a rescue mission that would end in death and disaster for everyone inside the garage?

She reached out and clutched the steering wheel. Mohammed was silent.

Coco tried to recall where she had last seen John Canada. Had he been sitting in his usual place on the floor or was he perched on the bench watching television? Had he been in the toilet? Was he lying somewhere on the floor now—waiting for a bullet through his head?

"Oh, God," Coco whimpered. "Oh, God."

"We know the two of you are in the front seat of the car," Aly yelled, sounding closer this time. "Don't move. If I hear the car door open we'll start shooting. Do not try to get out."

Coco's heart was thundering. Unconsciously she was turning the steering wheel as if it were the rudder of a boat swirling across a stormswept sea. She could feel terror in the car like a third person sitting in the back seat.

For a long while there was absolute silence.

It was as if the world had stopped and in the darkness Coco lost any sense of time. Her body felt liquid and floppy, out of sync with her metabolism. Panic was palpitating her.

"What's happening?" she asked Mohammed in a whisper when she could no longer tolerate the suspense.

"I don't know," he answered grimly.

Coco was twisting the steering wheel, rotating it first to the right, then to the left, in an attempt to control her destiny. Occasionally her hand bumped against something hard in the Ambassador's lap and absently she wondered if he had a gun hidden in the pocket of his tuxedo trousers.

A moment later the lights flickered twice and then came on again. Coco looked at the Ambassador in the bright glare of the overhead fluorescents and burst into tears.

Mohammed stretched out his bound hands and touched Coco's face.

"Don't cry now," he said kindly. "It's all over now. Don't worry. I think one of my crazy compatriots did it. I saw the fusebox over by the telephone. I think they were just testing the system for security reasons. Don't cry."

Coco straightened up and moved back into her own seat from where she could survey the scene outside. Below the car everything seemed exactly the same as before the lights had gone out. John Canada was still seated on the floor, seemingly shriveled and shrunk from the terrifying moments of darkness. Aly and Izzat were circling the garage, checking the overhead door to assure themselves it was still securely clamped against the ground. Coco saw Abass go into the toilet to examine the small boarded-up window.

Finally Coco collapsed back against the car seat and woefully rubbed her hand across her face to wipe the tears chapping her cheeks.

"Where . . . where did you get your gun?" she asked Mohammed.

The Ambassador turned and looked at Coco uncomprehendingly.

"The gun. In your pocket," Coco repeated. "I felt it when I was holding the steering wheel."

There was a long silence.

"I don't have a gun," the Ambassador said calmly, looking straight ahead.

"Oh."

Coco lit a cigarette for herself and kinetically tried to remember the configuration of the object she had felt.

Jesus.

Secretly she studied the Ambassador out of the corner of her eye.

Large organs did not necessarily fascinate Coco, but this was something else. Usually she craved movie-land settings and hokey atmosphere rather than metric measurements. Usually she yearned for dramatic scenarios, background music, elaborate stage props, and sentimental scenes rather than enormous physical equipment. Basically she enjoyed intrigue, deceptions, disappearances, disappointments, departures and tearful separations in rainy cities or socked-in airports. Atmosphere was her customary aphrodisiac. Still . . .

Right when Coco had decided to become more serious, more mature, more commanding, she was suddenly reduced to a pulsating, palpitating presence with no objective powers of reasons.

I will not—Coco swore to herself—let what I just discovered influence me in any way. That huge thing I felt
was a monstrous abnormality—an unreal apparition—
which should not have any effect on my basic political
views or values.

Was Coco going to regress into a counterrevolutionary person just because she had accidentally felt the
Ambassador's astoundingly obscene organ?

Of course not.

Was she going to capitulate to carnal curiosity?

Of course not.

But once again impressionistic images of life with an
Iranian lover who had a large staff, in both senses of
the word, began to corrupt Coco's brain.

"Excuse me," she said. "I've got to get out here."

The Ambassador seemed puzzled by her abruptness,
but he opened the door and climbed down so that she
could follow him. Once back on the ground, Coco hurried away from Mohammed and ran across the garage.

Abass and Aly were still pacing about, but when
the telephone rang everyone turned to watch Izzat answer it. After a moment it became clear, from the expression on Izzat's face, that this was the call for which
they had been waiting.

Coco stood motionless. Once again she felt as if someone had covered her mouth and nose with a fan of fingers that stifled her breathing and threatened her life.
Coco no longer believed the terrorists could maintain
their drill indefinitely. If the Shah refused to free the
prisoners or began haggling over details that would ex-
tend the discussions beyond midnight, Coco was sure
the men would blow up. Like Canada, she was coming
to believe the terrorists would panic or, with premedi-

tated precision, kill everyone in the garage in retaliation for the failure of their plot.

Finally Izzat replaced the receiver and turned around. His face was covered with sweat as he walked over to his comrades to report the conversation. Ambassador Mohammed stepped forward in an effort to hear Izzat's words, but a moment later the three young students began to yell. They crowded together, alternately embracing each other and shaking hands, shifting between laughter and cries. After a while, Izzat broke away and walked over toward his prisoners.

"The Shah has capitulated to our demands!" he announced. "Our comrades are being put on a plane right now." His voice cracked and he took a moment to recover. "They will telephone us when they reach Algeria, and as soon as they are safely installed with our people there, we will leave here for Dulles Airport with Ambassador Mohammed as our hostage. There's a plane waiting there to fly us to Algeria." Then he glanced guiltily at Aly. "But first we must release both Americans," he said. "The Shah made his agreement conditional on our releasing both of them."

Coco felt a rush of tears spring to her eyes and, too weak to wipe them away, let them roll down her face and salt her lips.

"We won," Izzat said, shaking his head slowly with proud disbelief. "You," he said curtly, nodding at the Ambassador, "will be released in North Africa."

Coco looked over at Mohammed whose face had settled into a fierce mask. His eyes had the guilty glaze of someone who had inadvertently injured a loved one. He was clearly grieving for the Shah.

Suddenly Canada approached Coco and reached out

for her hand. For the first time she felt him emanating an authentic affection and she smiled as relief engulfed her.

"Oh, I'm so glad," she sobbed. "So glad." She flung her arms around Canada's neck and pulled herself off the ground to kiss his cheek. Then, sliding down the long length of his body, she walked over to Izzat.

After a moment's hesitation, Izzat accepted the hand Coco extended toward him. "You did it, Izzat," Coco said softly with a strong sense of pride for him. "You did what you had to do. And you won."

"I know this has been hard for you," Izzat said gently, "but you'll be free soon."

"So will you," Coco whispered drunk from emotion. "So will you . . ."

In a moment of mutual accord, they moved together and Coco lowered her head to press her wet cheek against Izzat's shoulder. Then she looked at the other two students.

"I'm glad," she called out to them. "I'm glad your friends are going to be freed."

Abass, preferring to conceal his emotion, shrugged indifferently.

Aly turned away.

"How long will it take them to reach Algiers?" Coco asked Izzat.

"Six or seven hours, I suppose."

Coco whisked her jacket sleeve across her face to catch the drippings from her nose and then turned to the Ambassador.

"Well, Mohammed," she said. "What do you think?"

His eyes indicated supreme resignation. "What does it matter what I think?" he asked wearily.

Coco reached out and took his bound hands in her own. She didn't know quite what to say.

"Well, at least you'll be in your own part of the world again, Mohammed. And I'm sure they'll send you home as soon as you reach Algiers."

"No, they won't," Mohammed said grimly. "Once they're safe they'll kill me. They'll use me to ensure their safe passage and then shoot me."

"Oh, I know they won't do that," Coco protested. "The Algerians won't let them double-cross the Shah. I'm sure the Shah has it all arranged to have you flown home directly from the airport in Algiers."

Mohammed shrugged with morose disbelief.

"And they'll know that if they kill you, there will be reprisals against their families. Really, Mohammed, don't think about that. Of course I'm sorry you can't be released here with us, but I know it will work out all right," Coco said. "Actually, I'm a little surprised Canada and I don't have to go to Algiers too." For a moment she wondered if she felt a drop of disappointment about not seeing North Africa. Then, dismissing the notion, she touched Mohammed's cheek gently. "Everything will be all right," she promised.

But as she turned away, she saw Izzat and Abass standing beside each other with their arms raised over their heads.

Coco couldn't understand what they were doing. Slowly she turned around. Aly was standing directly behind her with his gun extended from a quivering arm.

"You aren't going to sell me out," he said quietly to the Iranians who were only a few feet away from him.

Coco looked at the Ambassador and Canada who were also edging toward the wall, lifting their arms above their heads. Briefly, Coco wondered if she should do the same thing, but then, feeling shy about such a melodramatic motion, decided against it.

"You can't release the Americans because this one belongs to me." Aly said. "I'm not going to let her out of here until I get what I want."

Coco felt herself start to unravel internally. All the adjustments she had made to accept her situation began to disintegrate.

Now she began to think more politically, blaming the times for her trauma. It was all the injustices of previous decades which caused her present peril. Generations of indignities had produced political egocentricity. Now every people had their own priorities. It was the political ME decade. Everyone was out for *me, me, me. I want. I want.* I want my rights right now. How could there be cooperation, let alone civility, with such rampant vengefulness?

Coco felt Aly approaching her from the rear.

His gun touched the small of her back like the offering of an amorous man.

The cold hard object bumped her softly and coaxingly. It was the same soft nudge made by the dumb animal each man carried between his legs. Coco could remember Gavin embracing her from behind while she washed the dishes or stirred something on the stove. Clearly everything men carried in their pants pockets felt the same.

A revolver was just a technological advance over the penis—detachable and more deadly. No wonder the world was caught up in an arms race which the male sex had created. Men had developed guns as extensions of their groins. Indeed, they had modeled their automatic pistols along the same lines as their penises and went around shooting them off whenever and wherever possible. Violence was obviously an obsessive and intoxicating substitute for sex.

"Go," Aly said from behind Coco's head. "Go over and get their guns. Take the guns out of their pants." He waved his free hand at Izzat and Abass. "Right now."

Coco started to walk. She approached Izzat first and their eyes met.

"Keep your arms up, Izzat," Aly growled, "or I'll shoot you. Don't try to touch her."

Nervous, Coco reached out toward the side pocket of Izzat's Levis. As discreetly as she could, she began to wedge her fingers inside the stiff material. Her fingers inched downward until she felt the handle of his gun.

—What is it with these guys and their guns and their dicks—she thought wildly as she slowly tried to extract the revolver without injuring the other object in his pants. What had made men externalize their genitals in such a fearsome fashion?

When she looked down and saw the gun in her own hand she felt both revulsion and terror.

"Hurry up," Aly shouted. "Get the one from Abass."

Coco walked over to him.

At least his coveralls were loose so the pockets were more easily accessible. She reached inside the left one. For a moment she couldn't distinguish what she was feeling and thought that Abass had two guns until she realized her mistake. If she survived this experience, Coco would be penis-shy the rest of her life. She would never be able to disentangle or disassociate those two objects in her mind ever again.

She was now holding one pistol in each hand. They

were both file-cabinet grey, cold, heavy, and ugly. She waited docilely for Aly to take them away from her.

"Come on," he said. After confiscating the two weapons, he began to pull her backward.

"What do you want?" Coco asked fiercely. "What do you want from me now?"

"We're getting into the car," Aly said, raising his voice so the others could hear him. "I'm going to keep her up in the car until you call the President and say you won't release the Americans until the Israelis release their Palestinian prisoners. I'm going to hold her hostage until you do what I say and I'll kill her if you don't."

Aly began pulling Coco through the oily slush on the floor.

"Please," she said looking at his petulant profile. "Please, Aly. I don't want to go up there."

His fingers dug into her arm as she slipped and slid through the oil which formed pools inside the water puddles.

Aly was walking backward so he could watch the Iranians.

"I swear I'll kill her if I don't get what I want, and then you won't be able to make your exchange. If I kill her the Americans won't keep their end of the bargain."

"John," Coco called. "Help me."

John Canada started to make a forward motion before Aly waved his gun at him.

"No one come near here," Aly yelled, pushing Coco toward the boxes. "Don't come near the car until you've got the President to say OK."

With his gun, Aly prodded Coco onto the boxes and into the front seat of her Monte Carlo. Then he scrambled inside and crawled over into the back so he was sitting directly behind her. Opening the window he stuck his gun outside, pointing at the men across the garage.

"Do it," he yelled. "Get on the phone and do it . . ."

He concluded his command with a gunshot.

Coco smelled smoke and felt a bullet blast out of the car. She couldn't see where it hit because she had instinctively lurched forward so fast that she hit her face against the steering wheel.

Oh, no!

This she couldn't handle. This was going to tilt her right over the edge. She was going to freak out in a wail of shrieks. She was going to become one long, shrill scream.

"Coco!"

She lifted her head.

Mohammed Mohammed had run halfway across the garage.

"Coco. Are you hurt?" he yelled.

"Go back," Aly roared out through the window. "Get back against the wall. All of you. Stand next to the telephone. Izzat! Call the President. Right now!"

Mohammed Mohammed wavered, looked up at the car, and then began retreating, slowly, toward the telephone.

Coco collapsed back against the seat. Now that she was in the car she was glad that the two Iranians were disarmed. At least they couldn't start taking pot-shots at the Chevy, trying to kill Aly in order to recover Coco. Indeed, she had probably saved her own life by sticking her hand down both the Iranians' pants.

Then her bravado melted and she was flooded with incredulity again. She couldn't believe the whole thing.

Her face became wet with tears.

Suddenly Coco knew she was going to die. Somehow or other she would be shot. Gavin would have to come to the city morgue to identify and claim her body. The police would pull Coco out, in a drawer, from their bureau of bodies and fold back the sheet so Gavin could say "Yes."

Yes. Oh, yes!

But where would Gavin bury her? The Burmans had never bought any burial plots. Where would he inter her body? Under the azalea bush in the backyard where they buried the extra house key?

Certainly Gavin wouldn't have the time or presence of mind to do any comparative shopping among city cemeteries. He would probably just go out to the sub-urbs where burial plots were cheaper according to some inverse correlation between distance from the inner city and cost. There was no way the Burmans could afford six feet of land in Georgetown. Given the current infla-tion, would Coco have to be buried beyond the Beltway —out among the department-store warehouses which ran furniture sales on national holidays?

Oh, God. Not that. Not there.

No wonder Russian short-storyists kept using plots about plots. There was much meaning buried in such material—a multitude of ironies to be mined. Certainly Coco's family had understood the nature of the problem for they had been making monthly payments on burial plots near Chicago for decades now—knowing that a family that was laid together stayed together forever.

"Get started," Aly yelled toward the men clustered around the telephone.

Perhaps Coco should try to do something.

Perhaps she should excavate the bicycle lock from beneath the front seat and throw it at Aly's face.

Then, suddenly, the lights went off again.

Coco froze.

Now what?

Now what would everyone do?

The blackness was profound.

The fear inside Coco was even darker.

Aly didn't speak or move. There were no sounds outside the car.

Coco held her breath and stifled her bodily sounds as she edged off the seat and curled up in a ball on the floor. She could see nothing but she could smell the dampness of the car carpeting which, for some reason, reminded her of her children.

The telephone began to ring. Unconsciously Coco began to count. Two times. Six times. Twelve times before it stopped.

Then she felt herself falling through space.

She thought she was fainting or dying.

Undigested food rushed up into her throat as the car plunged downward.

Blood rushed to her head as the Chevy settled on the ground, rocking in the ruts of the hoist.

Someone had lowered the lift and dropped the car.

Coco's body was quivering.

"Okay. We're on both sides," Izzat shouted. "Throw the guns out the window, Aly. Right now. We've got you covered."

"With what?" Aly yelled.

"The machine gun."

Coco heard three metallic thumps as Aly tossed the guns out the back window onto the ground.

"Put on the lights," Izzat yelled.

The darkness disappeared.

Coco stayed on the floor.

She heard the back door of the car open and a shuffle as Aly got out.

"Are you okay?" Izzat asked, sticking his head in through the front window as he had done the morning before when Coco came into the station for gasoline.

"Yes," she answered feeling weak and nauseous as she wiggled back up onto the front seat.

"Stay inside," Izzat said. Then, reaching into the back, he grabbed Coco's blanket and threw it at her like a parent tossing comfort into a crib. "Lie down for a while."

Coco did as she was told. She didn't want to see what was happening outside the car. She knew Aly had been disarmed, unharmed, but she didn't want to witness his humiliation—his self-hatred and rage at the others. His coup had failed and she knew he wouldn't be able to accept that gracefully. He would feel he had betrayed his Palestinian friends in Jerusalem.

Coco slowly stretched out on the front seat and pulled the blanket around her body and over her head so she would see no evil, hear no evil and know no evil.

When she awoke it was afternoon.

The Midas Muffler clock read 1:30.

Coco sat up and looked out the window.

Aly was sitting, unbound but sullen, on the rear-wall bench. Canada and Mohammed had their hands tied behind their backs again. Abass was rolled up in a sleeping bag on the floor and Izzat was fiddling around with the Coke machine.

Coco got out of the car and walked over to Izzat.

"Well, that was something," she said to him.

Izzat smiled and kicked the side of the machine.

"So, is the deal on again?" Coco asked.

"Yup. We cooled Aly out," Izzat said nonchalantly,

as if they had only had a verbal quarrel. "We made some future plans with him."

"Well, then, can I call my family, Izzat, and tell them I'll be getting out tonight?" Coco asked.

"OK."

She walked toward the telephone, giving wide berth to the place where Abass was sleeping and skirting Aly on the bench. Rummaging through the debris at the bottom of her purse, Coco recovered the remainder of her loose change and put all of it in her jacket pocket. Then she deposited three of her last nickels and cautiously dialed her home number.

This time Gavin answered, and Coco broke into sobs. It took some time before she could explain she was crying with relief—that she was still safe and slated for release that night. When Gavin shouted out the news, pandemonium broke out in the Burman house and Coco's children began picking up various extensions, fighting and howling for possession. They spilled their joy through the telephone wires into her ear. They cried with love and excitement. At one point Coco detected a fist fight when Nicky tried to take the extension away from Mike, but gradually everyone quieted down. Then Coco told them how glad she was to be getting released and how much she loved them. Even Diana seemed to sound excited. Finally Coco promised to call them back a little later and everyone blew blossoms of kisses into the telephone.

But the minute Coco replaced the receiver, the telephone rang and she automatically answered it.

"Hello," she said, looking over her shoulder to see if there was any reaction to her initiative.

"Coco? It's Dave Macintosh. How you doing?"

"Oh, hi, David. How did you get this number?"

"I watched David Schumaker dialing it over TV. Did he reach you?"

"No, but maybe he talked to someone else. There's been so many calls I couldn't keep track of them all. Is anything wrong?" she asked.

"Well, I've got all the hard evidence we need," he said. "I'm ready to go public with the whole thing based on what I discovered last night."

"What was that?" Coco asked wearily, feeling an unexpected rush of self-pity. Why did she have to continue worrying about *everything* even when she was a hostage?

"Jesus, what an ass I am," David groaned. "I'm so shook up I didn't even ask how you are. But I did hear over the news that you were scheduled for release tonight . . . that the Shah accepted the deal . . . or I never would have called. I'm really glad for you, Coco."

"Thanks, David. But I can't stay on the phone too long because there's probably a lot of other calls coming in."

"Oh. For sure. But listen. The reason I called is that I found out Diana's been in on the whole thing. I found two complete sets of books in her desk—one has the records of the real data and the other the doctored version."

"Whew." Coco expelled her breath. "Well, I guess we're just going to have to blow the whistle on both of them," she said slowly.

While Coco could enjoy the idea of exposing Diana Whitcomb for being the opportunist she was, the prospect of angering Lionel Hearndon was intimidating. Ever since Coco had discovered her boss was afraid of women, she had been terrified of frightening him.

"Yeah," David agreed. "You're right. But listen, Coco. I was thinking. Since you have so much public visibility at the moment, I thought it would be more effective for you to make the charges. You could just call up someone from the *Post* or the *Times* and tell them the whole story. The *Post* would love it. They haven't had a really good scandal in years. Just think—Fraud Found in $5 Million Dollar Social Science Institute Infelicity Index."

"But won't they want to see some proof?" Coco asked.

"Probably. So just tell them they can pick up all the evidence they'll need from me over here at the Institute. I'll just stay here and wait for any requests that come in."

"OK," Coco said.

There was a long emotional silence on David's end of the line before he spoke again. "I want you to know something, Coco. I think you're a terrific person, I really mean that. God bless you."

Then he hung up.

Coco rested for a moment before replacing the receiver.

Yes. David was right. Coco *was* terrific. Here she was living through a personal nightmare and she still had enough spirit to fight crime at the same time. Coco Burman still had the strength to join arms with progressive people from all walks of life to struggle against all kinds of tyrannies. No matter what else was happening, she would not allow Lionel Hearndon and Diana Whitcomb to perpetrate a fraud on the public. Coco Burman would blow the whistle on any such official illegality.

Wearily she walked back to John Canada.

"You're not going to believe this," she said, sitting down beside him near a puddle of water with an oily rainbow running through it, "but remember what David was saying at Diana's party? Well, he just uncovered evidence that proves Diana was in cahoots with Lionel in falsifying the Infelicity data. David's got the proof that Hearndon was upgrading the numbers."

"You better be able to back up those charges with some damn hard evidence before you go public with anything like that," Canada said testily. Coco stared at him. After all the hours of hardship, John Canada still looked scrupulously clean and exasperatingly organized. He was clearly the kind of man who ate the same thing for breakfast every morning and who probably cut his toast diagonally before buttering it. It was clear that Canada's civility was evil.

"Well, David got the original printouts and the ones Hearndon gave him for final programming," Coco said.

"They show Hearndon exchanged one set of numbers for another. It's out-and-out fraud, and I'm going to call the *New York Times* and turn them onto the story."

"You better think it through, Coco," Canada warned.

"I have," Coco answered. "I told you over at Diana's that I didn't believe everyone was as happy as the Index showed. Jesus! 76 percent satisfied with the quality of life in their cities!" she said sarcastically. "69 percent happy with the performance of their government! You'd have to have fallen out of a tree not to know how miserable people are." She stopped ranting. "Why are you trying to cover this up?"

Canada looked directly into her eyes. "Why do you think?"

"Because you're the chairman of the Social Science Institute board and because you've got to get Senate clearance for your presidential appointment."

"Right."

"Well, I think that sucks. Why should I care if you

get to be on the Council of Economic Advisors? Why should I trust you with a big government job if I can't trust you to blow the whistle on some semipublic, semi-private survey research?"

Defiantly, Coco got up and walked over to the battered telephone book dangling from a chain on the wall. After thumbing through the Yellow pages, she dialed the number of the Washington bureau of the *New York Times* and asked to speak with the reporter who covered federal agencies. A young man picked up an extension and grumpily said his name was Dillon Baxter. When Coco identified herself as one of the Gulf station hostages, excitement overcame his boredom.

"How you all doing in there?" he asked.

"Oh, pretty good now," Coco answered. "But actually I'm calling about something else. See, I'm an editor at the Social Science Institute and I've been working on the National Infelicity Index for almost a year. Anyway, yesterday our research director discovered that the original figures submitted to the Institute have been altered so as to indicate a much higher national felicity rate than actually exists. David Macintosh now has copies of the original data that proves Lionel Hearndon was keeping two sets of numbers. You know what I mean? Like two sets of books?"

"Uh-huh," Dillon Baxter grunted. "But let me ask you this. Have you heard anything further since the Shah accepted the terrorist demands?"

Coco paused. "No. Not since early this afternoon. But about this other matter . . ."

"Uh-huh," the reporter repeated. "Well, I'm going to make a note of this and give it to my editor as soon as we're off the phone. But listen, what's going on inside there? Have the terrorists bullied you at all? Were you manhandled? Did they let you make contact with your family?"

Unconsciously, Coco began to scratch the inner side of her right wrist where some eczema was erupting.

"You know this National Infelicity story is a real scoop," Coco said in a severe tutorial tone of voice. "Lionel Hearndon has gotten two and a half million dollars in federal grants to run this study, and now there's solid proof he's been perpetrating a fraud. It's possible someone—either in the government or from one of the corporations that supported the research—paid Hearndon to falsify the numbers. This is *really* big."

"I know, Ms. Burman, but it's not of quite the same magnitude as your kidnapping. *You're* the real story today. You might not know this, but Washington is absolutely paralyzed. The sky is *full* of helicopters. Traffic is bumper-to-bumper. People are glued to their TV sets. We've got four reporters down there at the Gulf station and now I've got you on the phone and all you want to talk about is a social science report you're editing. What I want is a little local color—you know, a couple of details or some personal impressions about your experience. After all, you were the only woman inside there and you're quite an attractive woman."

Coco hung up. A second later she was flooded with regret at not having asked Mr. Baxter how he knew what she looked like. Had Gavin produced some photograph of her after all? Was some picture of Coco which she hated now flooding the media?

Upset by her own vanity, Coco sighed and recommitted herself to her crusade.

During the next hour, she telephoned the Washington *Post*, CBS, NBC, and the wire services. Of all the calls she made, her first to the *New York Times* was the most rewarding. The other men she spoke to were even less interested in what she had to say than Mr. Baxter. Upset to the point of frenzy, Coco went back to borrow some more change from Canada.

But when she saw the familiar smug expression on his face she felt a surge of rage.

"Listen, John," Coco said, threateningly. "I'm having trouble interesting the press in our little Social Science Institute scandal, so I want you to make some calls for me. I want *you* to call the *Times* bureau and ask them to investigate the S.S.I. story. You've got enough clout to make them listen."

"Are you kidding?" he grimaced.

"No."

"Well you must be on dope or something, Coco, because I wouldn't lift a finger to launch that little story."

"Well, if you don't do it, John, if you won't help me expose Hearndon to the press . . ." Coco cast about for an appropriate threat and smiled as the right one drifted into her head, "I'll tell them that we've been lovers for years. I'll smear your name across the front pages of every paper in the country. And you know damn well that's the kind of story they'll pick up in a minute. I'll blow us up into a first-class scandal."

John Canada looked at Coco calculatingly and then turned away with a dismissive gesture.

Now Coco felt fresh resolve starch and stiffen her will.

This was too much.

Enough.

No more.

When she returned to the telephone she dialed the White House number. "I must speak to the President," she said firmly to the switchboard operator. "This is Charlotte Burman. I am one of the hostages at the Gulf service station." It was almost as good as saying the "Senator from Connecticut" or "the Senator from Wyoming."

"One minute, please."

"This is the President," Jimmy Carter said.

"Hello, Mr. Carter. This is Coco Burman. I mean, Charlotte Burman. I'm one of the hostages over at . . ."

"Yes, of course. I know," the President said wearily. "I suppose you've heard the good news. We've made the final arrangements for your release as soon as the plane from Tehran lands in Algiers."

"Yes, Mr. President, and I'm enormously grateful for all you've done." Coco paused and took a deep breath. "But I have just one more small favor to ask of you. I hope it doesn't sound too presumptuous, but it's something that I feel is quite important. You see, I'm an editor at the Social Science Institute where we've just completed a five-year study on Infelicity in America."

"On what?"

"Infelicity. Unhappy people."

Jimmy Carter laughed. "Well, they seem to study everything these days."

Coco laughed too. Jimmy Carter really did sound quite sweet. Perhaps the fact he had deregulated natural gas shouldn't be held against him. Perhaps Coco should be more forgiving about his inability to handle Congress. Perhaps Jimmy Carter really did believe that cutting back social welfare programs would halt inflation.

"Well, Mr. President," she continued, "the thing is—this study, which was half funded by federal funds, is going to be very important when it's released, but our staff project director just discovered that the director of the Institute changed some of the census figures. Dr.

Lionel Hearndon committed fraud with federal money and I'm afraid that there's going to be a cover-up . . ."

"Now Mrs. Burman, please calm down. I think it's admirable of you to be concerned about such matters under such extraordinary circumstances. And I'm actually pleased as Punch that you've telephoned me because I've been wanting to chat with you about something else. I don't know whether or not you know this, there've been some hints of it on TV, but mostly it's appearing in the newspapers. I'm referring to some . . . speculation . . . about why you and John Canada were together Friday evening. As you know, gossip of that sort puts me in a very difficult position and I'd be happy to have your personal assurance, as I've had his, that your relationship was, and will continue to be, only that of colleagues."

Coco's eyes widened. There was no doubt about it. The President of the United States was sticking it to her. He was not going to discuss fraud at the Social Science Institute before discussing her relationship with John Canada. The whole thing was mind-blowing. Apparently Jimmy Carter really couldn't abide the idea of any extramarital activity and he was dealing with the issue in a button-holing, arm-twisting, half-Nelson, Lyndon-Johnson sort of way.

"I have always believed that the sanctity of the family is reaffirmed during crises such as these," Jimmy Carter continued, with the drone of a friendly family pastor. "Don't you agree?"

Coco realized that he was not going to let her off the hook until she foreswore introducing any adultery into his administration. He was not going to back down or let go.

"Well, of course," Coco said sweetly. "I understand and agree with everything you're saying."

"I'm sure you're looking forward to being reunited with your family," the President said warmly, "and I know Jean Canada is anxious to see her husband at home again."

Coco grimaced. "Oh, for sure, Mr. President. I agree completely."

"Fine then. Now that we understand each other, I'll assign one of my White House aides to check out the situation over at the . . . Social Science Institute, is it? Just don't worry about a thing," President Carter said. "We're going to have you out of there as fast as possible. You just stay calm until you're released and then we'll worry about this survey problem afterward. Needless to say, I'm relieved to know you will sever any . . . social relations with Dr. Canada. Also Rosalynn and I are looking forward to having you and your husband come by for dinner some night soon."

The President hung up.

Without speaking to anyone, Coco returned to her nest in the front seat of the car. She needed some solitude in which to think. After all the horrifying, albeit humanizing, hours of being a hostage, Coco suddenly saw her situation as an opportunity rather than an ordeal. The offer she'd just received from the President of the United States was alarmingly illuminating.

Coco had finally—for reasons beyond her control—accrued some clout. Because Jimmy Carter saw her as someone who could hurt him politically, he was willing to bargain with her. Because Coco was now able to produce gossip which could injure the President, she had been cut into the political process. Because she could manufacture a scandal that would rock the government, she had been given a piece of the action.

Now she could make waves, deals, and demands.

Just because the Shah of Iran, who had told Barbara Walters women were inferior to men and thus unable to govern, had decided to ransom his Ambassador didn't mean Coco Burman had to go along with the gag. Just because a bunch of male world leaders had made a political deal didn't mean Coco had to cooperate. Just because a band of young terrorists had decided she was no longer vital to their interests didn't mean they could just toss her back into the world where she would have to scurry about picking up all the loose ends of her life—which obviously would have unraveled further during her imprisonment. Just because the men were finished using Coco didn't mean they could just throw her out into a crowd of cranky cops, quacks, cranks, queers, and crazies who would want to question, examine, interview, acquire, or exploit her.

Were they kidding?

After twenty-four hours in the Gulf garage, Coco would be behind in every aspect of her life. As soon as she got home she would have to go to the grocery store to replenish their food supplies and check all the batteries in their smoke alarms. She would probably have to spend a lot of time trying to revive her plants which she had forgotten to ask Gavin to water. She would have to go to the laundry, the cleaners, and the shoemaker. Of course she would be back among her loved ones. She would be able to see her children once again. Coco would be able to kiss them and love them and help them when they needed her. They would have their real mother instead of a young administrative assistant taking care of them. But Coco would also be back in the same personally frustrating, socially isolating, and politically alienating existence that had imprisoned her before her capture.

Actually things might even be worse. If there had really been as much public speculation about her relationship to John Canada as Jimmy Carter had suggested, Gavin's psychogenic aspermia might be exacerbated by suspicion. After a few days he would begin pummeling her again, pumping away like crazy all night, so Coco could never recover her lost sleep. Dark circles would develop beneath her eyes. Worry wrinkles would appear. More grey would grow in her hair. She would be too tired to think clearly. She would be unable to orchestrate any media coverage of the Social Science Institute fraud. Obviously Lionel Hearndon would fire her the minute she was free and Coco would be unable to find another job. She would be forced into writing some Sunday supplement story about her experience with something like "Fear Of Dying" as its title.

And all she had was Jimmy Carter's private—and probably privileged—promise that he would have some aide check out her story about the National Infelicity Index. John Canada would do all he could to suppress the scandal. Diana Whitcomb, either out of love for Gavin or rage at Coco, would help in the cover-up. Lionel Hearndon would try to discredit both Coco and David Macintosh. Powerful establishment forces would cut off any investigation and successfully cover up any guilty tracks or traces.

It would be David and Coco against the social science establishment.

Why should Coco trust Jimmy Carter? How did she know he'd come across and do the right thing?

Coco would obviously have to blackmail him into ordering a Justice Department investigation of the Social Science Institute's National Infelicity Index.

She would have to use rumors of her romance with John Canada as ammunition to threaten a scandal and thus secure her own demands.

# CHAPTER ELEVEN

This was clearly the moment for Coco to change the course of her life. She had learned a lot in the last few days and the President of the United States had moved her from a state of political ignorance to one of influence. She no longer had to let herself be used. She could take a stand.

This is it—Coco thought, picking up Mao Tse Tung's book and rubbing the cover as if to release the genius from within. She did not have to remain an object all her life—a hostage to other people's demands—detained or derailed according to the special interests of special groups.

Coco, too, had some individual and class interests. At least she could try, while she still possessed some prisoner-power, to rectify some of the wrongs that plagued her. Coco could issue some ultimata requesting reparations for her imprisonment in the form of federal assistance for her neglected neighborhood. She could get Gavin and the children to agree to some drastic domestic changes, John Canada to pledge his support in the fight against fraud at the Social Science Institute, and Jimmy Carter to promise some governmental reforms.

All she had to do was threaten to create a scandal that would ruin Canada's reputation and tarnish the image of the Carter administration.

Coco opened the *Quotations from Chairman Mao Tse-Tung* with the inspired motion of a person seeking direction from the Bible and looked at the first passage that caught her eye.

> We should rid our ranks of all impotent thinking. All views that overestimate the strength of the enemy and underestimate the strength of the people are wrong.

Was that Mao's message to Coco? Had Coco been thinking impotently—feeling victimized and vanquished by circumstances she *could* confront and, possibly, conquer? Were all the sexual, social, mechanical, and political disorders she experienced only the result of her own impotent imagination? Did her feelings of help-lessness only perpetuate her powerlessness?

She flipped through several more pages.

> We should check our complacency and constantly criticize our shortcomings just as we should wash our faces or sweep the floor every day to remove the dirt and keep them clean.

Coco felt power surge through her.

> Unite and take part in production and political activity to improve the economic and political status of women.

Coco could indeed free herself right now.

Reaching under the driver's seat, she extracted the blue vinyl bicycle lock which she used to secure the car hood at night. Looking at the chain she realized it represented freedom. She was the only one who knew the combination, and the terrorists could not leave the garage without releasing her and Canada first. If nothing else worked, Coco could chain herself to the

227

steering wheel and remain there until the White House and her family agreed to all her political and personal demands.

Yes, the time had come for the system to yield to Coco Burman.

Feeling like a newly emergent nation, she replaced the chain beneath the driver's seat. Now Coco, like Namibia and Zimbabwe, was ready to step forward as an equal among equals—to take her rightful place in the political world of opportunistic operators.

Excitedly she opened her purse and took out the little notebook once more. Because she had used it so often, the cover was tearing away from its spiral spine and only a few clean pages remained. But ideas were rushing helter-skelter through Coco's head and she was anxious to record her lists of grievances.

Quickly, from the notes she had already written to Gavin and the children, Coco composed a master list of domestic responsibilities that each member of her family would have to accept. Then, pausing to think for a moment, she tried to pick her public priorities. Since few of the social services in the Adams-Morgan community actually worked, Coco could start anywhere.

She could certainly request better staffing in her local post office. Sometimes it took an hour to purchase a book of fifteen-cent stamps simply because there weren't enough Spanish-speaking clerks to help all the Latinos who used the local post office as an international bank for underprivileged, unemployed, unregistered aliens. Latin men (whom United States Immigration officers sporadically picked up for deportation on Sunday afternoons during Spanish-speaking soccer games on the Mall behind the Washington Monument) and their wives—ashen and aging in shabby, corset-tight winter coats—daily formed endlessly long lines to buy money orders for export to their native lands.

Slowly and painstakingly, the Spanish-speaking customers would spell out the names of some even less-fortunate relatives waiting—on some hot, dusty road lined with lush tropical flowers near a shanty post office in Malaguay or Guadalupe, for that meager money order issued from the cold, grey, understaffed substation on 18th Street near Columbia Road. After laboriously negotiating the purchase, they would insert the money order in a soiled envelope brought, preaddressed in a sad sprawling Spanish script, from home, and start the agonizing process of registering the letter. During the past Christmas season, conditions in Coco's post office had considerably worsened, because the Latinos who, out of necessity, had to wrap, tie, and label their gift packages with public scissors, twine, and marking pens, blocked all avenues of approach to the STAMPS or PARCELS windows and generally jammed up the local U.S. mail system.

Coco uncapped her pen and began to write:

1. Two more Spanish-speaking postal clerks must be added to the Adams-Morgan substation on 18th Street and a second money-order window must be opened.
2. Due to the large number of welfare checks coming into 20009 there is a good deal of mailbox theft as well as the actual stealing of whole mailboxes. Because of this, some credit-card companies—BankAmericard to be precise—refuse to mail credit cards to anyone living in this zip code. I believe this is discriminatory, if not unconstitutional, and that the Senate subcommittee on postal affairs should hold hearings on this situation.
3. The main post office MUST paste a new schedule—telling the time for weekend and holiday service, as well as the location of the nearest mailbox with later

229

pickup hours—on the 18th and Columbia Road mail-box to replace the one that was torn off. The U.S. Postal Department must also either *find,* or *invent,* a new glue that can't be peeled off. There should also be a special investigator assigned to spot check this mail-box at night to see if the pickup truck really stops there (I believe there is a tendency among certain mail-truck drivers to skip mailboxes in lower-income areas because they feel that the letters from poor people aren't important), and if any winos or druggies are pissing down the mail chute late at night since PEPCO took away our streetlight on a corner which has ONE OF THE HIGHEST CRIME RATES IN THE CITY to save energy without—repeat—WITH-OUT informing the neighbors!

Coco paused to think for a moment. Remembering the long harrowing Christmas season when the main post office had lowered its employment standards and affirmatively hired inexperienced part-time seasonal personnel who obviously disposed of—rather than de-livered—letters, Coco considered asking the President to turn the postal service over to a private cor-poration. She hesitated only because she was unsure whether such a demand was politically progressive or regressive. Also, since Amtrak couldn't get its Metro-liners anywhere on time, Coco wondered if a private concern could run the mail service any better than the government.

Uncertain about her position on this matter, Coco decided to hold back on any further postal demands until she thought through the entire situation.

4. When the C&P Telephone Company makes a refund for money lost in a pay phone, they should send fifteen cents in *cash* rather than a refund slip that can only be

cashed at a bank (which is a drag) or applied to the next telephone bill—if you remember to do so.

5. The appropriate federal regulatory agency should stop Griffith Consumers from taking customers off the Budget Pay Plan if they fall behind in their payments because what's a budget payment plan for except for people who have trouble paying exorbitant heating bills on time?

6. The American Express Company should be federally restrained from putting PERSONAL AND CONFIDENTIAL on their billing envelopes because everybody knows what that means.

7. There is absolutely no rationale for department stores making all merchandise purchased on sale, final. Why should they? People make more mistakes during the chaos of a clearance than during normal shopping periods and consumers shouldn't be penalized for that. Also, department stores that negligently forget to give credit refunds for returned merchandise should be penalized with fines paid to the customer.

8. Adams-Morgan needs a complete twenty-four-hour-a-day day-care center with a professional staff, fascinating play equipment, and a tender after-school tutoring program. I want a place to leave my children that is nicer than home!

9. Adams-Morgan needs more food stamp outlets and a Metro station built at 18th and Columbia Road, N.W.

10. The U.S. should stop supporting fascist regimes around the world.

11. The D.C. Police Department should make public-service announcements over TV as to when they are holding their annual stolen-property [bicycle] sales.

12. The U.S. should stop corporations from manufacturing carcinogenic products and other environmental pollutants.

13. Restaurant computer machines that devour credit cards with overdue balances should be banned and made illegal.

14. The National Institutes of Health should study ways

of upgrading the social and sexual images of middle-aged women.

15. By federal regulation, all gynecologists should be forced to warm up their instruments before conducting pelvics, and schedule their appointments sequentially, rather than simultaneously, apropos the recent ruling about overselling airplane reservations.

Coco smoked a cigarette and relaxed for a while before continuing.

16. The D.C. Motor Vehicle Department should be prohibited from withholding license plates on the basis of unpaid parking fines. There is a difference between scofflaws and poor people who can't afford to pay. No "Denver boots" should be placed on any D.C. vehicles with less than fifty dollars worth of outstanding parking tickets.

20. The Justice Department should investigate the possibility of criminal extortion within the Service Maintenance Contract Departments of large local retail stores (such as Sears, to be specific). Nationwide chains sell defective appliances and then intimidate customers into buying insurance—the rates of which are jacked up each year so the customer has to pay more and more protection money. Perhaps the government should put a price freeze on these contracts, like the old rent control program, until a criminal-extortion investigation is conducted.

There was a sharp rap on the car window. Coco stifled a startled scream when she saw Izzat peering in at her.

"Telephone for you," Izzat said grumpily.

Coco jumped out of the car and ran over to the telephone.

"Hello," she said, suddenly aware of Abass, who had

been asleep the last time she saw him, advancing toward her threateningly.

"Coco?"

"Yes." She looked up at Abass who was now standing alarmingly close to her. "It's for me," Coco explained guiltily. "It's just my husband."

"Make it fast," Abass growled. "And you can't talk on the phone anymore."

"OK," Coco nodded.

"Honey," Gavin groaned. "Who's yelling at you? Are you OK?"

"Yes, Gavin."

"Jesus, Coco. J just got rid of that dippy dame, Diana. Boy, is she flaky! It wasn't bad enough that me and the kids were falling apart, but I had to deal with her on top of everything else. Oh, Coco. I love you. I couldn't live without you, honey."

"Thank you, Gavin, that's sweet of you to say. But listen. There's something I have to tell you. I'm not sure I'll be coming out right like I said I would when I talked to you and the kids before."

"Honey! What happened? What's the matter?"

"Well, Gavin, I've got some . . . business to take care of."

"What do you mean? Why can't you come out?"

"Well, it's complicated."

"Don't you *want* to come out, Coco?"

"It's not exactly that I don't *want* to," Coco corrected him gently. "But as long as I've been in here for twenty-four hours already and everyone's already been traumatized and everything, I thought I might as well try to accomplish something. See, I've sort of cooked up a publicity stunt so that I can make some demands of my own to the President. You don't know any of this yet, but David Macintosh found out that Lionel and Diana have been changing the numbers of the National Infelicity Index so that Americans would appear to be happier than they really are. But when I asked Jimmy Carter to investigate the thing, he didn't sound like he'd really do it. So I decided that unless he promises me an investigation, and announces it over TV, I might not come out right away. Do you understand what I mean?"

"I think so," Gavin said slowly. "I mean, I'm trying to follow what you're saying."

"See, these kids—Izzat and Abass and Aly—have really been persecuted, Gavin. Their friends and relatives have been thrown in jail and SAVAK watches every move they make here in this country."

"Coco. You don't have to convince *me*. I've never been a big fan of the Shah's."

"I know. So then you can understand why I'd like to take a political stand and make a meaningful political statement of my own, if I can. I mean, I've learned a lot since I've been in here, Gavin. I've learned a little Zen and a little Mao and I'm even beginning to understand what Eurodollars are."

"Who's teaching you all that stuff, Coco? John Canada?"

Coco ignored the question. The fact that Gavin had focused his suspicions on the wrong man was ironic because it was Mohammed Mohammed who was now watching Coco with jealous concentration, sensing she was having an intimate conversation with her husband.

"See, all I want to do is show people that Americans aren't that different from other underdeveloped people. I want them to see that an average American, like me, can recognize the contradictions in our system, too. Do you know what I mean?"

"I do, honey, but I still don't want you to start any trouble after all the arrangements have been finalized. Izzat and his friends might really get mad at you for gumming up the works. I mean, if everyone's ready to leave and you start making a fuss, they might get mad enough to hurt you—right when it's almost all over. I love you, Coco, and I just don't want anything to happen to you *now*."

"I don't think Izzat or Abass or Aly would hurt me," Coco lied. "I think they'll understand. And I really do believe that the only way to improve our system without an armed revolution is through educational actions like the one I'm planning."

"Well, . . ." Gavin said doubtfully.

"Also, Gavin, I want to keep things equitable. I don't want to ask the government for anything I wouldn't ask from my own family. So I've made a list of some domestic reforms that I'm going to ask you to accept in a very formal way. I mean, for instance, since I've done all the laundry for the last fourteen years, I think you should do it for the next fourteen. Things like that. In fact, I've itemized everything about the laundry—like the fact you have to empty every thing out of everyone's pocket before putting clothes in the machine, and that you should turn all the bluejeans right-side out, but leave all the underpants and jockey shorts inside-out the way you peel them off because that keeps the heavier soiled side exposed. I mean—if you agree to do the next fourteen years of laundry, you have to do it right and you have to pin dirty pairs of socks together before washing them, even though I did read in a magazine that some manufacturer's going to start producing socks with snaps on the cuffs. But until those go on the market, you'll have to stick to our safety pin system. Actually, I have all the laundry instructions written down for you. But would you be willing to sign a list of domestic demands like that?"

"Well, sure, Coco. Of course."

"Also, because I've had plenty of time for thinking in here, I worked out a new individualized color-code system for personal items that tend to get mixed up with other people's which I want you to administer. It's a new procedure in which everything—key chains, toothbrushes, socks, tennis balls, boots—everything will be identified by a particular color that belongs exclusively to one individual. In other words, all of Josh's things should be white, Nicky's brown, Jessica's yellow, Mike's blue, and yours black. That way you wouldn't even have to pin the socks together before washing them or roll them up into sock-balls for the drawers, because each person will be able to wear any one of his or her socks with any other since they'll all be the same color.

"Yeah." Gavin said.

"Also, the boys' briefs and boxer shorts should be marked on the inside waistband with an indelible pen of the same color as their socks so you won't have to unroll those little labels in the back to see what size they are to find out *whose* they are. An X in the proper color will instantly identify the owner. I also think you should buy key chains that match each persons' socks and the Xs on their underwear so everyone knows whose key is whose. Also, everyone should buy a new toothbrush to match their socks and Xs and key chains. I mean, would you be willing to administer this new color-code system and get it functioning?"

"Sure, Coco."

236

"So you'll sign on to everything, even if you haven't read the whole list?"

"Sure, honey. Sure I will. But now I want you to calm down a little and get some rest and promise me you won't rock the boat. Promise me that."

"OK, Gav. Kiss the kids for me. I'll see you soon."

Coco blew a kiss into the telephone and hung up the receiver.

Briskly she walked over to John Canada and looked down at him, with what she hoped was a suitably disdainful expression, as she explained that she was going to issue her own separate set of demands to the President.

Canada's forehead recreased itself into the roadbeds of his previous frowns as he listened.

"You dumb broad," he finally sputtered. "You're going to get all of us killed." He rose to his feet. "You're not going to pull a Patty Hearst number on me now," he said vehemently. "It's bad enough when an heiress joins the guerrillas, but a goddamn, middle-aged JAP . . ."

"You're going to have to push for an investigation of the National Infelicity Index," Coco said coldly, "or the shit is really going to hit the fan. I'll tell so many stories about you to the press that the Senate will never confirm you. I'm not bullshitting either, John. You better believe me."

Then Coco turned around and walked back to her car. Settled in the front seat again, she reopened her notebook.

On the off chance that something might go wrong—like a shootout at the very last minute—Coco wanted to say good-bye to her children. She did not want to leave them only detailed consumer guides and advisory instructions about meaningless equipment. It was almost unbelievable that Coco had spent so much precious time and paper on such trivial drivel. Certainly her last message to her babies shouldn't be a laundry list. Oh, why hadn't Coco ever had the foresight to plant little love notes for her children around the house in unexpected places, hiding them away like those shy, semiliterate messages left behind by the cleaning lady who had once worked for the Burmans.

"Deer mrs. I brok yur ashtray. Kan I pay for it out of next wks celery?"

At least now Coco had a chance to say something real to her children. Even if she couldn't articulate any profundities, at least she could get some major ideas across. She could express an intent—like vague *Vogue* notions which were not supposed to be taken literally but only figuratively. Fashion editors didn't really expect working women to paste sequins on their eyelids every morning, but they did want to encourage the use of mascara at all times.

No. It wasn't too late. As the deadline approached, Coco would write only meaningful messages to her children, just as Mao Tse Tung had left appropriate aphorisms for his people.

"Dear Children: Each person should be responsible for his/her own self," Coco printed very neatly. "That is freedom."

She looked at it. She liked it. Indeed, other than a few words of wisdom, what else could she leave her kids? Her bike was too tall for anyone under five feet. Her umbrella pinched people's fingers and made blood blisters under the skin. Her Minolta camera was too complicated for a kid to load. Her little reading lamp had to be flipped over and shaken to turn on. Her blow drier didn't blow anymore. Her vacuum cleaner didn't inhale. What else could she bequeath? Coco had nothing of value but her own values to leave behind.

Inspired, she turned to a fresh page in the notebook.

"My darling children,

"Basically I believe you should turn our house into a commune and our family into a collective. All that means, really, is that everyone should take care of his or her own self while helping each other as much as possible. Like any liberated community, a family can work more cooperatively and live more lovingly if they redesign their priorities and goals."

Coco looked out the window. Certainly her kids were still young enough to kick conventional capitalist habits and, through auto-critical analysis, take a great leap forward toward becoming new men and women. Although she didn't want them to attempt producing steel in any backyard furnace, she did want them to learn how to use the outdoor rotisserie, which traditionally lay idle from one Fourth of July to the next. In case the oven broiler went on the blink or Daubers just couldn't fix the toaster, Coco wanted her children to know they could brown bread on the hibachi or cook colonial style in the living room fireplace which they all viewed as a decorative accessory rather than an alternative source of energy. Indeed, she wanted them to discard all the faulty appliances which could become fire hazards and devise new and safer methods of cookery.

Coco thought of the long list of domestic duties she had spelled out on the new assignment sheet for the children and wondered whether or not they would really perform their proper chores. Would it be necessary for her to mention any economic incentives? Was it necessary to introduce the concept of profit into the system in order to insure or increase productivity? Would her children perform without classic capitalist lures as incentives? But with what else could she replace money? What else was there? Brownie points? Celestial approval? Parental love—from a possibly dead mother? Coco couldn't think of any system of rewards that wouldn't require rigorous retraining in order to inculcate new values in her children. She decided to avoid the issue altogether and simply appeal to their best instincts. Indeed, the most effective way would be the binding wishes of a will.

Turning to the last page of her notebook, Coco wrote:

## THE LAST WILL AND TESTAMENT OF CHARLOTTE BURMAN

I leave everything I have to my family.

My husband, Gavin, shall be the executor of my estate but is not responsible for any debts that I incurred before I died—including department store charges.

All of my papers should be burned without being read first.

Any of the children's baby teeth which might be found in various containers around the house should be strung together into a bracelet or necklace by a professional jeweler and given to Jessica.

My final WISH is that all my children love each other very much, work to make the world better for everyone, and do anything they see which needs doing around the house.

Coco closed her notebook.

She felt spent—the survivor of an incredible epiphany—and exhaustion embraced her body.

She closed her eyes.

When she awoke, Coco realized she had slept for

several hours. There seemed to be an air of excitement in the garage and, feeling rested and restored, she climbed out of the car. Before speaking to anyone she went into the bathroom to wash up and carefully comb her hair before joining all the men gathered around the television set.

"What's happening?" she asked, looking around.

Aly seemed to be in good spirits despite the collapse of his coup, and he grinned broadly at Coco as if she had been his conspirator rather than captive. Beneath the straight fringe of his bangs perspiration gave his round brown face a leathery polished-saddle sheen.

"Carter's coming on to make his statement," he said. "The newsmen are very excited. 'Baba Wawa' says it's Carter's biggest political act since he took office and that the whole world is watching by satellite."

Coco smiled and looked over at the screen. There was the elegant White House Oval Room, clean, orderly, and neat—no dust under the President's radiators. His desk glistened beneath the TV lights. His presidential papers were stacked in short, even piles. A single pen stood erect in a handsome leather holder. Everything was Ready and Go for Jimmy Carter.

The prisoner, Coco Burman, was supposed to become a silent spectator.

Walter Cronkite's face crinkled companionably across the screen. "President Carter is preparing to enter the Oval Room," he informed the world with fatherly authority.

Izzat and John Canada leaned forward.

Quietly and inconspicuously, Coco moved toward the telephone.

This was her big moment. She had found the road to freedom. She would not be turned back.

Of course it would be a while before Coco would discover whether or not her newfound freedom was real. First she'd have to find out what freedom really meant—if it were metric, linear, or something else. Then she'd have to wait to see if Aly and Abass and Izzat were actually flown to freedom by the United States government and if the terrorists really freed Mohammed Mohammed in Algiers. She would also have to wait to see if John Canada could liberate himself from his own liberal shibboleths and help Coco expose the Social Science Institute fraud. It would also take a while before Coco could determine if her family would reform itself, and then even longer to see if she could use new knowledge to create enough order at home in order to free herself to work toward a new world order.

Coco scraped the last nickel and dime out of her pocket.

Had she peaked or was she starting? Could she hang on to her new perspective of domestic and world affairs? Could her self-actualization become transpersonal and expand to encompass social and political involvements both at home and abroad? Was Coco in touch with her real powers and was power really freedom?

She dialed 456–1414.

"I'm calling from the Gulf station garage," Coco whispered to the White House operator. "I'm one of the hostages and this is an emergency. We have to speak to the President right away."

A few seconds later the President picked up an extension.

"Jimmy Carter here."

"Hello, Mr. Carter. It's Charlotte Burman again."

Coco looked over at the TV set. The Oval Room was still empty. "I know you're about to go on the air to announce the settlement, but after we spoke I started to rethink some things and, well, I've never had much political experience or power before . . . in fact, I've never had as much visibility as I've had since I got locked up in this body shop. But I found our last talk very educational because you asked me to do something for you before you'd agreed to take care of some legitimate government business. And that was very instructive because it showed me how *real* politicians work—how they get something in exchange for everything they do. So then it occurred to me that—well, here I am, locked up in a garage while the Iranian and Algerian and American and Israeli governments negotiate their own interests—and I suddenly realized that everybody was getting something except me. In fact, I realized how governments hold their citizens hostage all the time while they promote their so-called national interests. So then I decided that I had some special interests too and also the power to negotiate my demands for two very good reasons. First of all, I happen to have an especially sturdy bicycle lock hidden here in the garage and I can chain myself to the steering wheel of my car unless people pay attention to what *I* want. I mean, I think it's unfair that hostages get taken advantage of and never get anything for themselves out of the deal—any personal or political compensation. Secondly, if you don't agree to my demands and I get dragged out of here anyway, I'll just tell the world—that John Canada and I are lovers."

"Mrs. Burman! What are you saying?" the President gasped.

"I'm saying that unless you promise me what I want,

I'm going to create a sex scandal about me and John Canada. And I really mean that, Mr. President. So I've written down a few things I want the government to promise me as reparations. I'm sure Adams-Morgan has suffered severe financial losses during this seige because of the roadblock on Columbia Road, which must have cut off local traffic . . ."

"Mrs. Burman," the President of the United States interrupted, "as you can see if you've got that TV on in there, all the major networks are waiting for me. I just received a note from the NBC producer saying that they lost $79,000 in the last two minutes while waiting for me to go on. Why don't I just make my speech and then come right back and speak with you as soon as I'm done."

"Because Mr. President, I want you to announce *on the air* that I'm not going along with the deal—that I'm issuing my own set of demands and that I'm going to chain myself to my car unless those demands are met. I want you to make a public promise to me over TV that you'll investigate the fraud at the Social Science Institute and that you'll put some federal money into my community. So there's no point in you telling the world that everything has been settled when it really hasn't. And if you don't make these public promises over television, when I come out of here I'm going to tell so many stories about John Canada that he'll *never* get approved by the Senate. Also—my little news conference won't help you very much politically either."

Coco turned around. The five men were watching the television screen nervously, trying to figure out what had gone wrong.

"It's hard for me to believe you're making trouble

at a time like this, Mrs. Burman," the President said despairingly. "I've just received another note from CBS saying they're going to return to their regular scheduling if I don't go on camera within forty-five seconds."

"Well, Mr. Carter, I have my list right here."

Coco reached for her purse, but her notebook wasn't in it. Right at the moment when she needed it most, her notebook was gone. She must have left it in the car. She would have to wing it and improvise her demands.

Coco cleared her throat authoritatively. "Number one, I want a citizen's panel, including a representative number of Adams-Morgan citizens selected from the black, white, and Hispanic communities, to review the U.S. military budget and see if some of that money can't be redirected to a few local projects which need federal funding very badly."

"Oh, Lord," the President moaned.

"Number two is that I want an investigation of the American banking establishment to see why they're decreasing interest rates on savings accounts while increasing interest rates on small business and personal loans. I also want a Senate hearing on current bank loans to South Africa."

"Oh, Mrs. Burman!"

"Number three. I want an investigation of the S.A.T. testing system which upsets our American youth. Four: I want the FCC to check the possibility of including people's zip codes, along with their addresses, in the telephone book and to find out why people with 232 exchanges—most of which are in Adams-Morgan— can't get pushbutton phones. It's my guess that this is a racially inspired restriction based on geopolitical factors. Number five is that the people of Adams-Morgan do *not* want any more speculators coming into our area. Low-income residents need a banking agency to negotiate low-interest mortgages so they can buy homes they've rented for years instead of having those houses restored and sold to middle-class suburban refugees."

"Mrs. Burman! I promise I'll meet with you immediately after your release to discuss every possible way of expediting your suggestions. Won't you trust me?"

Coco looked over her shoulder at the THINK METRIC sign. Did THINK METRIC mean HAVE FAITH? Should Coco trust Jimmy Carter since most of the American people apparently did.

Still, they had also liked and trusted Richard Nixon.

The President interrupted Coco's silence. "I'll have my personal secretary phone you back the minute I finish my speech and you can dictate your list to her over the telephone."

"But you *have* to announce it over TV, Mr. President," Coco said. "Just say that I have this list of demands and that you've agreed to do everything you can to meet them. You also have to say you're initiating an investigation of the Social Science Institute—at the insistence of John Canada, your own appointee."

"I can't do *that*, Mrs. Burman."

"Or else I'll say I've been sleeping with Canada in Lincoln's bed at the White House," Coco said threateningly.

"You wouldn't do that, Mrs. Burman. What about your husband?"

"I'll worry about him," Coco said. "We have a special arrangement."

"All right," the President said reluctantly. "You've got me over a barrel, I'll do it. Go watch me give the speech. But I'm truly sorry you're making a mockery out of our settlement at the very last minute."

He hung up.

# CHAPTER TWELVE

Excited, Coco ran back to the car, found her notebook and replanted it securely in her purse. Then she returned to sit down on the floor with the others to watch the presidential address.

Halfway through his statement, Jimmy Carter made the promised announcement of his separate peace treaty with Mrs. Charlotte Burman of Adams-Morgan.

It took a while for the terrorists to understand exactly what Coco had done, but then Aly became incensed. Apparently feeling that Coco had publicly humiliated him by negotiating a separate peace, which he had been unable to do, he jumped up and ran toward her, flailing his arms and shouting in Arabic. Izzat, who also looked angry and upset, tried to quiet Aly so he could hear the rest of the President's speech. Only Abass, who had previously shown little interest in Coco, seemed mildly amused by the initiative she had taken and smiled slightly as he watched the television.

Coco meanwhile had curled up under the wood bench that ran along the rear wall of the garage.

The fear she felt during Aly's violent reaction continued unabated even after he sat down again. He was still muttering loudly in Arabic despite the "shushing" hisses made by Abass and Izzat, and Coco's anxiety mounted. But right as Carter was about to conclude his speech, a piece of paper was slid across his desk and, after reading it, he quietly announced that the planeload of Iranian prisoners had just arrived safely in Algeria.

Then the President looked directly into the camera and spoke to the terrorists.

"The official exchange at the Gulf garage will commence within the next ten minutes. Instructions about the proper procedure for exiting will be announced to you by the police."

It was a terrific television moment and Coco, too weak to rise, remained on the floor, wilting with relief.

The realization that it was only Carter's second surprise announcement that had deflected Aly's rage and saved Coco from some unknown fate created an emotional circus in her head.

Within seconds of Carter's disappearance from the television screen, an electronic bullhorn began blaring outside the garage. An official-sounding voice began to give orders: The two Americans were to come out first—through the sidedoor—and walk toward the gasoline pumps. As soon as they reached the pumps, the terrorists and their hostage were to come outside and enter a police van parked by the side door which would take them to Dulles Airport. The voice on the bullhorn repeated the orders twice.

Chaos erupted inside the garage. Izzat began running around, trying to find certain things he wanted to take with him. He began yelling at everyone and Coco huddled farther beneath the bench, afraid to get in anyone's way. Abass and Aly were scurrying about repacking items into the satchels which they were going to carry. Ambassador Mohammed stood silently beneath a sign saying TIRE CENTER watching the confusion.

Coco remained in the shadows as the commotion continued.

Eventually John Canada came over, and grabbing Coco's hands, pulled her up and led her to the exit. Then he stood close beside her until the other men had collected their gear, gotten out their guns, and gathered together at the door. Canada was the only one sufficiently calm to throw back the bolt.

"OK. Go on. Start," Izzat grunted to Canada, including Coco in his commandeering nod.

Canada opened the door and gripped Coco's forearm.

But at the threshold Coco suddenly broke loose and turned back to Izzat. Throwing her arms around his neck she embraced his tight, tense body for a moment.

"Peace," she said, hugging him against her. "God bless all of you."

"Go ahead, Coco," Izzat said roughly, mispronouncing her name so that it sounded like cuckoo. Then he shoved her back to Canada.

Coco's head was swarming with sensations. She was only half conscious of the door opening and John Canada leading her outside into a wall of lights.

A cheer came up from the darkness beyond the Kleigs.

As Canada pulled her along a shoveled pathway, Coco turned her head to watch Izzat, Abass, and Aly, clustered close behind Mohammed, shuffle out of the garage and scurry like a many-headed monster up into the rear of the police van. They pulled the doors shut behind them, and the van immediately roared across the driveway and out into the street.

Only then did Coco turn and look forward. Gripping Canada's arm and leaning against his shoulder so that the President—if he was watching—would squirm a little at the dangerous possibility of Coco making a public spectacle which would embarrass the Carter administration, she began to walk.

Adjusting to the lights, she scanned the crowd of faces as a fan of microphones rose up like a fist in front of her. Knowing that Gavin and the children wouldn't arrive for another few minutes, Coco looked at the crew of media people who were now surrounding her.

From all sides voices were pitching questions:

—How did she feel?—

—What was the first thing she would do when she got home?—

—How had she been treated?—

—What did she think of her captors?—

It was the same kind of stupid question the press always asked—off the point, out of line, and out of order.

Coco grimaced.

The police were struggling to keep back the reporters, but one man, holding a Pacifica radio microphone, plunged forward.

"What were the demands you made that the President agreed to?" he called. "What did you ask for?"

Tossing her hair back from her face, Coco lifted her head and looked directly into the blinding lights, totally unconcerned about her appearance. After twenty-eight hours in the garage, she was completely focused on the fact that she had a captive audience and a great deal of information to transmit as quickly as possible.

"I have several things to say," she began, aware that Canada was talking to another group of reporters behind her.

"First of all, I want to say that I hope both the American and Iranian governments have acted in good faith and that our . . . captors and the 123 prisoners from Tehran will receive sanctuary in Algeria. I also hope that the Algerians will see to it that Ambassador

Mohammed is released to his own government—which they deserve.

"Secondly, I want to announce that the Social Science Institute's National Infelicity Index, designed and directed by Dr. Lionel Hearndon, is a fraud. Dr. Hearndon has falsified official documents and altered U.S. census material. As a member of the Social Science Institute staff, I am ready to testify to this and produce the documentary evidence which proves Dr. Hearndon mishandled federal funds from the National Endowment for the Humanities as well as private money from a matching grant made by Mobil Oil."

—How did he change the data, Mrs. Burman?—

—Are you charging him with fraud?—

—Do you think he'll face criminal charges?—

Like sheep, the reporters fell into line, following each other's train of questions.

Coco ignored them, knowing enough to appear reticent about details so as to keep them interested.

"Thirdly," she continued, trying to blot out the shrieking sirens and stagey sound effects of the hyped-up crowd, "President Carter has agreed to investigate, and, hopefully, remedy certain local situations which cause infelicity among Adams-Morgan residents."

"Mrs. Burman, aren't you exploiting your accidental kidnapping to pressure the President? Aren't you superimposing your own political interests—or agenda—onto this totally separate event?"

"Yes. Definitely," Coco answered firmly. "I am definitely trying to exploit the circumstance of my imprisonment to draw attention to other oppressive situations here in Washington, D.C. I hope to become an effective force for the betterment of local government in the District."

"Has this always been a legitimate concern of yours?" a young blond reporter asked.

"Of course, because I'm a citizen of this city and have been injured by the system for a long, long time. I will now read to you the list of demands to which President Carter promised to address himself. We will be commencing negotiations on them within the next few days."

Suddenly, CBS, ABC, and NBC microphones were shoved in front of the one marked Pacifica. Coco was picking up a national—rather than natural—audience and she felt power and potential surge through her.

Like a veteran, she pulled the notebook out of her purse and, turning slightly to avoid the glare of TV lights on the paper, began to read her list of demands.

# ABOUT THE AUTHOR

Barbara Raskin is the author of two previous novels, *Loose Ends* and *The National Anthem*. A journalist as well as a novelist, Ms. Raskin has written articles for many national publications. She was one of the founders of the Washington Independent Writers organization.

Ms. Raskin lives in Washington, D.C., with her husband, Marcus Raskin, and three children: Erika, Jamie and Noah. She is currently at work on another novel.